ASTEROID IMPAIRED

RIGHTEOUS AMERICAN FICTION: VOLUME 1

Co-edited by
Alexis Hall, Catherine Sullivan
and Benjamin Weissman

PRINTED IN THE UNITED STATES OF AMERICA.
ISBN 1-881616-82-7

AVAILABLE THROUGH: D.A.P.
Distributed Art Publishers
155 Sixth Avenue 2nd floor
New York, NY 10013
phone : 212-627 1999
fax : 212-627 9484

PRINTED & BOUND BY
Thomson-Shore
Dexter, MI

ILLUSTRATIONS
Jim Shaw

DESIGN
Simon Sharpe

IN MEMORY OF

Wendy Lewis Moore

AND

Kevin White

contents

the introduction:
To be Asteroid Impaired is to free fall from one hallucination to another--to live and work, to study and float in a little corner of sweetness, the shimmering mindbend of Pasadena. If there is a glitch in the system, if a bubble or a scratch appears without warning in the light bulb of your brain, be grateful. Something is letting you know that you are among friends. Within the pearly black gates of Art Center College of Design, the little art school by the freeway, a wanderer such as yourself will find the cheerfully troubled, a muttering mob, a pack of flaming fiction writers. Beware of the asteroid. It is hard and ugly. With our delicate hand and lovely eye we welcome you. Hi.

Vincent Johnson

Excerpt from "The Autobiography of my American Soul"

n Hell we see our mothers so lovingly clean the various sized pipes of the smoking and smouldering men, men who will no longer be punished for the vile and putrid acts they witnessed and wished for themselves and often did perpetrate upon the potent faces, lips, hair, teeth, tongues, necks, bras, breasts and eyeglasses of mothers and soon to be mothers still living on earth for the present. All of the Mothers here were currently receiving their just and duly earned punishments — which they must suffer (never enjoy!) and try to finally suck to a dry dust the bones of the anti-life until their exists not a single man or drip in the ever flowing, never diminishing, abundant replenishing forever of permanently eternal sex time crime. Of course this Entry to Hell for males could and would truly be a fall one experienced on one's own, like a single water drop into the Black Well that is our Mother's Soul, but only if each were taught repeatedly to despise the male inhuman body and be repulsed by even the the thought of Oral Eyes, as well as the seething pure hate for those who sought the enterprise, such as those unfortunate souls whose wives vomited upon being requested to make such a performance on the bulkhead. But, as we know, there are with all Earthly Hells euphoric Heavenly worlds of escape. Sniff, if, in eternal time, the Mother with tears in her hair and eyes discovers a way to make palateable the demonic three tongued lusty crimes of the vendors of lumpy love pearls, (how would you choose to survive?) then finds a brilliant way in her mind to actually stay alive despite her eternal inprisonment before the endless male lines, she will have formed the tools sufficient for her to escape her mind from the salty worlds of self hate and venomous remorse, and when she returned again in a new body to Earth she would grow up now in wealth and good health and reward herself with an easy job of life long work of shooting men in the face with a sawed off pump. BLAM! "You're the son of someone I knelt!" No longer would she be one of hell's residents — she would pass out through the unloading docks through to the Hellgate — onto the pearly white milk crates of bodily heaven and murderous bliss! Of course I do acknowlege that the nightmare cycle of putting up with eating shit in order to give pleasure to others — Especially a Black Dog as unworthy even of his own life as your husband — would be even harder to break (except maybe across his face) if it were you too — Yes you too, since you are by sex the male, would know that somewhere in the span of all death in jail time, that you would be pushed forward in the line to take your turn and your time and be pampered and served by no one else but her. You would be responsible for bringing tears to her eyes meanwhile enjoying her vastly improved French speaking skills as long as you'd like, and as you knew, you know, that you would not could not back off because there was an endless number of men waiting to punish her, (a thousand husbands, they dreamed of it) so you stand weak and bent with your hands on her skull because, after all, This Was Her Punishment! And She's Doing Such A Good Job! Good Job — Good Bob, OH BOB...At the end of each end you launch and scream to God to let out your soul — you'd heard from the demon guard a resounding No! then your Hell Date ends too late and would start all over again. Since both of you two would recognize (or maybe not in a Catholic guise — then this story would have to be farted out!) each other at once and despite your Mom's pleadings for you to not strut your stuff and to instead fight for her dignity (even though on the Earth she was a...) "But Mother, they're so many—-they'll beat my skin off of me and jump on my heart until I scream the most Hellishly unimaginable scream and the devil will send me to an even lower level of human Hell and depravity! And then after all of that he'll kill me!"

"But son you're already dead!"

Instead of fighting you are driven and bound by the blinding lust to be orally loved by ANY female mouth — The Very Devil Himself reminds you of this and promises pleasures that will drown any doubt — and here: "Uh Goo-d!" once again your need for the highest form of depraved self approval love was about to be met let/wet out: What Lust, What Exquisite Pain! What Blinding Guilt! What Brutal Inhuman Agony! You Profane Absolutely Perverse Son-Of-A-Bitch! Isn't life a bowl of hot shit! I should shudder — All of you dogs want to be with my Mother! Go ahead bad boy, you've got her...But remember, as the cycle of Death and Life goes, on my next time Underground the deeper you stick size between my Mother's eyes the further I plan to stick length in your Mom's face. Are you ready to go to Hell with me, partners? And by the way, do you have a Father? No? Pray to God that you're without one. For the loading dock of male hell is not at all about Sex but Hellish terror and hideous fantasy double ax murders and winning the job of Executing yourself throughout Eternity. For the creative man this means you will die a different death each time, for the not so lucky you die the same horrible death over and over and live to know your fate and die forever after a while not from your fate, but from certainty. The balcony of Hell awaits us, Friends, Let Us Not Forget Our Past And favorite Glories. Now, hellward, to Bloody Victory!

Mike Kelley

Bee, Gang, P Eye

'm sorry." What else can I say. And I know these are only words; speaking them cannot make up for the immeasurable suffering I have heaped upon the world since I was born. Yet, only recently have I become aware that saying this simple phrase was even necessary. You see, I was unaware of what a beast I was. I was not conscious of this fact, I was living a lie. My dirty little life was a secret to me; the pond-scum of my psyche had been erased from the index of obtainable references. While my perversions were handed down to me, I was sleepily unaware. All the while I was. Yes, they were byproducts, of a lifetime of miserable abuse, an abuse which, in order to protect itself, hid in the deepest recesses of my mind. My recalled life, is only a screen memory, a cheap stage set built to pretty-up the slum of my true biography.

I was a happy child . . . what a laugh! Yet that is what I believed. I remembered nothing bad, so I filled the blanks in with family romance: with summers spent in the sun; with winters playing in the snow; with springtimes full of flowers - and, best of all, the falls, when I shared the companionship of school chums. I remember all of their sweet names. But they didn't exist. I've never had a friend. All of it is fiction, a pack of cliches culled from television and spoon fed to me with sugar on top. None of it ever happened. Instead, I grew up in a drum of toxic waste welded tightly shut. I was, in fact, never born. I still reside in the home of my parents: the dank, dark and poisoned cavity of my mother's and father's anal womb. This is an elastic architecture that stretches forever, encasing me always, even to the very ends of the earth and time.

But to the point at hand. You will hear enough of my sordid past shortly enough. How unfortunate for you, for I know that you are not in the least bit interested in my problems. But I must, to the best of my recollection (a recollection that, I remind you, cannot be trusted because it was formulated by brainwashing and torture) recount every disgusting tidbit of my sorry life. I must do this because my recovery demands it. My recovery has put forth the order: "Track down and apologize to all of those that you have treated wrongly in the past."

Interestingly enough, the first instance of cruelty that pops to mind is one against a "lower life form." This should not really be a surprise, and I reveal the incomplete state of my recovery in my shocked reaction to the recollection. I should be willing to face the fact that I am a piece of shit. Everyone at peace with the world knows it is all of one skin. This super-matter, this protoplasmic unity, treats all life as equally important. It turns a blind eye to the supposed hierarchies of life forms. Anyway, a disquieting image rushed into my mind all at once: I am putting a single honey bee into a small plastic pill container. Now, I am dropping this bottle into a pit being filled with wet cement. And now I watch as the delicate being is swallowed up by tons of hungry concrete. This hole, this abyss, being filled, was the foundation for an add-on to the house I was raised in. And how my heart sank as I realized I had just completed an evil and irreversible act. The honey-thing was now permanently encased in the soil, the very ground on which I was to spend the rest of my days. I have to stand on top of this site of my sin day in and day out, year after sorry year.

Ever since that eventful day I have been plagued by the image of that primal act, and an accompanying terror: my all-consuming fear of internment while still alive. As long as I have lived - since this time and perhaps, as we shall see, from even before - I have felt as if I were buried alive. I suffer every day from claustrophobia, a type so severe that even the air which surrounds me feels as if it is smothering me. How I wish I could turn back the hands of time. How I wish I could dig down and break open the tomb of concrete to release the poor bee, if only to give it a proper and respectful funeral. And, I would hope, in doing so, release the weight that sits upon my own chest, a weight so enormous it threatens to sink into and demolish the whole planet. I wish I could burn that house down, with all of its interior secrets. I wish I could incinerate my memory of all of the tinder of my youth. My greatest wish is for a cleared lot: a razed mind.

But certain embarrassing negative engrams refuse to die. There is a memory, for instance, of a group of photos of the very young Cher, dressed in Native American-style fashions, cut from TV Guide. They have been arranged on poster board in a weird composition, glued down with jism. And this fetish object became the center of a group of activities, the grounding point ... meant to ...

Oh, why go on?

In Catholic elementary school, I was often warned of the dangers of chumming around with Protestant boys. I was told of their warped views of our Lord's teachings, their callous disregard for the mother of Christ: the holy Virgin Mary, and the horrible fact that their "priests" did not practice celibacy. The protestant's inability to curb their animal instincts make them susceptible to the sins of the flesh, perversions of every kind. It is common knowledge that young protestant boys are chronic masturbators. And, sadly, the girls too. I heard of one neighborhood Lutheran girl, nicknamed Sugar Bear, who had to be taken to the hospital to have a section of broken-off hot dog removed from inside her. The boys are unable to keep their hands off themselves, and as they get older this libidinal urge shifts to anything else they can get a hold of: inanimate objects, animals, whorish girls, and, worst of all, dead things. Protestants are deeply resentful of the Catholic's ability to keep the temple of our Lord, our bodies, free from sin. They are envious of our holy restraint and thus seek to harm us whenever they can. They want to sully us as they are sullied. Their greatest pleasure comes from seeing a Catholic sink to their evil ways.

I heard all of this, yet I paid no heed. It was hard to believe that anybody could do the things my teachers described to me. Such practices were simply unthinkable to a truly Christian mind. The Protestant boys in my block seemed like regular fellows. Though I didn't know them well, they were friendly enough, and in one instance, a few Protestant boys my age stopped a teenage Protestant girl from beating me to a pulp. This bruiser was staunchly anti-Catholic and had tried several times to catch me. Finally, she succeeded and I was getting a severe "ass-kicking" until I was saved by these boys. Despite their own taunts, which I shrugged off as simple bravado, they let me go. For this I rewarded them with my lunch money. I had never seriously thought that this girl's cruelty was religiously motivated. Instead, I assumed she was an atypical juvenile delinquent. I was wrong. Religious prejudice, as I was to find out, was the norm.

Every day, I rode my bike home from school across the bridge spanning the Rouge River. In actuality, the Rouge River is little more than a stream, yet I loved to stop on the bridge and stare down into its green waters. Across the bridge, on one side of the road, was a fire station. Sometimes the firemen would be there, busily polishing the shiny red fire truck; but generally the station was locked up, as they were often out on call. Then the station had a lonely, deserted aura. On the other side of the road was a soda fountain/candy shop run by two old brothers. The shop was a vestige of another time, its proprietors being unwilling, or unable, to keep up with the current tastes of their young customers. The two brothers were mirror images of one another: they were over seventy years old, white as dead fish, thin and frail, and wore matching white soda jerk uniforms. They lived in their own world; neither one could understand a word uttered to them, and both were so feeble they could barely speak. All transactions had to be conducted in the point and grunt method. Also . . . their smell was intolerable. Consequently, the shop was nearly always empty.

The only people to frequent the place on a regular

basis was a gang of four young toughs from the local public high school. Their names were Meat, Eddie, Lumpy and Pee Wee. If the old men still had their wits about them, they would have closed their business long ago because these "customers" never paid for a thing and constantly demeaned the pair. I was unlucky enough to enter the shop one afternoon when this band of ruffians was there, and was horrified, permanently scarred, by the scene I witnessed. The pack of leather-jacketed thugs had trashed the shop, destroying all of the merchandize except for what they were eating or readying to carry off. One old fellow was still being slapped around and taunted, while his brother was laying on the floor, face up, having already been beaten. His pants were down around his ankles and his face was smeared all over with gooey chocolate bars. Meanwhile, the old fellow still standing was being marched around the vandalized store by Meat who propelled him forward with swift knee-kicks to his butt. Then, after a final powerful wedgie which elicited a howl of pain from the elderly gentleman, Meat stripped this old man's pants off too. Then, switchblade to his throat, the bewildered codger was forced to squat upon the candy-smeared face of his brother. The crew of delinquents stepped back and laughed uproariously, all the while pointing at the tableau they had created. This, the "shitty-faced candy-man can can," as they called it, was the finest scene they had ever devised.

If it wasn't for the fact that these scum were so engrossed in their foul play, I'm sure I would have met with the same fate as the two aged soda jerks. Blessedly, I escaped without notice. This was the event that changed my conception of the world. After seeing the brutal actions of these public school boys, I knew the world was not as rosy as I had before imagined. I knew now, I was in constant danger.

Soon my new world view was confirmed. After the soda fountain incident, I always rode my bike home across the bridge on the fire station side of the street, naively believing this was a safer route. Sometimes I would steer into the alley behind the station because it allowed access to a path that led down to the river's edge. This particular spot by the river was always deserted. I could while away an hour or so watching leaves drift by on the current, or read a book until the sun started to go down alerting me that dinner time was near. On this day, however, the alley was not deserted. On making the turn around the side of the fire station into the alley, I was set upon by a gang of seven or eight Protestant boys who quickly knocked me off of my bike and subdued me. These guys were my own age, younger than Meat and his buddies but just as cruel. Initially I thought I might escape with only a beating and the loss of my bike, but I soon realized these fellows had different intentions. They recognized me as a Catholic. I had stupidly forgotten to remove my tie after school. This article of clothing was a dead giveaway as to my religious affiliation; now I was doomed.

At first, they just slapped me around while taking turns riding my bike up and down the river bank. It was obvious they had no interest in stealing my bike, for they took every opportunity to run it into rocks and potholes until the frame was dented, the paint scraped off, and the wheels bent. Then they removed the seat from the bicycle and forced me to ride the damaged vehicle up and down the alley. They found this pathetic parade hilariously amusing. Because the bicycle wheels were so bent, and the surface of the alley so irregular, the seat shaft painfully poked me in the anus as I peddled. One of the despicable bullies then got the idea that I should perform this same trick "bare-assed." Their squeals of laughter intensified as they saw the increased pain on my face. The metal shaft bounced repeatedly against my naked and tender orifice until blood began to drip down and spray off the spokes of the wheels. Tiring of this game, they broke into two groups: one stomped my bike to pieces, while the other kicked me about the head and genitals until I was a bruised and bloody mess. I thought I was dead, but they were far from finished with me. No, they were not interested in destroying me, they wanted to destroy my faith.

One of the two groups dragged me, naked, several blocks to a garage "club house" behind an abandoned house. Above the door was a crude sign that read "No girls allowed." Its interior was decorated with strangled cats hung from the rafters, and three-gallon mayonaise jars, containing their "piss collection," were in careful rows lining the walls. The other group left with my wallet. When these boys returned, several hours later, one of them was carrying a small portable cassette recorder that I recognized as my own. The rest were carrying other objects of value taken from my home. They had used my school ID card to find my residential address and, using my own key, they had broken into and burgled my parent's house. Besides the standard items easily saleable on the street, they had stolen some religious articles. These were worth nothing monetarily; they had been taken only to defile. One of these objects was a ceramic statue, much loved by my mother, of the Virgin Mary. This, they took turns defecating on while forcing me to watch the despicable act. All the while they snickered about the "lie" of Christ's virgin birth. "The Virgin wasn't a virgin and neither are you," one of them snarled. He then sadistically "popped my butt cherry," as he called it, with the sacred statue.

Then came the most cruel twist of the knife. Turning me back over, they shoved my cassette player into my face and turned in on. Out of it came the unmistakable sound of my dog, Duke, whining in agony. With his face right in mine, one of the louts spat: "We've got your little dog, you fuck, and if you ever want to see him alive, you'll do something for us." I was beyond caring if I lived any longer, in fact I was hoping for death, but the sound of my dog's torture was unbearable. I was willing to agree to anything to prevent any mistreatment of my beloved Duke. The boys then produced a schedule of Catholic masses from my church. Another of them spoke: "We picked this up at your house. And look, there's a service tonight! We're going to fix you up pretty, and you're going to go and bring us back a host." I did not argue.

Stuffed into some fresh clothes, I was escorted to my church. The bells were tolling signaling the beginning of mass. In the pew, on each side of me, was one of my tormentors. Throughout the service, the cries of Duke preyed on my mind. Sickened as I was by what I was about to do, I felt Jesus would understand, would approve of any act that saved the life of one of his beautiful creatures. When it came time for communion, I knelt before the altar and received into my mouth the wafer of bread that is also the body of Christ. I did not swallow. Immediately, upon my return to my seat, I was led outside. I was then compelled to spit the precious host into the waiting hand of one of the monsters.

Back at the "club house," the real horror began. Faced with the perversions being acted out, I regretted my decision to follow my captor's orders. I would have rather died, seen my dog's death, even my parent's death, than the atrocities performed on the body of Christ that I was forced to witness that day. First, the entire gang had a "circle jerk," ejaculating en masse onto the host, an activity they sickeningly dubbed "cum on the cookie." Then, they took turns masturbating onto our Lord in another game called "Oreo," which called for me to suck the "cream" off of the host after each perverted act. Then they would flush the wafer out of my mouth by urinating into it as a group. The defilements escalated. I was forced to suck the host out of the anus of every one of them, one after another. Then they each took a turn pushing the host deep into my rear end by sodomizing me. Then they caused me to defecate our Lord out by giving me a Coca Cola enema - first shaking, then inserting the exploding bottle into my rectum. They repeated this action again and again until my sphincter was so loosened it ceased to give them pleasure. An old yardstick, the full thirty-six inches, was inserted into my rectum, then turned sideways. The ruler was rotated like a propeller, stretching my anal muscles beyond the point of contraction. When the ruler was removed my sphincter hung to my knees like a deflated inner tube.

I was barely alive when they introduced my dog Duke into the action, repeating many of the same offenses against him as they had against me. New tricks were introduced. Since my rear end could no longer provide any sport, they shifted their attention to my genitals. My penis was covered with bacon grease which the starving Duke eagerly licked. Uncontrollably, I became erect. How mortified I was at my inability to prevent this shameful occurrence. Thankfully, the erection did not last long. As soon as my penis stiffened, Duke would begin to gnaw on it as if it were a rawhide chew. The pain was tremendous and allowed me to regain control. Then the roles were reversed. Duke was held in position while Lickem Aid cherry-flavored powdered candy was sprinkled onto his crotch. I was compelled to lick up the sweet red material until Duke's shiny crimson penis swelled out of its sheath and into my mouth. Gagging, I regurgitated brightly dyed vomit all over myself and the dog. This game they called "seeing red."

At this, the zenith of my abuse, an incredible thing happened. While Duke and I were being subjected to torture, another group of boys were busy defiling the host. They had pinned the body of our Lord to the center of a target and were entertaining themselves by throwing knives at it. At the first bull's-eye, the host began to miraculously bleed and cry, alternating between shedding blood and tears. Despite the bullies best attempts, the miracle could not be stopped. When the host was chopped to pieces, it reassembled itself. When it was flushed down the toilet, it floated again and again back to the surface. Every time they turned around, the host was back in the center of the target giving forth its precious body fluids.

The Protestants began to shake in uncontrollable fear as a black cloud oozed out of a crack in the earth. Within this mist a portal opened, revealing the fiery pits of Hell. At the same time, a fluctuating image of Christ the Judge, and the wondrous bread that is also He, appeared in the sky. The perverts screamed, tore at their hair, wet themselves, and fell upon the ground flailing. Releasing Duke and I, they got down on their knees and begged for forgiveness. "That," I said, "is something only Jesus can grant." I instructed the gang to pick up the host and, together, we carried it back to the priest of the church it was stolen from. The fate of these criminals at the hands of worldly law is a story I will not recount; and their fate according to the laws of Heaven, I will discover only at the time of my own death.

Mother and I were abandoned by my father at the moment of my birth. I was raised by her alone, though we shared a small house with her three sisters: my spinster aunts. As an only child, lacking brothers, or even female siblings, my entire youth was spent in the company of older women. It was as if I had multiple mothers. Yet I craved male companionship and sought out fatherly role models, often with disastrous results. The memories of some of these attempts at male bonding are so painful that I have trouble to this day confronting them. In fact, in many cases I can only remember certain places or situations, while specific interactions remain beyond the grasp of my recollection.

I do remember a very kind elementary school biology teacher who took an interest in my sorry state. The anatomy of amphibians was a subject I was enthralled with; that, the mysterious properties of electricity, and Norse mythology, were my passions. This man and I would spend long hours after school working together on our special project: the dissection of frogs and the animation of their disembodied legs through the application of electric current. Before long, I was invited to visit him at his home, where he lived taking care of his aged mother. This crabby and demanding old woman was an invalid who had been confined to a wheel chair for many years. Her crippled legs caused her constant agony and in desperation she had turned to quack medicine for relief. Over the years she had acquired a large number of mail-order gizmos that supposedly helped ease pain through the application of ultraviolet light. My teacher (I'm sorry but I can no longer remember his name) would place attachments of glass tubing into an electrical holder that caused them to illuminate with eerie black light. The different tubes were contoured to conform to the body's various curves, and with these glowing purple bulbs he gently massaged the skin of his mom. She swore that this numbed her pain. I don't know if this was true or not, but I looked forward to the procedure for I longed to see the special light. I was completely enamored with the strange forms of the glass bulbs and the exotic lovely glow they produced. This light mesmerized me.

Like two youthful Abraham Lincolns, my mentor and I studied using this dim illumination as our candle. It's plum rays guided our way through the pages of books recounting the exploits of the old Viking gods and heros.

Then, one day, my teacher offered me his greatest treasure: his own childhood collection of rare Thor comic books. Thor was, by far, my favorite of all the super heroes. With his long blonde hair, strong muscular build, and perfect Aryan features, he was the image of masculine perfection to me. Frail youth that I was, Thor was all that I aspired to be.

I can recall vividly, my heart anxiously thumping in my chest the entire time, our descent down the rickety wooden stairs into my benefactor's cellar. I felt so excited; it was as if I were crossing the rainbow bridge into Asgard itself. This place we were entering was where the tomes of my desire were stored. I can still feel the dampness of the crumbling plaster walls; I can smell the musty odor of mildewed paper; I can taste the swirling dust upon my tongue; and I can see the massive antique chest just ahead of me. Its heavy lid slowly cracked open to reveal its secrets. All of this was illuminated by, charged with, throbbing purple energy. The room pulsed, I . . .

I can recall no more. All else is buried in the hidden recesses of my mind. My surrogate father is no longer a part of my history. Nothing tangible remains to substantiate my memories. After that last pregnant image . . . no more, no more.

The storehouse of my childhood recollections is peppered with many more half-forgotten tales of wrong turns taken in my search for a father's love. I will recount some or them, at least as much as I can remember, at a later date. But now I want to push ahead to my adulthood, and the most momentous experience of my life.

I left home at a tender age and joined the merchant marine, for this had also been my father's profession. And though it was not a conscious decision, I'm sure, on some level, this way of life was chosen in hopes of discovering the fate of my lost daddy.

The life of a sailor was a new, and pleasant, experience for it afforded the friendly company of many supportive men who were more than willing to guide me into manhood. Every voyage to strange lands increased my sense of comfort with the world; I seemed to be more and more a part of humanity. Then (I cannot face the misery of recounting the long and complex set of circumstances that led to it) I was dashed again upon the rocks of my painful childhood. For the winds of chance led me, long after I thought I had ceased to care, to the shores that held my long lost dad. Oh, what a painful delusion it was that told me that my soul was free of desire for my father! How I wish I had that mistaken sense of freedom today.

I found myself shipwrecked on a small speck of land far from anywhere. My home on this dismal island of solitude was a hellish cell made of cold stone. And the only other prisoner there, my cell mate, was my . . . my FATHER!

Our reunion was not a happy one. Unlike the Prodigal Son who was welcomed home with cries of joy, I was greeted with a sneer of disapproval. My father cared as much for me, the product of his loins, as he did for the handfuls of shit he threw out the barred window of our "home" every day. To make matters worse, the series of horrific events that led to my capture and confinement in this hovel, also resulted in the loss of one of my eyes. I was in a physically weakened state. With only a gaping, sightless hole on one side of my head, I was prey to my father's attacks. If I refused to follow his commands, I was blindsided. It was impossible to anticipate his blows. More times than I can recount, I found myself lying on the floor regaining consciousness after one of his surprise beatings. It didn't take too long before the pecking order of this foul coop was established. The prison was his territory and I was his jailhouse punk.

My food was his food. His work was my work. I was at his beck and call. And then there were those horrible times, and they were not that rare, when my father felt the "call of nature." Then the crushing blows would come upon my dark side and I would awake again to find myself sore from being "used". How loathsome! My father was old and ugly, but he was as randy as an old goat, and still quite strong. All of my moralistic arguments against the sin of incest fell upon deaf ears. Dad's logic was a simple one: "I spawned you, so you're mine to do with as I please." This seemed only natural and right to him. He was God in this domain.

A few moments of peace were provided by my father's own abuse at the hands of our captors. My heart was lifted by the sight of his torture, and the sounds of his cries and whimpers were music to my ears, for these were the quiet moments when I was free of his cruelty. This was the price my father paid for his domination over me. I, on the other hand, was never tortured by our keepers. I assumed that I was considered just too insignificant to bother with.

Strangely, we were the only men on this atrocious island. It was populated entirely by a race of white-skinned female natives. They never spoke to us and I do not know if they even had the power of speech. Every once in a while a high-pitched cooing passed from their lips, which I understood as a sound of satisfaction, but no other vocalization did they make. Their appearance was frightful. They were almost entirely bald, with only a few long strands of hair hanging off their scalps. But in other places they were quite hairy. They had rings of fur around their wrists and ankles. And they had extremely full pubic bushes, so even though they wore no clothing, there was the impression that their nakedness was covered by a pair of furry underpants. Actually, they did wear one article of clothing - a hat, much to small for their heads. This ridiculous item looked more than anything like a tiny flower pot perched atop their hairless domes. Their long noses hung like sausages over their top lips, and their eyes were beady and unintelligent. All of them were physically huge, with the physiques of football players, and each and every one of them had the same deformity of the arms and legs, the lower portion of which swelled out larger than the upper half in a bell-bottom manner. Thus they had huge hands and feet. They walked like apes, swinging their heavy arms side to side as they shuffled about.

On occasion a group of these women would come into our cell. Dad knew exactly what this meant and it sent him scurrying about like a rat looking for escape. All of his screams and cries were wasted on these brutes however. They easily cornered him, stripped him down and tied him, naked, to a cross. Then their "fun" began as they proceeded to degrade the old coot, poking and prodding him all over, in every soft spot and hole. They slapped his face until he blubbered, yanked on his dick, and fisted him with their massive arms, all the while cooing like a flock of pigeons. They seemed to have no interest in genital gratification at all. In fact, they exhibited no sign of emotion whatsoever. They approached my father's debasement as if it were the simplest everyday chore, and got no pleasure from it as far as I could tell.

At these times, I found my old sympathies for my father returning. After his torture I would nurse him back to health, and my childhood love for him would swell again. It was sad to see this mighty oak of a man reduced to a little gray mouse, and I did my best to make him strong again, even though I knew he would show me no gratitude. As soon as he was strong enough, my abuse resumed.

The most unpleasant thing about witnessing my father's mistreatment at the hands of the natives, was seeing him made subservient. After all, he was my father, and it didn't seem correct that he be put into the submissive role. That was my job, both as son and as jailhouse punk. Then it dawned on me, perhaps the island women did not torture me because they perceived me as female. My submissiveness to my father told them as much. I was, in a sense, one of them.

But, unlike them, I was truly female for I was a nurturer. This is why, despite the many reasons to not do so, I sought to help my father become well after his abuse at the hands of these "women." I had a biological imperative, an interior core of tenderness, that forced me to care for him. The women of this island were phallic women. Their war with my father was over symbolic power. Their's was a struggle to become the LAW. And I, as the only real woman on the island, was the prize in this game. Their whole existence became centered on taming the old patriarch. He was to be "pussy-whipped" at all costs. I then realized, it was my duty to strengthen him, to bolster his position of male power, and thus preserve pure and natural femininity as exemplified in me. Otherwise, "bad mothers" would take over. Their example would become the norm, and femininity would be forever spoiled, to be preserved in a perverted form. So, when my father was again strong, I approached him with the big question: I asked him to take me as his wife. "Forget," I said, "that cold woman who was your wife and my mother. Forget the surrounding hordes of phallic torturers. I will be your mate and I will bear you a child, and your power will live on through me, even after your downfall."

And, despite his father's cruelty, this child will be sweet and loving. I will make it so. This child will be the embodiment of love. This child will be the Messiah.

Kevin White.

Heliotropism

In a small bedroom late at night, Brooklyn is chewing on Cecile's shoulder, trying to put her in the mood. She feigns only a slight interest.

"Did you take a shower?"

When she asks this he stops and looks at her, somewhat hurt.

"What do you mean? Of course I took a shower, I took a shower an hour ago. Do I smell or something?"

His tone sounds defensive and just a little bit paranoid.

"Well, actually..." she adds, now a complete stranger to him, not even looking him in the eyes. "I don't know what it is, I don't usually smell foul, it's strange..."

At that point Brooklyn's mind seized up with anxiety, the nightmare was beginning. She was starting to pull away from him.

The next day Brooklyn goes out for a run, and ends up walking most of the time because he feels incredibly heavy and weak. He realizes that he has felt this way for years, but hadn't really paid it much notice. To him it always felt as if he was carrying some extra baggage. It was a constant state of his psychical being so familiar to him as to be almost non-existent. Cecile's comments, although indicative to Brooklyn of a much greater change in Cecile's perception of him, forced him into a violent confrontation with the issue of his own obesity.

He decides to go to the doctor, convinced that he is suffering from something other than weight gain. Cecile thinks he is crazy for thinking this, and grows increasingly disgusted with him, openly avoiding him.

Brooklyn goes to the doctor and tells him what he

thinks is wrong with him. The doctor is reluctant to do anything at all for Brooklyn, but Brooklyn convinces the doctor to give him a physical, analyze his blood, and take some x-rays. The doctor does these tasks, barely able to conceal his annoyance for Brooklyn, whom he regards as yet another over weight hypochondriac.

A couple of days later Brooklyn returns to the doctor's office for the results of the tests. There are six other men in the office besides the doctor, and Brooklyn quickly realizes that there is something really wrong. Everyone in the room is looking at Brooklyn with an expression of disbelief. Without saying anything the doctor turns out the lights and turns on the x-ray viewer.

The x-ray image looks like a poster for some modern dance company. An emaciated naked figure is holding a spastic pose that looks something like a diver springing out of a fetal position an instant before he strikes the water. This nebulous figure is superimposed over the figure of a man standing, with his arms down to his sides. The transparency is a brownish-yellow color.

Brooklyn steps towards the light table, looking closely at the face of the man in the strange pose. His father's corpse is wedged inside of his own body. None of the doctors know who it is that Brooklyn has inside of him and this thought makes him feel a little better, a little less self-conscious.

The doctors seem to be concerned for Brooklyn's health, they talk about operating to remove the corpse, they completely skip over the how and why of his condition. When they find out that Brooklyn does not have health insurance they decide to postpone operating indefinitely.

When he leaves the hospital he walks back to work through the park. Half way through the park is a small glen. Brooklyn sits on a bench on the edge of the glen, partially concealed within the forest canopy. His new psychical identity consumes his thoughts. It seems to him that his father, the new addition to his identity, is listening to his every thought, and every feeling.

Brooklyn goes through an intense rush of emotional pain every time he lets himself think about his present condition. This cripples him somewhat. He barely makes it back to his work, where he feigns sickness and leaves early. He shuffles slowly back to the apartment, getting there just as Cecile does. She manages a small smile for him, briefly, and then lets herself in, leaving the door open as she enters the apartment like some unwanted garment she is throwing behind her, to the ground.

When Brooklyn tells Cecile about his medical problem, she gets angry with him. She thinks that he is making up a stupid sick story and it pisses her off, she won't even look him in the face. He insists it is true.

"Call the doctors and ask them, they will show you the x-rays!"

He is pleading with her, as she readies to leave.

"What is wrong with you?! Huh? Why do you say stupid shit like this?! You're overweight and you smell! Deal with it!" she says, finally allowing herself to openly show real contempt and disgust for him.

After she angrily packs a bag and leaves him alone in the apartment, he sits in the living room and stares out the window, in shock. He tries to recall when, and how, he managed to get his father's corpse inside of his body. After a long while he concludes that it must have happened sometime shortly after his father's death six years earlier.

In his mind he travels back to that time. He sees his fathers funeral, and all of the relatives. He bends over to look into his father's casket, but he cannot fix on the image of his face, somehow he just cannot see it, it is almost as if his face were being purposely blurred, like they do on television. He looks for a long time at the fully clothed body inside the coffin. The whole image looks like it was projected onto glass. The idea of a faked representation of his dead father strikes him as being absurd.

He remembers being very thirsty later after the funeral. Back at the house, he drinks more than a gallon of water and falls asleep, feeling very bloated and heavy.

Brooklyn wakes up the next day and goes over to stay at his mom's house. He tells his whole family the new development in his life, and they prove to be very understanding. His grandmother offers to pay for the operation, to remove his father, saying that she has always hated his father, and she didn't see why Brooklyn should have to carry his corpse around inside of him.

His mom seems to be disgusted by the whole thing and his stepfather doesn't seem to care one way or the other.

The three operations take over a week, and he spends another three weeks in the hospital recovering. When he wakes up after the last operation he asks the doctor what they have done with his fathers corpse. The doctor tells him that they have "disposed" of it.

"Who gave you permission to throw away my father's body?"

Brooklyn tries to sound upset, but finds himself to be too sedated.

"Your mother signed the release form for the disposal of your father's corpse three days ago, I am sorry, I assumed you knew."

The doctor tells Brooklyn that they had to cut up his father's body into twelve sections to get it out of his. He describes, with as much emotion as one would use to describe the carving of a Thanksgiving turkey, the methodical dismemberment of his father.

The action of tearing apart his father's corpse has left Brooklyn in a lot of pain, for which he is prescribed copious pharmaceuticals, all of which make Brooklyn feel sick and unfocused.

Altogether it takes about two months for Brooklyn to completely recover. He is left with seven large scars. The longest scar, an eleven inch scar about an inch thick, stretches across his stomach just below his belly button. The pain, except for a little bit of lingering stomach pain, is all but gone by the time he leaves home to return to the city.

Brooklyn moves back to the city by himself, finding his own small place and getting work as a lifeguard at a public pool. He doesn't feel any lighter after the operation, and he still cannot manage to run very far, or very long.

After a while he gives up on the idea of running and switches to playing golf, which seems to require a lot less strain.

Brooklyn grows into a comfortable existence as a slightly overweight golfer, alone except for the occasional night out with his golfing buddies, and trips home to see the family. He stops thinking so much about his father, and the operation and begins to concentrates more on his own isolation.

A year after the operation Brooklyn runs into Cecile at the supermarket. She seems shocked to see him so self-confident and content. All of the self-conscious bitterness about life that she remembers in him, seeming to have disappeared.

She finds herself very attracted to his aloofness and he responds to her flirting automatically, as if it was some behaviorism he had learned and forgotten. They spend the whole weekend in his apartment getting re-acquainted, and talk constantly on the phone during the week. By the next week-end she has all but moved into his apartment.

They are back together, as if nothing had ever happened.

There is a certain lightness between them this time however, something that was not there before. It is as if any reason they might have had for disliking each other (before) had completely disappeared. She simply no longer found it necessary to ridicule him because of his weight, and he no longer pretended to be his father.

Motor Fleet Safety Supervision

hen I came home the hat was sitting on my pillow. Mom clanked somewhere out in the yard. She must have put it there while I was away, thinking it would be attractive to me. The pillow must have seemed an appropriate place to put it, to her mother's mind; she reasoned that since the pillow was a place where my head was kept for an uncertain amount of time nightly, that if she put the hat in that place exactly, then I would understand that I was supposed to put it on my head. I removed my shirt while keeping my eyes on the hat. It was a wool cap, the color of bark and leaves, resting slightly on the pillow. The bed was squat and low to the ground, covered in a quilt sewn together from pieces of other blankets. I felt the hat on my head, then pulled it off and held it to my face; the texture was rough and the wool tickled my nose with hundreds of small hairs, a vague shape under my eyes. A bit rougher than the hat on my pillow. It felt hand as opposed to machine-made. It smelled like oil and the sharp citrus of old insect repellent.

The old man died upstairs in my bedroom. He left his mark on it, in a quiet way that could be sensed as a feeling if you sat on the bed and were still for a while. It looked like the room of some old man. The ceiling was too low for me, and the floor slanting. The place where his bed had been was marked by four indentations rubbed into the floor by the bedframe's feet. My mother always slept in the guest room on the bottom floor, her old age not allowing her to get upstairs. Before she moved here, with my father, the old man had died suddenly of unknown things in his sleep. His wife then sealed off the

44

entire top floor with cardboard and trash bags, and the raccoons and ivy took it. When they broke through years later, there was a small tree growing in the hall, at the top of the stairs, some thready sapling sucking up the powdery inside light. The whole bottom floor had grown a fungus of garbage piled in drifts. After they took the woman away they looked behind the kitchen door and found the old man's teeth and fingernails, glued to cracking paper, an entire set of teeth glued in yellow caulk (perhaps they had been dentures), and the nails from ten fingers and ten toes. I kept my own nail clippings in a little jelly jar hidden carefully in the wall.

My mother got jealous when my friend Sue gave me the hat, which she had made herself. Mom tried to distract me from it with the other hat. Sue's came in the mail, wrapped in tissue inside an eleven by fourteen manila envelope. A note told me that Sue had made it with my head in mind, and I thought of this when I wore it, the thicker band around the bottom not as tight as it should have been and flared out like the bell of a trumpet. The wool was itchy, even through a thick head of hair. I wore this hat when it was warm outside and the little hairs of the wool seemed to poke through my skull. It did not absorb sweat.

Once, a little girl ran up to me in a park. She had been frightened by something and was crying, and she mistook me for her father. Her little arms wrapped around my thigh, she wailed and the her face was shiny with tears. Words tried to form themselves in her mouth, to name the bad thing, but she couldn't speak. When I didn't move, she looked up at me and our eyes met. Her small face frozen like a photograph of someone laughing. A thread of drool stretched from a damp spot on my leg to the corner of her mouth. She stopped crying abruptly, just let go and ran in the other direction, and my hat fell on the ground.

I picked up the new hat from where it sat on my pillow. It was old and stiff and a fume of mothball smell escaped from it and made my eyes squint. My mother chopped at the weeds in the yard with a bent knife tied to the end of a broomhandle. She used to pull weeds with her hands, when her back could still bend. When I was a was younger I would help her, down there with her on my hands and knees, listening to the roots as they popped and broke. During these times the tedium changed and felt important. The bucket was an old aluminum one that could have worked as a hat, if it weren't so big, but as it was it only rested its rim on your shoulders and made things sound hollow. The bucket was usually full of dirt and weeds. When I peed in it just to see what would happen she saw me do it and talked to me for a while about proper places that had been set aside to urinate in; now the bucket is flattened under the woodpile. Her knifeblade cuts neatly the tops of bright green weeds but leaves the roots behind, undisturbed. Every once in a while the broomhandle will swing up and back to her shoulder, and rest, while she stares straight ahead for a while into some memory.

This morning when the yellow light shot through the window and woke me, Sue's hat was gone. Just the empty space where it had been, the dust on the top of the dresser gone in a ring where the hat's brim had sat, and that was all. I opened the dresser drawer where I had hidden the one that my mother left for me on the pillow. It fit too tightly, squeezing my head and insisting that it was a poor substitute. I pulled on the clothing from the day before and went outside to confront my mother.

She was lounging in a chair behind a giant rosebush. The black dog named Fish was napping beside her, and when I approached it opened one eye to watch me. Fish looked stumpy. He was one of those dogs that show up from unknown places and decide to stay. He looked as if he'd been kept in a small box during his puppy years and not allowed to grow properly. His legs were too short, and his head too big, and his body too barrel-chested, and a huge bag of testicles dangled and knocked between his knees. When he was younger he was a passionate dog, and killed many cats, but he was allowed to stay for some unspecified reason. He would chase and catch them with strange speed, and shake them to death, his scrotum swinging. My mother's legs were stretched out before her and her hands hung loosely at her sides, a book called Motor Fleet Safety Supervision rested beneath one hand, on the ground. I had no idea where the book came from. Her head lay on her shoulder at the end of her bent neck, the mouth was slack, a small drip of spittle hung at the corner. After I had said Mother three times, she awoke slowly, and then peered at me in a sleepy way. Her fingers twitched above the book, and her eyes looked quickly down at it. She was realizing that the book was out in the open, where anyone could see it, and this seemed to bother her. I reached down and picked it up. It was hardbound, blue, with large, blocky yellow letters on the

cover. She seemed very uncomfortable about my handling of the book, but she didn't try to prevent me from
seeing it. She looked away, and fingered the wooden arm-
rest of the chair. She studied the yellow side of the house
next door. I thumbed through the book. It was all about
managing commercial vehicles, such as delivery trucks,
with an emphasis on safety. On the cover was printed the
claim that it was the first book of its kind, published in
1967. My mother had risen. She took the book out of my
hands and tucked it under her arm as if it was a newspaper. Fish looked up and blinked at us through the white
gum in his eyes. Mom patted his head, which made a
thump sound under her hand. The dog's neck gave way
under each blow, and his eyes squeezed to thin slits that
made small bulbs of mucous ooze. She squeezed my
shoulder with the same hand that had been used to pat
Fish, and I tried to search her out with my eyes, looking
for some clue. I asked her about the hat. She scratched
around in her thoughts for a moment, then began to
speak about the necessity of hats, and the good places to
wear them, certain areas for men to wear hats and certain
ones for women. Women could wear hats most anywhere,
because a nice lady's hat was an attractive thing to have
on one's head, something with a wide brim, maybe a
feather. Women had the right to almost unlimited hat-
wearing, whereas men were disallowed from wearing hats
indoors. There was a powerful and ancient reason for
this, one which she could not quite remember. However,
the danger here went far beyond bad luck, and we should
never forget or be flippant about such serious matters.
She gave this information slowly, as if she were trying to

make a small, simple-minded child understand her. After she went inside I never saw the book again.

The socks came a few months later. Sue had made these as well. They came with a piece of paper wrapped around them like newspaper around a fish. It was a note that said they were to be worn with the hat, to keep it company. They were the color of red leaves. Sue must have knitted slowly, working not with appearances in mind but instead focusing on how fully the thing she was making would fulfill its practical purpose in someone's life. Its strong construction and ultimate usefulness were her main concerns. Only as an accident did the objects become beautiful. They seemed to be self-confident. They were beautiful in an absolutely secure way. They said: fuck you, in your plastic-spun fibers, slug. When I wore the hat it appeared to be not so much a hat as some result of advanced scalp evolution that had grown up out of my head in order to keep it warm. It looked like it was supposed to be there. When I wore the socks at the same time as the hat, some sort of invisible circuit was completed that made me feel especially pleasant.

Not long after the socks arrived, my mother began to show a little preoccupation with undergarments. I think socks can be considered undergarments, and so did she; about five pairs of woolen socks appeared in my drawer reserved for underwear. Sometimes alone, sometimes in wads, they were included casually in the drawer as if they had always been there. They snaked around under boxer shorts and lay on top of them limply. I was usually wearing the original pair of socks and they never stopped itching. I thought that, over time, the itchiness would become less noticeable as the tiny wool fibers were bent and flattened and glued down with wax from the my legs and feet. This was not the case. They were hearty socks, and refused to be aged. After a while they began to feel as if they were growing into my legs and becoming new soles on the bottoms of my feet. The parts of the socks that touched the insides of my shoes and the ground became thinner and tough. So far my mother's decoy-socks had been unworn.

Around this time she seemed to notice her own footwear more often, the house slippers that had come to be bleached white with age like old wood left in the desert and reduced to porous bone shapes of what it had been. She was constantly fingering her feet through holes in the slippers, which she carefully enlarged with small sticks. Her underwear became a distraction for her, and she dealt with this by leaving them behind her on the ground, pulling them out of her dress and impatiently over her shoes. She did not wear stockings. The streetcleaner had begun to scare her. I was reading a book on the front porch, she was fondling some azaleas near the sidewalk that ran in front of the house. The streetcleaner was a block away, vibrating, brushing the street like a carpet steamer, shooting hot steam onto it, then scrubbing, then vacuuming. Mostly in the gutter. The pretty layers of oak-leaves that had assembled there, much like small rocks on the bottoms of streambeds, would all be gone, sucked away. As the noise became louder my mother cocked her head suddenly while grabbing an azalea. She squeezed the flower gently between the thumb and the tips of her fingers, watching it as it sprung back elastically each time she compacted it. Her head drifted to a tilt towards the left and all her movement stopped for a moment. Then she walked slowly away from the hissing, as if she needed to move in that direction anyway, but I could see beneath the skin of her face a little suppressed terror. Later she would not discuss the streetcleaner. She said *what?* each time I tried to ask her about it in a new way that might get through. I always had to be careful in my wordings of things because of the fact that she would frequently mis-understand me, running as fast as she could in the wrong direction, meaning away from whatever we had been talking about, focusing on some insignificant word that she misunderstood and which now demanded all of her attention. I might say something like: the display of prizewinning large vegetables was interesting, I guess, but the people who grew this stuff weren't there, so it seemed like the huge zucchini especially just sort of happened, on its own, without the help from an actual person, a real dirty gardener... and I'd go on about how much I admired folks who were so dedicated to their craft as to make things so big that they served no real purpose, but she would stop listening at the point where I had said dirty, and repeat the word over and over to herself for a time, dirty dirty dirty dirty, and shake her head, and look at me accusingly and a little hurt, thinking that I had meant dirty in a bad way, and then I'd have to spend the next five minutes convincing her that I didn't mean dirty in that way, and by that time the mood would be gone, the story having become limp and tiresome.

I found my mother naked. She was standing in the middle of the living room, next to a brown leatherette chair that reclined. She was looking out the front window, the kind that they call a picture window when they are trying to sell houses. There was a bath towel in her hand. She stared out at some people on the opposite sidewalk who had just emerged from a church. There were two older women in dresses and hats with little girls, one each, also in dresses, tugging and swinging on the older women's dresshems. The two women were discussing something, each holding the wide brim of a pretty straw hat that shaded her head from the sun. Then they finished their conversation, and parted, each walking in the other direction, each followed by a little girl. I looked at my mother. Her blank expression did not change. She was still as the furniture around her. Her skin was bright white with dark blue leaf-veins; wrinkled and sagging, all the elastic was gone. Her bottom drooped loosely, transparent hair poked out from beneath her underarms. The skin on her face was a soft bag that did not seem to be holding her head together very well. Her nose was pointy, like mine, but a little smaller and whiter. I went into her room to get some kind of clothing for her, and came back with a nightgown. I slipped it over her head and it fell easily down around her, trapping her arms. She stood there, in a cotton tube. I put my face directly in front of her and peered into her eyes, which seemed to notice me and focus, the little diaphragms shrinking, but still she did not move, or speak. I took her hand and led her to her bedroom, even though it was only early afternoon. The room smelled like it was being held together with dried saliva. I lifted the covers up for her and she got under them.

The yard in back of the house was once a garden that was a huge vibrating and throbbing green thing with flowers and many-leafed tentacles, where a small army of dogs had been buried. Whip, the oldest dog, was the first to be planted. There is a brown photograph in a little gold painted frame propped up with a deck of cards on the dresser in my mother's room. In it my mother and father are standing over a low table on which lies Whip, covered in some pale flowers and ivy. Around this sit other dogs, panting and slobbering. In the photograph there seems to be not much sadness at the funeral. My mother is smiling, using her young muscles, long before the whiskers and spots appeared on her face. Her smile seems to be something that had settled on her mouth after saying some clever words. Whip's head lies slightly tucked in toward his front legs, his eye open and glossy, having caught some shard of light in the photograph. She seemed to be imitating the photograph now, curled up on her side in the bed. She mumbled something about her brother, my uncle Eli, who had had a stroke and forever after was only able to say the word damn. In reply to any question, he'd answer with damn, and he'd sit in bed and sort of stammer the word to himself. A bad stroke must be like a frost that falls suddenly and jells your last thoughts or words, keeping you trapped in some moment that has long since past. He would visit when I was a child, before he was old and confined to a bed. Whenever he went through a door he would say okay to himself, the word carried on an exhalation of breath, sort of like he was resigning himself to a repeated and unavoidable experience. As if he was always about to jump into a very cold lake. He'd say it after a short intake of air, and then let it come out with the used breath. I saw his fat body of stinky old man skin falling through doorways and breaking pointy-sided holes in thin crusts of ice and dropping slowly through fathoms of water so cold it had become black syrup. I looked again at the photo of the dog's burial. Uncle Eli hated all dogs. One of them, a gangly blue hound with a long body, had decided that Eli should get extra love, and made it a point to hover around him and lick any exposed skin, in spite of the fact that he told it to go to hell. The hound seemed to become more encouraged by each of Eli's rejections. Once Eli kicked it when he thought that no one was looking, putting the point of his blunt foot in its ribcage. The dog just whined quietly. I saw this from rear of the yard, where I was involved in some kid's plan. I never told anyone about what I saw. I assumed that it was something that would be better left untold, and I thought that in the telling I would somehow become involved in the actual violent act. Eli was frustrated at fate's choice of words for him to repeat indefinitely, but a little satisfied at the same time, because the word suited this frustration. I thought that, in his brain, a little piece of lint had gotten stuck just after damn, making the needle jump back again and again to amplify the same sound. The word was getting fainter, worn out. Each time he spoke it was softer. Soon his mouth would open, and instead of noise, little puffs of dust would come out.

I got down on my hands and knees and looked under the bed. There was a small bank of stale bread crusts mixed with dust balls, and my hat. I took the hat, leaving the dry things alone, and left the room, because my mother had fallen asleep.

Alexis Hall

No Sweetness Here

The syrup was pale brown, contained in a recycled plastic jar. Scrawled in what the men of the family had adopted - permanent shaky hand, were the words 'syrope simple'. I took the blue cap off. I stuck my finger in and licked, licked. This was supposed to be liquid sugar. No sweetness here. This phrase was to stick with me for twelve long days. I sniffed for alcohol, not a trace. Some can be deceptive. Vodka is practically odorless - stop! I threw the bottle down with a thud - my job is not to be an interrogator of old men on the brink of death. If he wants to get up at five in the morning and move pots, shuffle around with a champagne bottle, what right did I have to deny him? Old and tottering my grandfather had grown even meaner than my memories had allowed. I grabbed several odd shaped lumps of sugar and wished they were gold that I had been putting away, a pile of golden nuggets. But what would sweeten my coffee - the liquid which counteracted the effects of my tranquilizers...When I arrived he had only instant, single servings, Nescafe, atrocious to my mind. Even more atrocious was to be in France, less than an hour from Paris, in culinary heaven and eat frozen food. I didn't touch it on principle. Sometimes I refused to eat at all while othertimes I threw together the contents of jars with a grudge. Canned artichokes - normally a decadence, were spat on in my mind. Processed. Vulgar. I couldn't stand it any more.

Subtly, to my mind, after five days of such eating and two days without dinner - a vague protest which didn't even get any attention - I suggested that we go out to taste the neighborhood food. A simple village meal. Let's go where the farmers go. Let's eat like the peasants. I'll throw on my overalls, romp in the mud as an apéritif. I walked for hours wanting to be anything wanting to be a farmer wanting to live in a small house work hard and lounge around the French countryside moaning about the crops.

But a digression: I asked in the sweetest voice possible, "Do you think we might be able to try some of the local food while I'm here? Nothing fancy, the most provincial...I'll treat. I would just like to taste something besides my own cooking." I was already nauseated by my own ingratiating tone. I yawned and almost didn't even finish the thought.

"It would be hard to find a place where the village people go. They are smart and eat at home. Restaurants are too expensive. They go out one night a year to celebrate. No, the villagers are smart - they are thrifty. We have to be thrifty."

I cut him off. I like to think that he was shocked by my dismissal. I didn't want to hear his phony theories of the end: the world economy drowning on false currency, no one with a savings account or a shred of morality, all proven quite effectively by the lack of dining out on the part of the farmer. Yes, time's were hard. The end was coming. He was glad he wouldn't be alive to see the havoc this culture created...I cut him off mid-stream shaking my head rather nodding it as if I'd heard it a million times - the oldest cliché in the world. As tired as: wear clean panties...don't swim after eating...that which doesn't kill you...wine clears the blood(his favorite)...a penny saved...I rolled my eyes, packed a book, a flashlight, a

Dictaphone, a scarf, heavy sunglasses, thick jacket. I gathered all these things quickly. He was microwaving a vegetable or wrapping string. With my thick glasses on, I beat it.

"Please don't wait for me for dinner. I'm not hungry." He just nodded okay and continued with his task of heating the internal life out of that artichoke. Of course he had already basked it in lemon concentrate.

I walked through the village with vigor. Never before had I had so much energy. I had never been so alive with anger. My limbs seized with it and then I did something frightening. With my glasses on and a scarf hiding my hair - masking my already insignificant and unknown identity, I began to gesticulate with my arms. And then I heard a voice raspy, a voice which wanted to fight and didn't fight fair: "Oh yeah, you old man. Take your dirty old pans hauled over from Long Island. Take that and your diluted water, your rubber band collection, frozen entrees - take them all and stuff them up your ass! You don't have any friends except the ones you buy. This isn't about ambivalence anymore, old man, oh no we have strayed from that. That requires some bit of love and you offer none. My feelings are dead, cold like your heart or the money you sleep with. The same chill blood barely pumps to our limbs. Cold, cold and mean. *You ought to have a baby from a sperm bank. Having children is nothing people make it out to be special but one's born every second. Women used to lean against a tree and push it out. Those babies are fine and the women have saved fifteen hundred dollars...Art is dead. Real artists know how to paint hands. Look for the real artist by the hands. Practice makes perfect*

Art is dead. Only a bunch of tricksters left. Friends of the curator. One big ugly teeming incestuous scene - and none of them can paint hands! Not one of them has the least bit of talent!

My ranting stopped despicably. I couldn't draw hands or noses and I too had complained about the phenomena known as "couples shows". The same group of lovers, in the same show, different name, spouting post-modern bullshit. And none of them can draw hands. How I want to be a couple and refer to thoughts by "we". "We went to the store...We thought it was going to be... " How quickly I would adopt that pronoun, that plurality, and shed in one fluid moment that brassy "'I'". The dark side of subjectivity could be flung off as easily as a silk rain coat. I, walking in this field, arms raised, have too much of the excess - too much I, a team of ME's. A team that is against me. My brain is not my friend. It thinks of ways to torment me. If I was in a couple, the sum of the parts bigger than the whole, then I would have an external source to argue with. Then I could be calm, relaxed in my fight for sanity. But now I have these parts, very interesting, never a dull moment- battling among themselves. Parts which require all of me. But all of this is totally besides the point. That I happen to agree with him separately for different reasons regarding the art world doesn't mean that we are of the same mindset.

"I really wanted to come to France to eat canned foods. I wanted to come to watch you penny pinch and raise your finger at me - *do you want to take the next train back, young lady? Do you?!'* Yes! I would be delighted to never see your face again. See, this is not ambivalence. I see through it all to your mean heart. To your rotten string pulling and it won't work. Take it and shove it up your ass, your ass, your ass!"

Once again I am struck with shock. Last night we fought about Di and Charles's maid writing a tell all book. I was outraged. She had no right to publish such a book. She was paid well for her privacy.

He said, "Why can't she? Perhaps she was treated badly."

"Well then she shouldn't have taken their money. She could have walked away. Why write to humiliate them? Is she that broke, morally? She could have at least threatened them or tried extortion before airing their dirty laundry." I was adamant. If she had been in the living room I would have strangled her - taken her head, short tight curls, sipping champagne - and bashed it against the stone fireplace. I would have. I found my face red and angry, my heart tightening and this isn't a good way to go out - irate about a tattle-tale maid.

He had cleared his throat and continued, suddenly mister softy, "Employees have the right to tell all. They shouldn't be expected to be loyal. Families should keep silent. Families should show loyalty."

I cringed. Looking back to see if anyone had heard me yelling as I paced, ranting... looking back at these pages- utter proof of my lack of loyalty, my desire to tell all of the most banal gripping details to anyone that would listen- to the wind. Can you hear me wind? I can't paint hands and I hate him.

I would write a tell all book. I would even stretch the truth a little to make myself look better. I would admire the form, laugh at my own jokes. I appreciate every detail, notice every indentation and intonation. Nothing passes me by. I am there to amaze myself. I ruminate on word plays and the awkward tension created by none other. When it is really bad I say "what a feat to make something that appears to be so bad, what a wonderful thing to pull off. What subtlety that takes. What a hard thing to master!" But now the applause has stopped abruptly and the work has shown itself naked and ugly for what it is. No longer cute no longer under that bright spotlight which washes out wrinkles and puffy eyes we are in Bloomingdale's now in the changing room trying on bathing suits. Every dimple and pocket once seen as curvaceous and lovely take my breath away. Is this me? These mirrors must be mistaken, pebbled to cause insecurity. Fluorescent lights posit me in harsh reality. I can not escape the honest glare that stares at me, pointing to my death really. I accelerate in time and see myself wishing for those saggy thighs because all of the fat is gone. I've shriveled up, wasted away. I've been buried alive.

Mitchell Watkins

Speed

hilip was the scion of Palmetto's wealthiest family – a disadvantage he had worked zealously to overcome. With an entymologist's discerning eye he surrounded himself with the most malevolent specimens the town afforded, commuting to the slum-ringed city when this limited supply proved inadequate. Consequently he had crammed an inordinate amount of artistic experience into his years, being the first of our gang to catch VD, the first to do time, the one whose drug consumption was the standard all ours were measured against and humbled, took their leave.

But a couple of years had passed, and as fate had it I ran into Philip on a street corner in Los Angeles, three thousand miles from the state of our birth, the thirteenth of the original union, fifth of that second nobler and brief union. A face from home was a friendly face, history aside, and in the jet saucers of his dilated pupils I detected a reciprocity of this goodwill. So I had agreed to drive him out to an amphetamine lab in the desert, what I envisioned to be a favor substantial enough to smooth over past misunderstandings and allow me to bow out forever on a good note.

On the appointed day I met him at the arranged apartment, at the agreed-upon hour. He carried a pair of duffel bags whose menacing bulges left no dispute as to their contents. Accompanying him was a large hunchback who was introduced as Dave. "He's just for in case things go wrong," Philip reassured me, and shaking his hand, I was impressed by the massive pythons of muscle squirming beneath his forearm's tattooed foliage.

Once in the car my two passengers' furtive glances

quickly escalated into a frantic search underneath the seats, into the AC vents, the compartment, anywhere else there might be bugs or cameras. As it was explained to me, the DEA had stormed their apartment in a sting operation the previous night. They found drugs and guns, as well as the five thousand dollars entrusted to Philip for today's purchase, yet miraculously had left as abruptly as they entered. "Fucking unbelievable luck," Philip concluded, and my eyes embarked on what would by the day's end become a well-worn path from road to rear-view mirror.

"So I got to take you to this Mexican bakery down on Beverly. They sell Valiums, Clonopins, Quaaludes, all that shit over the counter. You have to know what to say, but I'm cool. They're only like a dollar each." He reaches into his pocket, dry-gulps the two horse pills he's pulled out.

"You got to check out this thing I'm working on." He unzips one of the bags on the floor. A banana clop flops out.

"Keep that stuff put up while we're on the road. Why'd you bring those anyway?"

"Oh shit, no I mean this," he retrieves a tattered spiral-bound and zips the bag back up. "And those are for, well, I mean, you never know what can happen at these places. You know, all those psycho biker types. I saw 'Pulp Fiction' a couple of nights ago, and man I'm not taking any chances. Here, look at this," he says, holding the steering wheel so I can devote all attention to the microscopic diagrams and text cramming the notebook's soiled sheets. "No, it's not the Necronomicon, it's the perfect city. I designed it — the...perfect...city. It's all here." His voice hints at, then snowballs into hysteria, leaping octaves with each word, higher, faster, "highways, sewers, transportation, all supply and demand." Try hard as I may, skepticism still leaks out of my face, and he grabs the notebook out of my hands and thrusts himself back onto the seat, exasperated. "Well, it beats this shit."

I share a childhood invention. "Check this out. I designed a ski lift, but at the top, a scythe swings down and decapitates the occupants. Then it dumps them and they fall into a big pit. OK, forget it."

Dave, having nodded off, snaps alert in the back. Indeed, it is only the back that is awake, the cerebellum, that reptilian legacy responsible for smooth muscle control and decisions no more evolved than fight or flight, the part of the brain just up and behind the back of the throat that good suicides aim for. He and Philip commence to argue over lost keys, narcs, and whether or not drugs will be legalized in the perfect city.

It is there I drift off too, daydreaming of all the world-encompassing egocentric schemes generated by the weak, the addicted, and the insane. I find Philip's relatively unambitious, or perhaps my imagination of it is such. Life proceeds as normal, with but a few notable exceptions. Showers of grief-stricken girls imperil the traveler, should his route lead under any edifice of a height substantial enough for these jilted lovers to end their misery from. Cheated landlords and innkeepers leave lodgings exactly as they were, preserved with the same adoration parents show for the rooms of dead children. Innumerable churches and cathedrals have sprung up to house the relics dropped during his wanderings—cigarette butts, blackened spoons, and so on.

"You know I'm six circuits old?" Dave queries, jostling me back.

"No, I didn't."

"Yea, a circuit's longer than a whole lifetime. It's getting clean in prison, coming out, getting thin again, and getting so fucked up you do something stupid and go back. I get jobs in the kitchen, so I eat well, lift weights, you should see me right when I've come out. It's a whole new life."

"So technically, you haven't completed the present circuit, right?"

"Yea."

"And so each circuit is a new existence, a new life? I mean, wouldn't that put you pretty close, parallel to your actual age in years?"

Philip chimes in, "Or even a lot younger, like a baby! You're two years old." He continues on, and this taunting begins to make me feel vulnerable, a feeling concentrated in the section of my neck exposed between the seat-top and headrest. I realize by Dave's unswaying gaze that I am to be held accountable for instigating this turn in the conversation, no matter how antagonizing Philip becomes. More importantly, while listening to them argue I begin to suspect that Philip does not know Dave neither very well nor very long. Philip abruptly ceases berating and after a moment feebly bleats out, "Those pills are fucking me up. I...can't...feel...my...face."

Still we head deeper into the desert. I have always interpreted the hard look indigenous to Westerners as the product of generations of failure, their ancestors not pioneers so much as fugitives, seeking in each new frontier, be it Tennessee, then the Mississippi, buffaloed plains, and finally desert, the prosperity and comfort denied them. My pet theories aside, I just never could understand how someone could journey thousands of miles to the promised Pacific and then stop a hundred or so shy and say I'm not going any further, I'll live in this goddam desert. Maybe it was gold or something, I just don't know.

An hour or so passes until Dave instructs me to exit the highway. Dave is the one with the directions, as the lab operators are friends of his. Philip has never been out here, or for that matter ever met these people who are going to give him such a good deal.

We drive through a town, and through twists and turns convoluted wind up in front of a one-story stucco house, indistinguishable from all the others lining the streets of this quiet neighborhood. I drop the two of them off along with their bags, Dave supporting a limp and disoriented Philip on his shoulder, and drive up the street to wait at Taco Bell as per Dave's instructions. Parting, he assures me that it will only take five minutes.

Five minutes is about the length of time I maintain my fragile inconspicuousness at Taco Bell; for the remaining hour and twenty-five minutes I weather the increasingly hostile and suspicious glares of the employees. Watching the people come and go it dawns on me just how large a role meth plays in these places. Mike Davis or one of those guys said something about it being the major source of revenue for desert towns. Of particular interest was a couple and their nine or tenish son, whose eyes hinted at intelligence and curiosity. The father had ugly purple tracks along his neck, and looking at the kid, I thought: intelligence is by nature self-destructive. Avid reading fosters reticence in a child, for each situation stirs redolently of a thousand others, and such limitless possibility cannot be smitten by a wisdom age has yet to provide. Of this comes the introvert, for when this reticence draws upon him the scorn of his peers, he will curse this innate diffidence, and here commence the black hours of soul-searching and self-dialogue. Yes, I realized looking at him that intelligence is self-destructive. Thankfully I have avoided this pitfall altogether.

Finally they come in, Dave, with what could pass as his twin. Philip is not with them.

"Hey, what's up? Sorry we took so long, uh, this is my pal. Call him Harmless, 'cause he's anything but! Ha!" The two high-five and giggle.

Harmless speaks up. "Phil's back at the house, we were out and had to funnel him to another place. But he's back, he's waiting there for you. You want to get your car?"

No two ways about it, Harmless gives me the creeps. It's like seeing someone and instantly realizing that your ancestors have fought, and generations upon generations will be shamed should you not take up the grudge.

"You know, I'll wait here. Go get Philip and bring him back. I've got to get out of here ASAP, um, people are waiting for me."

Dave stares at me, trying hard to conceal his irritation. "Huh. Alright, then why don't you wait here with

Harmless while I go get him," he says standing, agitated, and walks out, finishing his sentence from in front of the window beside our seat.

"Damn man, you've pissed him off. So what do you do?" Harmless asks.

Now worried for my well-being as well as Phil's, I think for a moment for something to say that would be significantly intimidating, something truly bad ass that would strike fear into his heart— a mercenary? A communist?

It came to me suddenly, the answer which would assure him of my desperation. "I'm a poet," I chirped, and as I saw his countenance briefly darken I knew that the ruse had worked, and he was indeed afraid.

"Really?"

"No, well not really. Actually I study military history."

"Oh, OK, that's cool," he says, obviously relieved. "I do too, not real serious, but you know. You like the South?"

"Would I be wearing this Confederate buckle if I didn't?"

"Is that real?"

"Hell no, it's just a replica. I been metal detecting battlefields and campsites for ten years trying to find a real one, though. I'm from Palmetto, south of Atlanta."

"Really? No shit! I'm from Columbia, South Carolina."

"The mother of secession?"

"Damn right!" Harmless howls, glancing furtively out the window. Motioning me to bend down he leans across the table. "Look, let's go out and get in your car and we'll go to this bar where we can talk privately. But we've got to go now, alright?"

I am happy to leave, and on the way there, we talk of Sherman's barbarity and Grant's brutal operational strategy. To my great delight Harmless listens patiently to my spiel about the parallels between the Army of Northern Virginia and the Viet Cong.

"Oh, sorry to interrupt, here, turn left." We pull into a mini-mall. "Just park in any spot." I stop and turn off the car, noticing that there are no bars around.

"Look. I'm not going to let you go down with your friend. He's a fuck-up, so big deal? You're better than that."

"He's not going to make it, is he?"

"No. He's already gone. You're the only loose end."

I see the parlor of his parents' house in Palmetto, the framed pictures sitting on the piano. "It was a damn fool idea to come out here, huh?"

"You almost got yourself killed, son. For nothing. Money."

In the gap of silence I vainly try to conjure up the patron saint of fucked-up situations, Andrei Vlasov, the Soviet general who, captured near Leningrad and facing certain starvation in a POW camp, formed and led the Russian Liberation Army, fighting alongside the Germans against Stalin. Of course, he was hung from a meat hook in Red Square after being repatriated by the Americans at the end of the war, so his advice always has to be tempered with discretion. On this day, though, he is silent.

"Get out of here, man. I've got to go back to the Taco Bell," he says, getting out.

"I won't forget this, Harmless."

He stops and looks back. "This is one goddam thing

you'd better forget all about." The door shuts.

I sit for a minute, knowing that later, it will be necessary to remember having done so, paused that is, when I dream, or write about it, this my last and greatest betrayal. Then I crank the car and drive back to the freeway, where I, like the settler, left my misery behind me in the East, and headed towards the ocean, further and further away from the bleached bones which even now lie indicting me from the shifting sands of the desert.

Catherine Sullivan

The Red Perils of
Voluminous Green

ff the bus and onto the beach, I feel kind of strong once again. Yes, I've found a spot near the lake where I can lay my towel down and show the suckers, show all the Uncles and Aunts what a real hard try is, what a girl with cancer does on a Saturday at the lake when all she needs is some sun a little Vitamin D to soothe the swelling kneecaps that keep her walking day after day. Off the bus and onto the beach, I'm spreading my towel out and it's hard. A hospital walk is only railing to railing, bed to toilet, toilet to wheelchair to railing. I'm not used to this, but the feeling is good, I know I can do it, I can set my chair up by myself. I do it happily, anticipating all of this swimming and sun. Hot sand blows in my mouth and burns the bottoms of my feet, but I can take it, everyone knows I can hang on! I laughed at the nurses as they gave me their warnings, I ran far away as their voices tapered off. The voices of sick kids made me run faster, "forget the nurses" they told me, "you can play it, you can walk tough, you're our Bubblegum and Bones, we're sending you out, to have some fun, we know you can do the day alone."

The cancer kids back at the death room are thinking about getting it together, and they've singled me out because I won't wear my "MAKE A WISH" ball cap. "I've got no use for a star and a rainbow, I prefer the pentagram, the axe!" They like the way my chemo wig fringes over my ears, the way I cut it, blunt, just above the nape of my neck. For this, they've made me their leader, a mascot with a say-so, an emblem - hunched, sickly, dangerous. They follow the aloof posture of my illness and mimic my words - heavy with insight, hot with bad grammar. We're black with cancer, in all parts of the body - in our eyes, noses and tails. My cancer is the fastest, so every smoke or step I take inspires them, but lately things have gotten very bad. The pain gets worse and I beat my bedpan, I pound out slow dull rhythms and no one listens, neoprene nurses work their shifts, take their turns. The pain is strong, I fall and they wake me. Their nicotine fingers are fresh and extended from a late coffee break. Punching in, punching out, they don't care if it hurts and it kills me, there is no consolation so I thirst for a bloody revenge.

Here on the beach I'll greet the sun, the source of my cancer. Alone on the beach I'll try to release the pain into a laugh or maybe a nice little swim. The kids chose me because I've been around the longest, I've earned my sick house schoolyard seniority. The kids are extreme and they like my fast cancer, they know, "You don't mess with Bubblegum and Bones, don't you mess with her cancer, don't you mess with her disease!" Bubblegum and Bones is at the beach! Bubblegum and Bones found a place for her towel! Bubblegum and Bones forgot her shoes today, but like a swift little vagrant she worked it out with two french-fry trays and some bikini string.

Now I'm a powdery kid in a nice pair of sandals and as I troddle by the people, like vultures they squat into position covering their sore and scaly asses with cocoa butter and burying their feet in the sand. It's getting darker in this hot place, but I'm blinded by the glimmer from white teeth that peck and lick on tinfoil fried chicken held hot and greasy in the hands. Tender flesh pulls away from bones bubblegum-easy, oh, how they'd love to get their claws into me! They look at my thin silhouette, they see it skulking, yes, I'm a mean kid and I've got them drooling, the sky is a luminous green and they hunger for a sacrifice. Someday they'll have me, at some point I'll let them do it but they'll only get a taste of blood from the end of my chain of command!

I pass and my strut is getting weaker, it's pure aspiration, a force too tough to manage. I need to catch my breath and sit down. I'm thankful for this towel, but it does me no good because I've picked a bad spot. I'm paralyzed with panting, and the sun is gripping down. My umbrella won't open, its telescope parts are stuck together, held firmly in place with soft grains of sand. I was minty-fresh a minute ago, but now my blood thickens into an oily slick. I've got what it takes to watch and wait, but dammit I want to do it from a shady place. The pole moves little as I grasp and pull, finally I get it, falling on the towel in the shade. Surprisingly, I'm composed as I complete the final trick.

The heat works up a sandy haze, I've mastered all of this moving and pain. It's time to toast leisure's commencement with a cigarette. I blow my smoke hard in a low tar salute to some Italian sisters I knew at age three. I watched them in long skirts, earrings and little curly haircuts, in the cold on a cobblestone road, smoking tobacco rolled big as Daddy's finger. Little suckers, I knew I could be tougher. At the playground, I'd take a drag and prop my leg up on the sandbox, looking kind of worldly in my polka-dot cap. Blunt teachers with nimble rulers saw me there, powerful, but never smacked my fingers knowing that Bubblegum and Bones was bellicose and sick, something for sure to fear.

Smoking and thinking always takes me to hacking, but this sign of my passing isn't a vex. I know I'll get my cakes and ale. I know that when the bubblegum really starts to fall off the bones, the kids'll put me in a tight box, dig a hole, and throw me in. They'll bury a unit, no ashes to sprinkle and scatter! I don't want to be everywhere, a part of all things, spinning out of stinkiness, randomly rubbing off on the next generation of kids. I'm not happy with tiny rubbings, never to know one another. I'm after something centrifugal, the flip side of a dispersal - because dying is too much like a minor sneeze. I'm trying to have fast fun with my fast cancer, for the kids. I want them to know that I was smiling when I made my last little "achoo".

Spring and sunshine took my hacking to laughing, ah, it's such fun to hold my lacy kerchief. I giggle, I dab at innocent mucous falling on my pale yellow towel. It's such fun to mop up the piles of voluminous green. In the shade of my umbrella, the sun tickles under, I'm ready to give over to a hot white daydream. But I smell pizza and can see it dripping, served up by two tall orders - volleyball people with bronze auras and long legs. Walking tall, carrying hot plates, their shadows pass over. I peak out, squint and crouch beneath the eclipse. At the net, they bend and sit on white terrycloth stiff with a dried Coppertone funk. How great they are in rubber thongs and mirrored glasses - the unkind sun ripping sparkles from yellow hair. Looking out at the lake and its glare, they sit, they eat and he kisses her. Mmmmmm. I can smell aftershave and I bite down hard on a piece of grape flavored gum.

They make a plan but I can't here the details. They lower their voices for fear I'll hear and ask to come along. I'll bet it's something great, a dark kind of plan with orgies and axes, pentagrams and beer! I scoot from under the umbrella, I want to get close to the net. Their talk turns serious now, and they put their pizza aside. I hear it all, no need for speculation, he tells her about murder, how they wil make a person die. "You stuff a sock down deep in her throat, hold her down so she chokes and chokes, eventually she'll stop breathing, that's when you throw her in the hole. Cover it up with some rocks and sticks, and tell the cops you can't remember where you hid the bitch."

I crawl a bit closer, and as the woman turns to face me, I see the amulet mole on her neck. Misshapen and brown, it grows and gets bigger. She gestures for me to come closer, "You know you don't have to hide." On the sand at her feet I can see her socks and they bear the stitch of my symbols - a pentagram, an axe, and a gold labeled bottle of brass colored beer. The mole widens and gets deeper, I know what she's doing. I'm afraid I've caused this, because of my staring they want to do me in! I lose focus on the mole and she brings a sock close to my mouth. I should stop all this thinking, the shovel sounds too soon! I need to get somewhere else quickly, he's running to help her, maybe I should go close to the lifeguard stand, close to the lake. I run to the water, I leave my towel behind, I lose my french-fry shoes on the way.

They don't bother to chase me, they just seize my

umbrella, giving a spit to the sand. As I run I chant fight-songs, words from the chain gang, the sick house barber-shop quartet. Our voices made sweet sounds low with determination. We were defiant and eager to win! I sing alone now and my voice cracks as I sing. Always in these moments I meet my inner demons, I charge the coleslaw mountain fighting a dripping shaky lip. I've given up the spot that I loved, and the feeling of defeat is great. I take it in the spirit of a war that I know will ultimately subdue me. On this earth it's a war that I'm bound to lose, but even so, I must act like it's one I can win. My sadness is both bitter and sweet, I like it and this is my reward. I look forward to the battle they'll have with my ghost. My death, my ghost, their prison cell, my disease. Yes, it's bittersweet as I'm likely to say. Standing on the coleslaw mountain I give in to my tears and cry, my chest is like jam, and on it falls one tear from each cheek.

I'm walking and crying now and I almost lose my all, when I hear bicycle wheels breaking, a pack of kids runs for the water, joyful in a thundering stampede. I'm prone to kids with shiny eyes and dolphin smiles, but what catches my attention here is a belly. A slight protuberance with a white patch, small curves and just enough give. I want to smile into the boy's eyes, I want to brush up against this patch. Here, the last tear falls and I follow my beautiful dolphin into the water.

I never tried to earn a swimming badge because the only place they'd let me pin it was on the front of that damned ball cap. Threads of moss rise from the foam, and I relish my refusal because I don't have to worry, this lake knows I don't know how to swim! With my ankles together and my toes curled under, I grab onto the moss and kick with my makeshift mermaid's tail. The moss is a tiny but powerful engine and it lovingly bobs me under and up. Speeding toward the boys, I heed the call for recreation, embrace the sport of water, as it sprays, as it licks.

I've never felt such moss, such green, or seen such gray overhead. A sea-storm at the lake begins to drop, and it tests all the weight in its wake. There's no need to panic because the moss hugs me tighter, dutifully following fins and flippers, tracking the white patch out to the middle of the lake. The sky gets darker and the Dolphins get dimmer, I can barely see them. They drift further and further away. Thunder sounds over waves that keep pressing my strength, my breath, my will to live. The wind and the rain churn hard and I see the kids bracing the storm too. The dolphin boys are tacking down, they've tied their boards together, and they curse at the waves that crush down on their makeshift ship. The lake is slick and lightning hits the target of its burning. I'm far away but I see the flames, the small smoked vessel, now they've got nothing and have to swim. The storm stays steady, and many gurgle under, I don't see my favorite boy, has the lake taken even him?

The storm finishes itself off after a laugh and a splash but for me its a sad bucket of rain. I can't see the dolphin, and my moss is fickle, it shrivels, turns black and moves away. After a few paddles and gulps, I'm a quick Titanic - heavy, sand-bound, under. Oh soundless water! Nothing but black overhead! It's tough to move, it's tough to see, but the sounds of thunder seem like nothing now that I'm heading for a sunken boat, a cozy vessel fit for the bones of a dead sick girl who can't even swim. I hear dull thuds, the sound of a pine pirate's box, a signal from my dolphin, calling me to the rescue. I don't know what will happen but I must start swimming! White bellied boy, I'll kick fast for you now, diving deeper, ever under, with my periscope eyes, and a line from the sick house, "You must always do your best to do what you can do!"

The poetry answers my prayers and through the volumes of perilous green, there it is, good as a pearl in the dank mouth of a clam. I flipper toward it, come up for breath, dive under again and watch as it hovers above muscles that kick, squirm, expand as they take in air. I nudge up against him, I'm a hard boat of bones, but I can be gentle when I want to be. Gasps and shrieks at first but then he gets used to it. He lets me feel my way around when he sees that I'm not a whale, or something with teeth. The storm is gone, but the water moves in slow circles, it moves with the boy who is now moving with me. Tangled in polyps, lapping at foam, the sonar is heavy, and with wave after wave of it, he fondles away at my baby-fine hair, with wave after wave of it, he sucks hard on my one special tooth.

I need to dry out after all of this mating and fun, and I want to show my dolphin babe to the kids at the net. We swim to the shore with a motorboat's speed, and as we get closer, there is something odd in the bubbles, something strange about his smile. On the beach I look at his sand-crust hair, he brushes moss away from my face. Returning the demands of his eyes, the Dolphin boy's lines try to cling to his phrases, his words don't make any sense to me. The words I want don't tumble from his lips, he has trouble breathing, getting his air. He looks at me and can only whimper and chirp, his eyes beseechingly look to me for relief. I've moved him to pain where the words should be, but when they come, they are hostile and he calls to the nurses, "There's something wrong with her, get her away from me!!" Getting his breath back, he's all human now, and as the nurses come running, a Dolphin ghost returns to sea.

The nurses spread out my towel, give me a blue ball cap and a needle and thread. The recreational director of our springtime outing is perplexed and annoyed, they don't know what to do with me. He works for the sick house and knows that I will not participate in any sports, lessons, or craft activity. He takes the cute kids for the posters and makes the others sew symbols on blue caps, vests and jeans. He's a parolee molester who exploits cancer labor. He's the lowest, but he's not lower than me! In the basement shops at the sick house, they hand out colored yarn and tell us to stitch things that make us hopeful, things that make us forget our disease. I have my own symbols, I will not start sewing, and I scream at the head nurse "I can stitch a fast rainbow bitch, but how about a pentagram, how about an axe!?" I was their favorite kid for the posters, but then I spat blood at the camera and started turning green. Ever since this, he's been coming on strong, tempting me with beer, then trying to iron fist me into the basement - underground. Here I work with the bad kids, my job is to keep productivity up, and employee absenteeism down. He gives me the strong arm, without success though, after all, I'm the girl that made a revolution set in.

It set in the day I stole a car and got a gun. I decided that was the day I would declare liberty. I went to an old folks home and kidnapped a granny and a little boy. I put them in the car, drove to the sick house, and made circles in the parking lot. I honked the horn and held my gun to granny's head. I wanted them to sing songs and praises, but the boy started crying and it was loud and it drove me crazy, but it fueled the revolution, revolving turns of violence, hatred and disease that had long ago set in. I shouted to granny, "You better get that kid singing or I'll start shooting." I waved the gun, but the boy wouldn't stop crying so he couldn't start singing. With this, granny's face grew whiter with fear. She couldn't speak to calm him, and as his cries grew louder, my circles got faster, my gun, closer to her head. With each circle his cries grew louder setting the stage for her death. Hospital maintenance men set up barricades, but gave up because my speed was wicked and when I felt it was time to stop, I waved a flag. Red, black and silver replaced the rainbow. The star was replaced by the pentagram, the axe.

I think this gave the kids a lot to think about. Problem children saw me pull up in front of the sick house, they saw me with my gun held to grandma's head. The kids fell in line as my patent leather shoes kicked out a revolutionary cadence they could relate to. They watched as the chemo wig set the tone, and made demands. They could see that although my gun was heavy, I held it firm with determined wrists and shaky hands. They saw me sick and green, bubblegum skin sort of hanging off of dull bones, yanking hostages from the car, mercifully setting them free. Granny and the boy ran through the flames burning from my tire tread circles accompanied by some big men from the SWAT team. They pulled up their belts as I shouted, "A gun and a car are as easy as bread, watch your back, I know where you live!!" I threw down the red force of a revolutionary fist and the kids got the picture, they shook their fists and clapped their hands. They snapped out of their suicide daydreams, chanting out all eight stories of the towering building, "Free the jean stitch sewers! Down with rainbows, stuffed animals and fruit! With the axe break down the prison cell! Let the pentagram cure the disease!"

The kids got the picture and began to resist orders. The dedicated began to beat up their mothers, shoving them up against the tiles on the kitchen sink. They grabbed their moms by the hair, punched them in the ears and reversed all the beatings, making mommy taste the buckle end of the belt she used to turn the original trick. As the kids get sicker, moms get punished by the smell of the hospital tubes hanging by the side of the bed. They live in fear that each time their sick children close their eyes to sleep, it may be for the last. My revolution satisfies as near dead ones whisper to loving mothers busy tidying rooms and emptying bedpans, "Mother, please get these floors cleaner. After all, this is the room in which I'll make my final pass." As for me and my final sweet dream of living, I want to be pinching the skin on my mom's chicken neck.

Godammit where am I? Wandering around with these thoughts that solve no problems, and I'm not having any fun. The man from the sick house casually drinks a beer, "There's no sign of your dolphin. He's waiting for another sick surfer, or dead girl who can't swim." The sun starts to set and I'm naked except for my chemo wig and this brand new ball cap. The people are gone, a break before nightime - bonfires, beer parties and sharks. I hear a small splashing, something calls me to the water. This time it's a wooden boat, nestled between two rocks. I'm tired, but I crawl to the boat like a crab. My face on wet wood, I hug its soft bottom and wait to become invincible again. I encourage the boat to float wherever it wishes. I want to drift with the will of the lake. It won't move though, it just shivers its oars, so I muster some hope and grab on. With all my strength I row past every floating turd, past every fickle fish, jet ski and neon smile. I row beyond all yellow hair to a mossy place in the middle of the lake.

Here I can see sick house buses pull up with coolers and tents, the stuff for a cook-out. For the kids it's one night of fun. Nurses with clipboards pull the kids and their IVs onto the sand, unstrapping them, propping them up. The recreation supervisor helps the kids with their tents. He knows that zippers are easy - on the tent, on the sleeping bag, on the pants and mouths of small children too sick to speak. Volunteers start fires and begin roasting weenies, taking occasional sips from bottles filled with tequila or beer. A nun with a guitar and a honey sweet voice strolls through the rows singing a song. It's upbeat but it will not excite them. For this the kids are counting on me.

But they listen to the nun and start singing along. I'm fearful because I remember these songs. They went with granola at breakfast, a folky palliative after a morning of advanced chemotherapy. It's too late for slogans, because they sing and they forget that illumination happens only after much blood has been shed! The water begins stirring. Something underneath cooks and it makes me feel uneasy but brave. I know that this is flammable water, this is beast and creature water that will take me under for underneath's sake. But I'm floating right in the middle, and I like this spot, it feels kind of right. I should bury my axe, signal to the singers with my pentagram, toast the revolution with a beer. Yes, it's dark now and my boat siezes on violent waters and threatens to tip. I'm back with a new feeling, the right kind of rocking, I'm definitely stronger as the gut of a new mass of land slides under my boat...sand...an island!! Stable land, paralyzing thoughts, a kingdom of kids where I'm not the king. I hear the sound of soft earth under strong feet. Indians...an unfamiliar culture moves onto the beach. Hands weave baskets of palm, liquor is chewed out of spit and roots, thumbs push fleshy walls of coconut shells making the meat loose and easy to eat. Oh dig me! Oh eat my bubblegum and bones! Lay your red, black and silver beads at my feet! I'll start you a revolution and you'll let me disappear on your island. Back at the beach it's a wicked solution - an unexplained seclusion or death. Bubblegum legends produce traces and sightings of bearded persons who look like me, sick little goddesses swimming with dolphins and healthy brown chests.

But where's the self abnegation one would expect from the king of the kids!? Am I green? Or am I red? I'll surely be yellow if I abandon the responsibility to my prison cell, to my disease. A sickening steam flowers forth from the island, the boat jerks and carries me back to the bonfires at the beach. Let the fires burn! Let the beasts roar! I'm the king of recklessness, of optimism, and I'll hold out for a real dolphin encounter, one I'll enjoy when our spirits have been set free. Only then will I nobly give myself over to a tickle from the moss, another lap at the foam from the lake! I cast the oars aside and begin to row again with the red force of a revolutionary sick kid. In the middle I get a good look at my options. The indians stand to my right, the campout is on my left, cooking outdoors for cancer's sake. I watch them both, back and forth, here it's clear that there can be no island solution. I must be a public figure, and with no time taken for me to get tougher, I start wielding my shit once again. Blood will be shed, there will be a belated beach coronation, I will be the king living or dead!

I rip a piece of wood from the side of the boat, spit, and gnaw the bark into a wishbone shape. A piece of gum chewed hard completes my slingshot. Now I'm hungry for blood and don't want to wait. I summon the moss, it anchors the boat, readies a platform fit for destruction, oration has now become passé. The Indians, a backdrop of solemn expression don't cry out at the start of my shooting, but the folks on the shore panic and scream, "There's a sniper kid with a chemo wig taking shots at the beach!" I've got to keep shooting so the kids will go crazy - and they do, they start shuffling, tapping their feet. They no longer sing with the guitar, they are stomping and clapping, paying homage to me. Quickly now, taking them all down, I'm a shadow of a kid on the base of a boat, the sum of a murderous prophecy.

Indeed, the kids are ready to fall, but everyone answers my call in a different way. Mothers can't bear to witness and fall to their knees and weep. Together they offer the spot, take a rock from my shot, chests falling onto the beach. The kids don't run from the smoke or fear death from my shots, their heads are bowed, they defer to me. I see them through the smoke and the flames as the bonfires join hands by the waves, by the sand. Although they are innocent, I have to keep shooting. I've got to make each one a swift kill. Getting it all, they swoon, they fall without the painkiller, without the IV. Twisting fast, grabbing the bottom of my boat, the moss shakes it and jerks me around. A born seaman I'm not. I drop my shot, falling to the boat's oaken floor. Damn moss! Evil green stew! Let me get the survivors, I want only the Indians to tell the tale! I'm not begging or praying, just catching my balance, but the water crashes over quickly, my moss, my once friendly chariot takes me too soon! I grab for my shot, I've got to keep shooting! Shooting, standing firmly, raising hell. But now I'm hell bound because the water is tougher and the boat is all the way under, in the water, and I'm following it down.

The sights have disappeared but I hear something like locusts, or vultures sitting on the crushed bark of the boat. To them my head is like a dead seal in the water. They want to chew it up, and scatter what remains for small fish in the lake, waiting for food and swimming around. But they will never peck on these bones because I pinch my nose and bubble under. The kids who've survived stomp with the locusts, they keep on tapping as the vultures flap their wings and fly away. They kick it out, the pattern I taught them, isn't the apocolypse all about having a beat? The Indians join in, putting sharp stone to wood, but this isn't just some rythmic conspiracy. Through the red volumes of perilous green, Indians carve statues in my image. No more worries because I'm breaking in gills and testing out flippers, no more worries because Indians on an island whittle away and think of me.

John Clarke

Blood Stories: Swan

n 1971 my mother went to England and came back with a picture of two big black swans with red beaks in a pond and one of my oldest brother, naked, taking a piss on Hadrean's wall. I thought that was really pretty slick. I always wished I had a picture of myself either as a foreign swan, or pissing on something ancient when I was tiny.

Mother got killed in a car accident in front of a grain elevator on her way to work one day. The elevator was huge and must have had enough grain inside to make enough flour for several billion pancakes for some chain like Denny's. I think of Denny's and mother in the same thought mostly. She could really enjoy half a Grand Slam — one sausage, one slice of bacon, one egg scrambled and a single flapjack. All on a Sunday morning. "Not too heavy," she was fond of saying, "just enough to hot the spot, and not cooked by anyone in the family."

When it was said and done, we didn't know what had happened, the ambulance on its wheels running into town, my father came back to where we were and told us to get a broom and dust pan to go get the broken glass out of the road where the Oldsmobile had taken its wreck. He didn't want anyone getting a flat tire. The wheat stalks along the road at the intersection looked all the greener as we left to drive home. No wonder she hadn't seen them. They were iron-ass stems with full-on heads, juiced up hormonally and experiencing the prime energy of scientifically steeped hybrid vigor. I would have floated on into the intersection myself and got my pelvis collapsed, brains spread quiet and flower-like over the steering wheel and windshield. There wasn't too much blood any-where in the car. I guess it mostly stayed inside her.

Saturday, June 6, was selected viewing day. This was the first time I saw a body all prepped up for God and the dirt. The different parts of the family all kind of showed up in different rides and at different times from different places. I'd been at home watching Planet of the Apes with a friend who wasn't invited to view, so I dropped him off at his mother's house on the way to the burial parlor. I didn't really want to go inside. I'd driven by this joint every time I'd ever come to town and I always thought it was fucked that the morgue in a small north-western town would have a southern mansion facade — pillars and marble and all with a huge pea-green neon sign pop-ping up on top informing us all that this was Burns' mor-tuary. Dead bodies were in there, odorless carcasses of geriatric Rotarians and cool, fast drunk dudes. When I finally got to the door, everything was dim inside. All of the family that were already there seemed like helpings of hot dish or something that had been waiting there, served onto separate plates. No one was feeling like the other, obviously, brothers and dads were here and there with their arms crossed and their sunglasses still on, and my lone sister was sitting on a tan metal folding chair doing a tearless whimper. This was in the side room, the main body-decorating room. Here, there were no deep velvet drapes and pews like in the real funeral room. No, the mother body was on a metal wagon with very large alu-minum wheels. Dad and us offspring were on a marble floor with a drain in the middle. No coffin as of yet. A sheet over lumps and bunches, turned back like it was a demonstration of how to tuck someone in. I went to her and stood over her face and tried to focus on her, my mother, on the point of her nose. I wanted to see light and have something let me know that all those Sundays at church and all the times that she'd told me that masturbation was Satan in my penis and elves in my fingers had actually worked. I wanted to know that the inside of her, that part of her nose, had, or was going to be, zapped out in a shriek of fuzzy hot tubing up into that part of the solar system where important religious guys hang out naked together, playing bagpipes and drinking milk. I tried to focus harder and harder and I started to feel sweat beading out on my chin and around my eyes. My ears were hot and pretty red I was sure. All I could feel was really roomy inside, but kind of full too, like my stomach was cluttered with a few small meals that were just hanging out and not too interested in turning into kiem and heading on down to the colon so that I could get some fat and energy. I think all my blood was down there and maybe even in my thighs because it sure wasn't in my brain. I was barely smart enough to feel embarrassed that I had been staring at a point on her face which hadn't been her eyes. So I tried to start scanning. But that seemed empty, and lazy too. Slow as can be up to the bridge of my nose and then a decision about which eye to look at first. Couldn't decide, couldn't think fast enough, clumpy in the head, dumber than a train. So I went back to her nose and jumped to the lips, it seemed easier that way, then the chin, and down again to that little part that dips in between collar bones , then to the hem of the neck of her dress. Drift back up and stare again. There was nothing in there. Nothing was gone and nothing was ready to go. All that my mind could get itself around was how it looked like all of her skin had been crammed into the stuff panty hose was made of. There was no fine hair on her upper lip, no lumps between her chin and the dip I was unsuccessfully focused on. Just all smooth and homogeneous with a half-way sheen that looked dangerously slick, they'd stretched her face back and clamped it behind her head and the pillow was hiding the apparatus and they generously brushed her down with the spray that janitors use to make those gigantic dustmops sticky to absorb dirt. That was all I could think of, when my head was empty I'd think it over once more.

It was just the same as the time I was painting this rich woman's master bathroom after dark. There were no windows except solid sky light and I was painting the back of the door. The paint was old and must have had some lead in it and it got to me and I started spinning this one image in the mind's eye like a View Master with only a single picture of a pile of used artificial insemination tubes I'd seen out by the fence that morning. The day before, we bred 13 Angus heifers and left the spent straws by the gate. The straws look like three foot long versions of the ones for pop and shakes at Burger King and at the time I'd thought how long it would take to get liquid to your mouth through one of them. Three seconds, possibly five, if you were a weak sucker.

Back with my mother, my thoughts finally moved on and I wondered if she was really up there and was indeed now omniscient like the Big Guy who was monitoring my petty, fucked-up mind, and was ashamed of how stupid I was that I couldn't even get below her skin. And if she was regretting that I'd plugged up her uterus for nine months and been the reason for yet another layer of scar tissue between her belly button and the top of her vagina. Interrupting my grieving, Mr. Burns the big mortician told me that he had to do another service in 20 minutes and that he was sorry, but I'd have to leave, so I did.

Francis Stark

Upon My Arrival

(So, you can't go home...)

A while back, obsessed with Westerns, I remember composing this simple sentence, which is anything but spectacular but finds its way, on significant occasions, to the right (contemporary) part of my head to echo there. Maybe I was missing my huge family home in Ohio, or was it Kentucky, where the dust can be easily kept under control, where you don't even think about its menacing presence nor are you for any reason left to consider its absence. This time it came when I was in the back of some lesser version of a Super Shuttle van on Christmas morning heading toward LAX. M. and I would be having some Christmas ham in Atlanta, once the sun was way down and we'd have worked up a fierce appetite reading so many magazines. I began devouring Vanity Fair way before we even boarded our plane.

Suddenly, or more like years after gross approximations and shabby eccentricities, it occurred to me that I was indeed, at this time, carrying matching luggage. Once when I was doing a lot of flying between Orange County and San Jose, euphemistically (and only after years of patience, realistically) L.A. to San Francisco, I had a whole set that actually matched but it was blue, not royal or navy or baby, a boring blue with fake leather trim, which was not black or brown but a poor rendition of oxblood, so that the glamour of having a set of matching luggage was completely undermined by this hideously banal (west coast preppy) color scheme which simply could not be worked into my own palate of that period (my not-blue period). So now that I look like a half-way sophisticated traveler it so happens that I'm only going to stay with someone else's parents (instead of my own) as opposed to doing some career thing on the opposite coast. One suburban living room "alternative" rock hero/genius etc. etc. brandishes harsh criticism of L.A. (as people of any ilk are prone to do) in a reference to "40 shades of black" ("so many fortresses and ways to attack..."). Well, I can't help it — it's the blackness of my new luggage that I like, I like it this way and my leather coat; of course it's black, new black things mix nicely with vintage items which happen to be black as well. I care so much. I feel unified somehow — adult in the way I had once hoped. Upon my arrival my airport image — my dashing cosmopolitanism — begins to wane. The anachronistic depression sets in, there is no teenage sex awaiting me yet I'm reduced to girlfriend status in boyfriend's parents' home. After I jump into a supine position on my boyfriend's teenhood bed, before thoroughly unpacking my lackluster luggage, my droopy, ambitious yet aimless youth flashes before my eyes, which I have now shut in response to the great sadness brought on by the inflated Oscar Meyer wiener hanging from the ceiling.

(I heart Southern California.)
I only imagined that I'm from Ohio (Kentucky) and that I ended up here on account of a yearning for the frontier. The furnishings in catalogues conjure up a home life kept fastidiously in order...and so it is that I have no home in Ohio [Kentucky] to return to or so it can soon be

deduced that I sprung from the dirt near a distinctive rock formation and was put into a basket on the back of an ass which took me to "town". (Someone once told me but I can't exactly recall who: "Try to realize that it's irrelevant where you come from — it's pure luck we have no burden of a heritage, you're more ambitious if you're not spending your time supine, running your delicate fingers through the grass in the shade of a leafy family tree.")

(You Have to Go...)
I've adapted to the reliability of a warm welcome no matter how ugly circumstances have become. Days before I cringe uncontrollably at the thought of having to confront the general morass of nastiness that surrounds the familial predicament of the moment. But I know, despite my general distaste for assessments like these, that "denial" prevails. It's like nothing ever happened. It's really like nothing ever happened. And then something comes up or goes down, however you want to put it and everything starts to figure in too tightly — all those things that happened, all the debauchery unwitnessed, it starts to threaten to come into focus — a grotesque orgy, you can almost hear the screams of the participants grow louder and louder, verging on a suffocating buzz unbearable even to the hard of hearing. When this is too much for me, when I'm almost certainly in the midst of such a horrendous possibility, I descend the tiny spiral staircase into the bonus room/basement.

(Mitigated Excess)
Detritus from dispassionate or just simply unmotivated

(heartless) commitments to certain styles and or just objects (i.e. kittens, owls, African violets, ballet, etc.) litter rather unintrigueingly the chilly basement. But you haven't seen the garage yet. It's not really the garage, because the real garage is for cars. It is for two new cars for the children, like brand new cars, and one gracefully aging cadillac, but only fits two so they have to kind of rotate, the two new kids' cars, because the cadillac always parks inside this garage that has windows and curtains, nearest the door that leads directly into the kitchen. The older truck which is a less gracefully aging vehicle is the father's car and it always parks in the drive next to where the boat is stored. It is an American truck, tan and brown. So the real garage, for the cars, it is not used for storage, except for storing the cars of course. The other place that feels like a garage is one of the rooms off the basement, like a tool room and this is kind of a sad place to go.

The way his parents' house shows time is that it actually passes by way of sending objects to the periphery, or when necessary, by sending already peripheral objects to the furthest possible peripheries. As it stands keepsakes too have shelf lives, central fixtures have no stability. But it's not as simple as the embarrassing evidence of trend indulgence. Only sometimes it is — like when she said "Use the green washer, it has more options" I knew it'd be Avocado green and that it would be "old" and when I did use it instead of the new white one I was drawn into the design of the knobs ("more options") and so on. This kind of disparity is simple to understand and delight in

— like when you see the 8-track tape player in the basement it is not so sad or disturbing. But something definitely is sad and disturbing, in and around basements, and it does, I suppose, have a little to do with nostalgia, but not the easy locatable kind (i.e. decade nostalgia).

(Refer again to the subtitle re: home)
It's all about tips of the iceberg, same iceberg different perceivable tips at any given moment. The thing that is so excruciating is the sameness and the repetition that doesn't know itself as such, perhaps from an optimistic point of view this could be considered something like renewal, as poignant and sublime as the forever annoying sunset/sunrise combo.

After jotting some notes down, I go back upstairs where M. is being reprimanded for having no shirt on while sitting at the dining room table. While waiting for this to come to an end or any approximation thereof, and for its effect on me to wear off (which takes longer), I go retreat to "my room", to the IBM Selectric directly under the Oscar Meyer wiener to make my observations into something. Before I know it I'm bopping down the carpeted hall, two new paragraphs in hand, towards the fancy dining room (as opposed to the daily dining room situated in the add-on area) where I know to find M., still shirtless, engrossed in Shelby Foote's 966 page Civil War "Narrative" (a mere one volume out of 3). "You're on a roll" he ventures, half-heartedly, for little can turn him all the way away from the aforementioned narrative, "why don't you keep going". I tell him I can only barely hint for

seconds at a time at my pervasive disturbance, that titil-
lating (in retrospect) excruciation, but I tell him in
cloudier, less articulate terms of course. I know that it
would probably serve me better, or rather, be in the service of more elaborate description further down the line,
were I to just make lists of those things that erupt daily
from their banality, shooting forth (down, up, out, the
direction is uncertain) but finding their way none the less
to my pool (puddle) of literary possibilities. Instead of
rejoicing in every splash, I emit a stink and fear like no
other I have known before, a stink and fear that resonates
throughout the day or days, giving me severe headaches,
nausea, and unproductive insomnia (not to mention the
breakouts it causes on my neck and around my mouth).
As I applied aloe to some of these blemishes, I got to
thinking how Henry Miller thought he looked kind of
Oriental and some people have said so about me — but I
think both of us just suffer(ed) from extreme puffiness
around the eyes. My father had an operation to reduce
the bagginess of his upper lids which was starting to
interfere with his already not-so-perfect vision. I would
like to have the operation now because I'm so vain, only
there's no way or body to pay for it — I won't live long
enough to see, however blurry, the day there are real medical reasons for surgery. I rubbed on some eye cream
belonging to M.'s mom, in a circular motion as directed,
and pontificated to myself further how I didn't think
"youth" was really an issue for Henry Miller — you know
he was so critical of American culture, what could he care
about youth? He could just dismiss that myth for something more religious and oriental. Now that was some-

thing I simply refused to do. I would much rather rot in my solipsistic cesspool of youth culture worship, growing old and bitter, nursing my has-been bed sores with a blistered dry cat's tongue blah blah blah. I would much rather engage in this shitty business of reflective doom and gloom than opt for some sliver of zen serenity. And so meandered my thoughts in the matriarch's pink bathroom complete with Laura Ashley wall paper.

(The revival of the gentleman — a starched collar fantasy) The nostalgia that feeds my dissatisfaction and dissatisfactory reactionary thinking proposed one morning, as I was buttoning my vest — a pinstriped one that for a moment with the striped shirt and rolled up sleeves made me look like a depression era banker or some lean abstraction anyway (as if I've ever even seen one) — the thought wouldn't it be nice were I a component in some coherent social clique, a small one, five or six (plus or minus a few peripheral lovers), gin drinkers, fascist and impeccably groomed. I would be in it by way of my fiance, as I am in the South already by way of him. Down here aside from being in the south I am feeling that definitely I am on the east coast as well. But still I felt homesick and a trifle depressed so I napped and dreamt of an ancestral pioneer woman. She said: "In the "west" it is demanded we live by a do-it-yourself credo, for example I didn't know I'd have to stain the table after I had it built and found it was easier to paint than stain" — a quicker, less arduous process I presumed, but all the true usefulness of the wood would be gone. She sobbed, "Bits of food stick in the paint — the paint cracks" etc. I kept thinking to myself "All this because one doesn't really know the first thing about wood or painting for that matter." Upon repainting, the surface builds a new texture attesting to its failure to live up to the standards of wood — this new texture is a relief map of deviation, of tiny appendices accumulating into a chain of micro-elevations. Near the end of my nap I ran a ponderous post-industrial finger over the disrupted surface and from my extreme distance, fantasized about the slowly emerging Rocky Mountains, not yet majestic or terrifying, with little of the smoothness and subtlety of the dying Appalachians.

But, it was during the gentlemen fantasy, which had more to do with feeling out or reveling in a kind of rigid structure which could support and enhance (as in showcase) my watery persona, a delicate yet persistently insistent persona, when I began composing a letter to a would-be friend about all the writing projects which have been consuming me lately — and then the real me, interrupting the fantasy, suggested that perhaps expressing myself (which could take considerable effort) isn't such a bad idea after all. Just find a willing reader — put all my eggs in one epistolary basket — then after the soothing rush of relief not unlike the one rendered in the, I think, David Lynch Alka Seltzer commercial, I could get on with the real business of writing. But maybe that could wait until I got back home to L.A., but probably it would have to wait until I got home to L.A. and then moved from my native California to a new home in the South, where someone could get some real writing done. But I didn't think I could wait that long — I would go to another set-ting in M.'s parents' house to lose myself in thoughts of southern domesticity (which never last more than 3-5 minutes).

(Later, back in L.A. and other unmentionable locales)
I was thinking it would be so funny for those figuring out the mysterious suddenness of my suicide to be hung up on why I decided to kill myself midway through a Balzac novel — and then it was even funnier when M. came home finding me perfectly alive, yet sulking profusely, with my place carefully marked by an index finger in his first edition that lay at my side on the verging-on-filthy sheet — I say "Balzac is such a depressing writer" and he offers, so knowingly "Who?", whereupon I glance down and realize it's Emile Zola I'm reading not Balzac at all.

L'Assommoir, the Zola novel, M.'s hardback edition, was not at my side anymore, but nearer my lifeless feet where its thick spine enabled it to stay clinging to the edge of the mattress, safely above the tons of crap, all that perversely personal crap, that littered the floor around my bed, which was technically no longer mine since I was now, finally, thankfully and peacefully, despite some vomit on my chin, dead. With me every scrap had the potential to become the object of an absurd resuscitation, meaning I didn't believe in throwing anything away. Incipient fan-tasies of being a literary pauper, a new wave vagabond, an existential minimalist always became less enticing amidst my mind's clutter of elaborately art directed possibilities whereabouts roamed the vixen, the 30's housewife, the dropout, the groupie, the professor — a waif, a fatso, a slut, a rebel, a winner, a loser, a babe, brain, a stoner, junkie, whiner, a woman. Now that heap of second-hand accessories meant to flesh out each aforementioned personal served simply as an obstacle to the two medics who came to save me. Neither of the muscular good-natured men whose hands brushed against my blue unenticing nudity probably ever considered that when first discovered a recycled signifier's recyclability is assessed as it passes through the Vaseline lens of my sometimes subtle, sometimes indiscriminate imagination. Knee deep in vintage clothing etc. they remained unaware of that seductive gloss which took over my life against my better judgement, that seductive gloss capable of reforming on the worn surface of just about any outdated person place or thing. They were unaware of the advanced sensibility necessary in rendering the garbage below valuable. They were just trying to save a little life, but they failed only because they were notified too late, not because my junk (so to speak) was an obstacle. Would they even take notice of my clothes or my furniture or any of my stuff, they were the types who looked at life from an entirely different angle. Me, I was glad to be rid of my belongings, those tangible fragments of corny narratives. But instead of bidding a fond adieu to the material world, I found I craved bigger, not-so-corny narratives and new belongings altogether. So, without knowing any wish, no matter how trivial or poorly thought out, was always within reach I ended up getting my first taste of the after life in a mall. I was embarrassed and alone, but thankfully invisible (I think) and I sat down on a bench and remembered so clearly M. saying with an unforgiving nastiness "Balzac?" and then I realized two things: number one, I probably didn't deserve M. and two, the mall wasn't a purgatory or even hell but my true idea of heaven. I would be on a perpetual shopping spree and love it because deep down, I was really just a suburban house-wife and now all my intellectual pretense was only a faint and almost painless memory, but nevertheless I felt sad about saying goodbye to my dual ambition of being cool and smart, so sad that I needed a shoulder to cry on, a sympathetic shoulder to cry on. You would think I would be able to communicate with M. but it wasn't working out that way, him being alive and all, so I ended up shar-ing a table near the Cinnibon place with a fatish kid maybe a few years younger than M. He too was a suicide, killed himself because his parents would never stop talk-ing about his disease, A.D.D. – Attention Deficit Disorder. "Do you know what A.D.D. is?" Me: "Yeah sure, I was just making fun of..." He glances pathetically downward. "...Or well discussing, I wasn't making fun of it in the way you think, I was making fun of it because I think it's a dis-ease I'd like to have had — I would've liked for someone to diagnose me with your A.D.D." "I think only kids have it," mumbles he. I started to wonder why my new friend ended up in the mall — on account of him being so "alternative" looking, but just in case he was a Tilt fanat-ic I didn't broach the subject — he seemed a little shook up, how rude of me to be so concerned with assessing his identity. But let's talk about the way he looked. His jeans fit him in a way that was reminiscent of a writer I know, in his heavier days, probably due to the distinct looseness at the knees and clumsy halt they came to at his worn black converse. His t-shirt which was oversized was not unlike one of my writer friend's select hypo-allergenic ones from a few seasons ago. I was looking at the boys back through the shirt, wondering if he was ever self-conscious about the fleshiness, as we went up the escalator even though we probably could've just, oh I don't know, flown. We leaned on the railing for old times sake. He was staring into the shop below at a girl, not your average mall girl. There at a rack straightening some dresses stood the reason he wound up at the mall. If only I could be so lucky to have such a sweet excuse. So even though he was shaken and verging on inaccessible (on account of an uncalculated reticence, or just plain not having that much to say, or maybe it really was his a.d.d that made him so flighty... "You know" his voice broke through my parentheses "I loved her. but she has a boyfriend, and he's in this band that I love." "Poor kid, how could you stand it?" "Because I didn't know until now." At this he sighs. I let out a tiny nervous squeak. A moment of silence. "So you really didn't kill yourself because of your Attention Deficit Disorder?" He nodded a half-ass nod. "What band is it?" "Pavement." "Is it the singer, she's in a relationship with the singer!!??" "Yeah, it's the singer, they suck now anyway — I just saw this video of them live..." Did I really want him to supply me with his reason for why they sucked now, here we were both recently deceased, alone, except for each other, and all we could talk about was Pavement. How embarrassing. How lame. Everything in death, like in life, was too stupid, and there was no escaping youth culture. I felt like puking but

I had already puked my last drop before checking out. "You know you look really familiar. Hey I think I saw you in that Pavement video, in the audience." "Well, I too had a thing for the singer of Pavement, but it wasn't like a love thing it was a delicate blend of admiration, inspiration and deluded kinship. I threw a tape of my band onstage to him once. So, like a year later, thinking he might remember that, I made another tape for him and wrote a little note, which was kind of sweet, kind of quirky, whatever and this time I was seeing them in a different city and I thought how cool if he gets another tape thrown at him and so on...so my friend and I go to the show and I see the singer, Stephen, out in the audience. I'm not thinking straight so I just go up to him. He's not looking toward me, so I call out his name, which is like the worst feeling in the world, I have to say, being a total stranger calling out someone's name who you don't really know yet you know, you know..." and here I looked at my little, or well, semi-big, friend and paused for about a tenth of a second and then launched back into the story "so he takes the tape which is all wrapped very deliberately in a special envelope type thing with special tape on it, special text, you know it's kinda subtle but he doesn't seem to care 'cause he just starts ripping open the envelope and I'm standing there like an idiot and he looks sort of at me and says I'll look at it as if to say get away from me now." "Jerk," my new friend says 'cause he thinks it's what I want to hear. "So, anyway, I know I jumped the gun, but oh well, then they start playing and I go right to the front of the stage because I've been to a billion punk shows and know how to pull this off while all these kids, well no offense, are a little soft, friendly or something, anyway I'm right there in front and Stephen comes out on stage and does some caricature of a rock and roll gesture jumping up into the air like he's out of control drunk, which you know he's not, and he lands right on his ass and I hear the crunch of plastic, the unmistakable sound of a cassette case being smashed, probably not on the video. So he took it out of his pocket and threw it down on the stage in what looked a little like disgust. I'm feeling very uneasy because of this. I don't know what I think but I'm embarrassed for being such a calculated fan, what a...well anyway they're getting into their set, the bassist crushes the tape again deliberately with his chic running shoe, I feel a bit hot and sick and find it hard to enjoy myself in this situation. Then they break into their radio hit, a sea of youthful faces beaming with excitement erupts, cheeks redden as bodies go passionately into alternative motion but I'm standing still — then I notice the guy who's been videotaping the show has turned the camera right onto the fervent audience. There's no escaping. I'm the one not moving, looking disturbed and a little less young than those in my midst." Now looking away I sighed and, realizing I was dead and stupid, and embarrassed, tears welled up in my eyes as I asked him "Is that what you saw, am I really the one?" "It's totally you and now here you are, what a fuckin' trip."

Ed Johnson

Calvary

rigg's car had become something of a prize to his social group ever since Marion's car had exploded in the parking lot last winter. Marion bagged groceries in the afternoons and two fully bedecked firemen had entered the store in the middle of his shift seeking the owner of the smoldering heap out front and for the rest of the week the boys had driven by the wreckage respectively or in groups of two bearing witness. The body had been painted beige and now resembled a large, bad egg blown up as a kid's prank. The hood had pitched itself upward in a grand peak, diminishing in smaller, erratic bevels before the blackened windshield whose cracks were translucent filaments from the outside and severe webs caked with the burnt stuff of the inside. The front seats were strewn with the ash of incomplete homework assignments and the particulate from the floormats nested in the craters of the dash. The seats themselves were something like burnt paint, bubbled and split, melted in spots onto the ochre foam of the cushions. And the softest inventions of the interior, quick to burn, had streaked the backs of the door panels like crackled fat. Vinyl had clumped into ropes descending from the headrests upon the charred curiosities of the floorboard: the quadruplet rinds of a basketball, a sunglasses case, the shards of cassette boxes. (It was from this mess that he would pry his rightful souvenir, the hood release lever, robotic now, with a tangle of gray uncoated wires spewing from its smudged shaft.) The car was already a piece of shit and everyone could agree to that so the explosion really took no one by surprise.

Trigg's car was still running, though its motley interior was becoming more ridiculous each day. Its window cranks and upholstery buttons had bleached sooner than everything else, including the dash that had cured so long in the sun its bulk had wafered and passengers had picked off in no order the constituent appliqués so that it remained tessellated like a numbered puzzle or a varicolored map. This car was their new mascot and those who saw Trigg could only approximate the significance of that car and could only demonize it as a feeble way of complementing what Trigg himself presented them with later that night when they would try to procure the tall balloon arch that framed the girl singer, the man in charge of events would say, hey guys, do me a favor - let me see when you get that thing on top of the Volkswagen. Trigg, up until their sophomore year, had worn daily a maroon nylon jacket with snaps at every corner and epaulets on the sleeves, a powder blue Oxford and amply soled athletic shoes with a black chevron on the instep and a tongue that covered the laces. He had since then amended this wardrobe only slightly, shedding the Members Only in favor of a black and orange dashiki.

It was in that car that he and Trigg had gone in to pick up the mushrooms for that evening, the others waiting, drinking beer at Cutter's house. The guy lived on the east side of town atop a knoll terraced by side streets and the main boulevard whose exits all gave onto fast food restaurants, grocery stores and warehouse clubs (in fact, had overlooked the first warehouse club in the city, 3 Guys later Big Lots whose ads had featured a fat man in overalls gazing to the tops of the high makeshift shelves

musing over and over "Ugly store, beautiful prices."
The owner had also been, to his memory, the first local
merchant to burn dollar bills on air as a testament to the
money misspent at the tills of his competitors.) A stand
of pines ran behind the shops but could not obscure the
coned roofs of water towers, gravel mixers and the tops of
oaks and poplars planted on the subsequent rise. The
glass buildings bronzed by dusk hunched in back of all
this like their upper stories had been cut and set afloat,
half submerged in what they truthfully oversaw, like the
fire trucks that would park upon the perimeter mapped
by the gravest trajectory, their cabs pointing up a small
hill appearing as bodies or forms on their way to becoming bodies, stretched and angled like the first animals
emerging from the ocean. Everywhere was the glow of
lights - gray, brown, and orange (the lights from the
house windows, the lights from motion sensing floods
perched at the apexes of countless garages, the lights from
fires, the lights from billboards, the brightest and most
famous bearing the initials of a coffee company that filled
from the bottom with timed rows of bulbs). This land-
scape was typical of the city's intermediate commercial
centers, but the trend had been of late towards a type of
streamlining quite different from the earlier ease of pre-
fabrication which had always borne the signs of incon-
gruity and topheaviness, the brick modules of the strip
malls capped by shiplike barn dormers and weather
vanes, the facets of the saddlebacked roofs dropping uni-
formly against the corrugated cornices. Before the man-
dates of sophistication it was not at all uncommon to see
a lifelike plastic cow standing amid the exhaust fans and

aerials. Everything now was brick agorae. Everything now was homologized by the flat line of their tops and the sinking line of their shopways; these pavilions ran together without distinction, the only clues to their construction being the bands of polychrome that delineated the attics and this last device was really only a customary conceit, the overhead spaces of the stores housing nothing but air. It would seem that anyone hoping to realize the bulk of these structures would be best advised to look at a preliminary pencil drawing or a watercolor. For despite a certain monstrosity, the complacency that the presence of these buildings elicited was a palpable token of their thinness.

They had no trouble finding the apartment, although neither he nor Trigg had ever been there, having never even met the guy until now (the name still unclear, a coworker of Cutter's at Reliable Music). The rooms were scattered with crush-proof boxes of reds, loops of guitar strings in plastic envelopes, empty crates, tuning forks, beer huggers (red ones with yellow print and yellow ones with red print), balsa wood dugouts and wads of laundry from which he would yank an oversized plastic bag of mushrooms.

See that, he said, those silver flakes on the stems, and the caps.

Yeah.

Underneath the hand brake lay a secret compartment of which an increasing number of police had forced them to make conventional use. Perhaps no one he knew would immediately attract suspicion, but Trigg had been deaf in his left ear since his fourth birthday and at times would finish words with the doppler h's so common in the speech of the fully deaf. One evening a county police officer with a harelip had detained the car in a parking lot and took Trigg's vocal idiosyncrasies for a mockery of his own, citing Trigg purely out of spite.

The church was to be appropriately dressed for the holiday though the celebration had been scheduled two days early as not to conflict with the larger spectacle uptown. Mylar streamers were slung around the aluminum placards of the parking lot lamps, all of them designating the lot by number and with scripture. These signs diminished onto stained and routed pickets along the sidewalk to the fellowship hall that in turn extended like a boot from the sanctuary. Most of the city churches had halls that favored high school gymnasiums - marbleized formica, blue three point arcs rimmed with trolleys of folding chairs visible through the lancet windows and then the classrooms — but the glass of this two story slab beheld conference spaces, gift shops and rec rooms. This annex saw the genteel habits of its congregation whose pastor every Sunday broadcast his sermon over the local television and radio stations, slowly surpassing the other evangelists in approval ratings. One morning he had awoken early to find on TV a young spotlit couple dining on either side of a cloth covered card table, their discussion laced with premarital banalities, a mutual uncertainty as to which utensil was the dessert fork, the man grimacing over the outlandish menu prices and an off camera crowd responding to all of this with subdued laughter. By and by their self-willed matchmaking emerged as divine administration, their compatibility decided by a tandem and supreme love of the Lord. The skit closed with applause and the light began following female choir soloists, classical guitarists and child singers until it finally illuminated the reverend, giggling from some joke furtively shared in the wings.

So many had been incorporated by the church, it soon became evident that a new place of worship was needed. A site had been provided against the groves and fairways of Scots Glen, and the construction of the huge crown was watched through the treetops by the group during their weekend parties amid the simultaneous building to the southeast where ivy was burned, ravines were evenly graded, cul de sacs were compassed and lots became the lowly forted arrangement of sumps, then the blonde sticks of timber, the reflective blocks of insulation walled up by brick or striped by clapboard and the rare occasions of chickenwire and fine stucco. When the construction was completed, the group moved to a field further south where only the lights were visible. Many teenagers aligned themselves with this rejuvenated manifestation of God, the wealthier ones' parents having made large pledges during the two year construction, the poor doing their part too, making gifts of the proselytizing T-shirts to their children (His pain, your gain; Catch the real wave: Jesus; God's Gym; Just Preach It). It had not been surprising to see many of them at the night's festivities, some serving cokes from a large camp cooler, others there with family wondering and later not caring if the group's unproctored presence was a plea for salvation or just mischief. The only attempted conversion had happened struggling with the doors and the bald man beside them made a special note of the church's erstwhile accessibility, Sundays above all days. He smiled, not knowing their condition or was perhaps guessing at it by a perusal of their wide open pupils and the inappropriate sunglasses that some had hoped to hide them beneath.

While they were sitting around the kitchen table dividing the residue of the drugs into equal piles, Marion - who ate his between soda crackers and refused to wash down the bilious aftertaste with some of the iced tea that the rest had swallowed quickly and unashamedly - had not even wanted to see anyone else and would later only talk to others individually, even when they were seated openly around the picnic table outside.

The tricolored bunting ran in parallel lines down the aisle clear to the other end of the church. Its wall of black plate glass reflected the wildflowers and the horse enclosure across the highway, the celebrants too diminutive and wrongly situated to be mirrored thus. There would be an apartment complex there maybe, like the one Trigg lived in after his marriage, six or seven spurs that drew around them creosote sided homes with thick balustrades and cut-out fanlights over the stairwells. At the ends of the complex would be the pools, game rooms, private stands of hoses and vacuums for car washing and laundry facilities. The dryers had shaken themselves loose from the wall the weekend of his visit and Trigg's wife's yellow workshirt hung through a rotted eyelet from one of the sophets, the logo above the breast pocket inscrutable beneath the wrinkles of a vigorous hand wash (a steakhouse, a shopping center, probably). The glass for now remained true to what it wanted from the present and gave no hints as to what it would reflect in the future. If it could, would it in all capital letters trace out words on its face like a talisman? Would it even now be able to make clear the peculiar encryption, MONKEY RAG, spelled from a jumble of plastic pegged letters common to the name of his apartment manager and the manager's son? The glass would most likely defer to the son himself, the son who stayed inside during the fall, being too incompetent to dress in anything more than swim trunks, screaming and splashing in the pool, going feet first underwater to the sadistic arrangement of pool toys he kept on the cement floor: plastic bags, metal trucks, toilet plungers. The glass would remind him of that second day when he had come to submit his application and the boy had answered the door naked, his tanned stomach distended over his fledgling genitals, not even beckoning his father toward the door. The father would bullishly appear with a white sock, tossing the thing at his child's lap as if to suggest that his little peter could slip inside of it. The letters of his name would be removed from the pegboard days after he actually left, the manager too busy trying to locate the rent money from apartment seventeen that had been discovered missing on the afternoon of his departure.

The group had followed the banners until they met the ground, sitting next to the expectant fire trucks and firemen who hoped that one of the orange or green lighted anemones would turn malevolent and shoot its quills into the crowd, but that had not happened.

Dennis Cooper

Guided By Voices

uke's at Scott's. Mason's home jerking off
with a picture of Blur's bassist, Alex. Alex's
jeans are so tight you can suss out his ass. It's
sort of nondescript like a kid's. Robert, Tracy, and Chris
are several miles across town shooting heroin. They're so
fucked up. Pam's directing a porn film. Goof is the star.
He's twelve and a half. I'm home playing records and
writing a novel about the aforementioned people, especially Luke. This is it.

"Robert. You screening calls?" Luke listened. "Guess
not." He hung up.

"They're still not home?" asked Scott's mosquitoey
voice. It tended to tremble, squeak, wheeze half-
inaudibly.

"Depends on what you mean by 'home.'" Luke smiled
mesmerizingly, he could just tell. Then he let his thought
patterns crap out to the music.

Guided By Voices: "Everything fades from sight /
because that's allright with me."

Luke's sweet, deep, a little paranoid, and perpetually on.
Newly twenty-five, he has shoulderlength hair, a thin face,
big, wild eyes, and a tall, narrow body disguised with
loose clothes. Scott, thirty-two, is an artist who shows
with a hip local gallery. Balding and schlumpy, with an
agreeable, unshaven face, he's overeducated, spaced out,
and extremely neurotic.

"Luke, you're too metaphysical for words." Scott
smiled... sarcastically?

"Whatever." Sometimes Scott totally weirded Luke
out. He grabbed for the phone. "I'll call Mason."

Scott stood up and clomped in the bathroom's direction.

"Mason," Luke said when a nasal voice answered. "We're out the door."

Then Luke sits for a half-minute, eyes glazed, absorbing Guided By Voices. Their fractured, archaic pop stylings are not to his taste. He's into trippy, computer built, danceable soundscapes. So he has a little daydream re: Chris, this acquaintance of mine, Robert's, Tracy's, and Mason's. Chris is a disturbed twenty-two year old junkie/porn star who looks like an elongated child. In reality, they've never spoken. In Luke's fantasy, they're at the used CD store where Chris works, and their eyes accidentally meet. There's a flash of recognition. It could be emotional, spiritual, sexual, whatever. The details don't matter.

Scott reentered the livingroom, sat.

"Deja vu," Luke muttered. He'd seen Scott reenter the room in that exact way before. Time was, he'd have suspected such thoughts were just fallout from LSD, DMT, Ecstacy... Now he knew they were magical.

Guided By Voices: "Oh, I... / wouldn't dare to... / bring out this... / awful bliss."

"Really?" Scott asked with his usual amazement. "You saw me walk in here before? We-ei-ird."

Once I dropped acid three times a day for a month. It was the summer, my sixteenth. My family was taking our yearly vacation on Maui, Hawaii. I'd made this friend, Craig, a local surfer with great drug connections. Every morning we'd score a few blotter hits, hitchhike to this remote beach, and spend the day zonked, hallucinating, babbling, and swimming around in the ocean. After several weeks, we started to lose it. We'd found this coral reef a short distance offshore. One day we robbed a hotel room, stole a truck, and transported the room's furnishings to the beach. We towed our loot, piece by piece, through the surf, underwater, and into this huge, cavelike nook in the reef, setting each chair, rug, etcetera in place, then swimming furiously back for the surface. Our plan was to live in this cave, rent free, far away from fascistic reality. It never crossed our minds that we wouldn't be able to breathe.

Mason was waiting in front of his building. Tallish and slim, he had a newborn goatee, tiny eyes, and an ironic manner. Seeing Luke's car, he gave a tidy little wave that was a bit self-parodic.

"Hey," the trio announced in a cluster.

As they drove, Mason declaimed about the beauty of Blur's bassist Alex, who'd just inspired a new group of his famous collages.

One afternoon we were hitchhiking out to our favorite beach when a carload of young Hawaiian natives pulled up. They half-jokingly ordered us into their car. On acid, we agreed. It was a known fact that most locals hated white tourists, whom they accused of gentrifying their island. They especially hated the hippies. And with our long hair and cut offs, we qualified. As they drove, the car's occupants taunted us. One whipped out a knife. I don't remember too well, but somewhere along the way they announced they were going to kill us. Craig played along. But I started crying and pleading with them, which I guess spoiled their fun, since they pulled the car over, and ordered us out. They drove off. We were safe, but I couldn't shake off my hysteria. For the next maybe ten or so hours I lay by the side of the road, convulsing, screaming, flailing my arms and legs uncontrollably, hallucinating so hard it was like being constantly punched in the face, while poor Craig tried in various ways to attract me back into the real.

"Is this funereal enough?" Tracy fed the new Guided By Voices CD into the player, and punched track 15. "There." She rose to her feet.

Out poured a charred, thudding song redolent of the early punk era, but sweetened, perhaps in production. Within seconds an irony-drenched vocal sliced through, and she returned to the couch, eyeing Robert suspiciously.

"Kind of," said Robert. Like Tracy, he was short, pale, watery-featured, and twenty. His deepset blue eyes were consistently sad, but his voice had a brittle, imperious manner, which made him unpopular, hence lonely. Hence that look in his eyes.

I've successfully blocked out those ten scary hours, but they were the worst and most profound of my life. I felt completely alone and lost. In my few clearer moments, between hallucinations, I believed I'd gone totally insane, or what people characterize as insane, and suspected I'd never return to the world, in which Craig, acting as the unofficial ambassador for everyone I'd ever known, saw me off with such bewildering tenderness. I wasn't confused. Despite my explosive behavior, I felt an unusual clarity. I knew more than I'd known, and yet, as part of this mental upgrading, I understood how this "genius" would isolate me. All that otherworldly information, so suddenly focused, available, etcetera had no accompanying language. But in describing my state, I'm unable to note more than its skimpiest outline. That's my point. How can I bring what I learned in that world into my everyday consciousness, then translate those thoughts into palatable terms, even assuming the knowledge is still in my brain somewhere? It's one of my big goals in life.

"Kick him," said Robert. He pointed at Chris, whose long, slight, androgynous body lay spookily still on the carpet. It had a Pieta-esque twist.

In the background, Guided By Voices blared away, giving the situation a tense, darkly comical spin.

Tracy shrugged. "If he's dead, he's dead."

"Well, what if he's dying?" Robert's eyes attacked hers, although, mentally at least, he was horrified, period.

Chris had been drugging himself in death's general direction for years, to his friends' mild amusement. In a way they were partly to blame, having offered half-jokey encouragement, supplying heroin, works... Not to mention their numerous, lengthy discussions of suicide and so forth. Tonight he'd crossed the line, it appeared. His "minute to rest", i.e. his little struggle with bad nausea had lasted... two unnervingly motionless hours, more or less.

Tracy dipped the pointy tip of her shoe into Chris's

black jeans and gave a very slight push.

Guided By Voices: "When you motor away / beyond the once-red lips..."

"Oh, shit." Robert stuck out his shoe, kicked. Chris slid a half-foot toward the door. His hands did little flip flops. The palms bloomed. His face sort of... slackened, is one way to put it.

Guided By Voices: "When you free yourself / from the chance of a lifetime..."

Among recreational drugs, only heroin and LSD access the sublime, to my knowledge. Still, their styles are completely dichotomous. LSD can make anyone brilliant, temporarily at least, but there's a catch, i.e., it also renders one freakish, inarticulate, an idiot savant uncomprehendingly jailed within the crude rights and wrongs of the world's "sane" majority. Opiates, on the other hand, tend to instigate a flirtation with death, which, of course, is a physical state one can only romanticize, which, as a consequence, makes one's flirtation with dying inherently profound, since "profound" and "unknowable" are synonyms, right? But serious opiate use can lead to actual death, and while dying lets users transcend their society's simplistic presumptions, it leaves the dead person's life and beliefs vulnerable to the lame revisioning of the long lived.

In the Whisky's dim men's room, Luke and Scott stood in parallel stalls, shaking piss off their dicks.

"LSD," said a weary voice.

Luke zipped up, did a three-quarter turn.

"It's Owsley," continued a tall, sunburned, skateboardy

kid with blond dreadlocks. His eyes radiated a cut rate malevolence. "Made to the specifications of the old hippie chemist himself," he continued. "So it's fierce shit."

One more thing while I'm remembering it. A year, maybe two, before my Mauian flip out — when I was fourteen, I think — I did mushrooms with five or so friends. One of them, Lee, a half-Korean pianist, began to hallucinate so furiously that he exited his body, or so it appeared, since his face lost all warmth and tore wide open, every orifice flared in a grotesque silent scream. The sight totally unsettled the rest of us. Well, all except for his girlfriend, who wasn't stoned, and who kept studying his wrenched, frozen face, then turning to us and whispering, with a huge, clueless smile, "God, I want to be in there with him." That moment really stayed with me, I don't know why.

"Wh-wha..?" Chris mumbled. He raised his head.

"Chris," Robert said, trying to sound unperturbed. "We should go. If we want to catch Blur at the Whisky, I mean..."

Tracy was hunched over, cooking a shot for the road. The spoon blackened, crusted up, etcetera in the tip of a skinny flame.

They each do a shot. Then they sprawl around for a few minutes, nodding out, nodding in. Robert organizes them into a unit that fits through the door, down the street, into Tracy's truck, which he insists upon driving, being a total control freak. On route, each one thinks spacily about death. To Robert, death is the enemy.

When it's a subject, he broods, period. Tracy weighs dying's positives and negatives. To her, death's synonymous with suicide, an act she contemplates every day as a way to... control her life? Chris just wants to die. It's been his lifelong obsession. To become dead as gradually and with as much intricacy as is humanly possible. He wants to feel himself fading away from one world, fading into what's next. There'd be a point, he imagines, when he would be simultaneously dead and alive. For that moment, however tiny, he'd know everything there is to know about human existence.

I'm playing an LP that came out the summer I took too much acid. As soon as the needle eased down on its crackly surface, that experience flashed back.

The phone rings. Shit. "Hello, yeah," I say into it.

"It's me." Luke was barely a rip in some distorted pop music. Blur's "She's So High," by the sound of it.

"Luke," I blurt. "Hey." I just totally fucking adore Luke.

"Listen, you won't believe this," Luke yelled. "Scott and I just dropped acid. But nothing's happening yet."

Chris works at a used CD store. For kicks he collects Children's Literature and acts in cheap porn films. Still, he's relatively asexual, not out of confusion. Sex just isn't an issue, except when he needs some quick cash, or wants badly enough to be friends with someone who's attracted to him. He blames drugs, which have helped him evolve. He's been stoned in one way or another since he was eleven. Drugs' pharmaceutical kick has circumvented whatever makes sex so supposedly sublime. Chris doesn't need people, or not in that lovey dovey, spiritual way. All of which gives him a slightly ethereal air. So he's kind of invisible, to most peers at least. But every once in a while, a certain woman or man will obsess on him. Mostly abject, artsy types for some reason. Being passive and drugged out, he's easily drawn into others' emotional gravity.

When Chris, Robert, and Tracy lurched into The Whisky, Luke hugged them, especially Chris.

Blur: "She's so high / I want to crawl all over her."

Robert nodded out, in for the band's entire set. Blur seemed fine, no big deal. He supposed they were cute. When the house lights came up, he asked Mason, who was both gay and intelligent, "What did you think?"

"That I want to have sex with the bassist."

I want to namecheck the record I'm playing, since its dated style is influencing my words. It's Donovan's Mellow Yellow. Donovan was an acidhead folkie who put out two brilliant, late 60's LPs, then kicked drugs, went New Age, and became the embarrassing twit whom his name brings to most people's minds. For a brief time he managed to translate the tone of an LSD high into exotic yet palatable songs. They're more souvenier-like than knowledgeable, but they do draw a sketch, however kitschy in tone, of that particular mental locale. Beneath their lame "period" surface, I can detect an eerie hint of enlightenment's siren.

Sunset Blvd. curved to the left... right... left... right... Its shapeliness made Robert want to get high, but what didn't?

"Can you drop me at Pam's?" Chris asked. He'd been slouched inbetween his friends, lost in forgettable day-dreams. I starred in one for a second.

"Sure." They'd stopped at a light. Robert and Tracy were trading fierce, miserable winces encoded with tons of interpersonal bullshit.

For years after my ten hour freak out, I wouldn't touch drugs. Then they filtered back into my lifestyle again, one by one. Except for acid, the mere idea of which gave me a mild nervous breakdown. Still, memory's weird. And there came this one night when... But I'm getting ahead of myself. Point is, some of the drugs I was using — pot, hashish, speed, mushrooms, Ecstacy — referenced my acid trip, but in a manageable way, sort of like documentary films do their nonfictional subjects. I would experience a shadowy form of the original freak out, and the proximity thrilled me. So I started to flirt with my lon-glost insanity, with drugs' assistance. Some nights I would wind up so mentally gone that my drug buddy friends had to slap me around trying to coerce me back.

As Luke drove, the freeway lost... something.

'What if the stars are the sky, and the sky is the stars?' Scott was thinking. He studied the windshield. '...If the blackness is solid, a wall, and the white bits are speckles of light that have escaped from whatever's just past that black barrier.'

In the back seat, Mason sat, eyes unfocussed, imagin-ing collages.

'...That's where the truth is,' Scott thought. 'In that whiteness the sky keeps away from our knowledge. What

if a 747 were flown into one of those specks?
Wouldn't... that..?'

One year ago, when I was writing for Spin Magazine, the editor asked me to spend a few days with an HIV-positive, homeless teenager named David and his gang of friends, then write up what happened. One of David's friends was a tall, blond, angelic punk rocker and part-time street hustler named Sniffles. He asked me to buy him, and, maybe because I was lonely and sort depressed at the time, I did. Thing is, he liked to be hit and slapped around, and, even though my imagination's a freezer compartment for violent thoughts, I'm a wuss. I was into crystal meth at the time, and before we went to bed I chain-snorted a gram. Crystal makes me psychotically horny. Sniffles had just dropped some Ecstacy, so he was feeling all warm and invulnerable. Anyway, things went a little insane. I intend to go into the details, just not at the moment. First I need to arrange a few things so I'll feel more at ease.

As soon as I open the front door, it's obvious. "Shit, you guys are really fucked up," I say, looking from Luke's stricken face to Scott's, to Mason's.

"Not me," Mason said. And he wandered inside.

Scott veered past my shoulder. "Oh, boy," he said, blinking. "Where's the... living room?"

Scrounging around in one pocket, Luke found, produced the last hit of acid. "Throw this away," he insisted. "Immediately."

It's spooky how Ecstacy floods one with indiscriminate

affection. It's a chemical lie. It kills thought, undermines sensibility. LSD, on the other hand, neatly demystifies sex. It can. I remember. On a great acid trip, you begin to realize the insidious way lust distorts almost every decision we make. Acid encourages us to embrace isolation, to disempower other human beings, especially their bodies. When LSD works, it makes clear how inane and addictive sex is, and how culture's overvaluation of physical contact keeps us from a true understanding of life and death issues. Maybe this lesson particularly struck home in my case since my fantasy life has been so sexual in nature and murderous in content.

"Later, guys." Chris, hugging himself to keep warm, trotted into a typical, faintly lit mini-mall. When he turned to wave bye, his friends' truck was a dot.

On the truck's staticky radio, Pavement's "Cut Your Hair" crossfaded into... uh, Guided By Voices?

"Let's fucking end it," said Robert. The idea arrived out of nowhere. Words just... formed, disconnected from everything else. He thought for a second then steered toward some oncoming traffic.

Tracy's eyes watered. "Okay," she said. And she covered her face.

I'll say this once. I'm extremely fucked up. It doesn't show, but I am. Over the years I've developed a sociable, generous side which I train on the people I know. It makes them feel grateful, which makes me feel purposeful. But secretly, I'm so confused about everyone and everything. Sometimes these moods will just come out of nowhere and lay me out. I'll curl up in bed for long peri-

ods of time, catatonic and near suicidal. Or I'll space into
a murderous sexual fantasy wherein some cute young
acquaintance or stranger is dismembered in intricate
detail, simply because he's too painfully delicious, i.e.,
through no fault of his own. But LSD cured this psy-
chosis, in hindsight at least. That's why I'm going to slip,
as "recovery" types like to say. Because for ten longlost,
jumbled-up hours I'd known a kind of... whatever, peace?
That's my current belief.

"Luke's so... amazing," I say, knowing that word's lim-
itations. I'm thinking about... well, pretty much everything about him "It's just overwhelming, you know?"

"You think?" Mason asked. "I guess I can vaguely
remember deciding so once."

Something about the black shirt Scott was wearing
made Luke sort of astral project into...

"Where's that kiddie porn tape?" Mason asked. He'd
crouched down by the shelves where I keep CDs, videos.

This is sort of a secret, but Chris and I are involved. The
whats, hows, wheres, whys will come along later. Suffice
to say, Chris is my type. Then factor in his death wish,
which is neatly aligned with my aforementioned dreams.
Problem is, now that my fantasy's so do-able, I can tell
how complex the thing is. I'm not just stupidly tranced
by the prospect of killing some boy during sex, even if
that great idea's been a bit too ignited by Chris's and my
interractions. Anyway, I'm sort of torn between Chris,
who accesses the evil in me, and Luke, whom I'm beginning to love in a pure, unerotic, devotional way that I
never would have thought myself capable of even four

months ago. And I have to make a choice, or I want to. Actually, I've made my choice. That's why Chris has to go, I don't know how.

A twelve year old kid stands around in Pam's studio, giggling. Marijuana smoke honks in and out of his freckled little nose. He has a delicate build and extremely black hair.

Chris shoots him a look of, well... sadness, bewilderment, jealousy. Some combination of those.

"Want a toke?" the kid asks. A shakey hand holds out the joint. "'Cause..." His eyes get confused. "... uh..." His jaw drops an unflattering inch, his eyes glaze. The whole face kind of... stiffens, as if it were made out of clay and Pam's place was a kiln.

Scott saw through Luke. Literally. The guy was a multi-hued mist. Luke, staring back, noticed something elaborately offkey in the world. Because Scott's eyes were too... dried out. When Luke wasn't there, beyond stoned, in a friend's livingroom, appreciating the fibrous texture of... what's-his-name's eyes, his view was blocked, thoughts mechanically consumed by a weird hallucination, i.e., he kept driving his car over a squashed, sizzling dog on some intensely overlit desert road. Really, over and over and over.

"Amazing," I say, studying Luke's gone expression. "How long..?"

A purplish-red orb strobed intently somewhere in Luke's universe.

"Don't ask me," Mason said from my kitchen. He cracked the fridge. I heard a beer bottle gasp. "First they kept saying how fucked up they were. Then they shut up completely. So... since they shut up, I guess. Twenty minutes?"

I'm studying the pill. "Want to split this?"

I've tried to reconstruct my acid-fueled nervous breakdown on Maui, because between brief bouts of horrified consciousness, wherein my difference from everyone else in the world seemed profound, I saw such intense things. Have I said that already? But the experience is lost, or polluted at least, by a bevy of earlier trips, and some later "flip outs," say my insane sex with Sniffles, or my entanglement with Chris. The memories are weirdly inseparable, blurred, I don't know why. Maybe there's something to getting incredibly stoned then having sex with self-destructive young guys that resembles the world acid showed me. But there are differences too, which I hope to define.

Robert was maybe just maybe one quarter alive but... Tracy was definitely dead. No fucking doubt a-fucking-bout it. Because she was... upside down?

Guided By Voices: "The hole I dig is bottomless / But nothing else can set me free."

Tracy couldn't... quite... think, but she could sort of, um, sense a kind of... haze, hiss. "Um..."

Robert moved his head very, very slightly. Oh, excellent.

The skin on Luke's face was a fog. Scott could see, or almost see, his friend's skull, or, more specifically, that curious object which certain historical types once so lazily labelled "the skull." It was more like a pkhw... Words failed Scott. A filament? But weren't words too complex to manipulate properly? Luke, for instance, meant nothing compared to the word "Luke," because it defined a million people named Luke. Or take love. Love was the world's favorite word. But it was also a lie that human beings made up to avoid actual knowledge, which was itself a lie. Or cancer. Cancer was a word that encapsulated a thought which had never reached clarity, which was why the disease was incurable. If Scott could think clearly from morning 'til night everyday of his life, he would never get cancer. Oh my God. It was so fucking simple. No, it was.

"So what's going on, Pam?" Chris lets out some smoke. "Here, take this." He hands the joint back to the kid, who pinches, looks down at it.

"Nothing." Pam's gazing daydreamily at what's-his-little-name, who's very slowly tamping out what's still around of the joint in a nearby ashtray.

"So," Chris says, turning to the kid. "What's your name?"

"Huh?" The kid blinks himself away from some thought asteroid. "What?"

Goof, aka Nicholas Klein, is a horridly parented twelve year old. Before he got sucked into drugs, his whole life was nightmarish. Now he's okay, sort of. Good sense of humor. Hence his nickname. Still, one shouldn't let oneself get too attached, because he's dying. Right now, unbeknownst to him, thanks to some undiagnoseable problem in one of his heart valves or something. But it'll

155

work out okay. No one will miss him, and, thanks to a brief stint co-starring in kiddie porn videos, he'll leave behind a vital body of work that'll only be more resonant with the knowledge he's dead. Trust me.

Robert was haze, on the inside at least. Thoughts sort of... frittered around. Skinwise, forget it. Might as well go ahead and die then... live... like...

Tracy: xklijmpprtizk...

Robert just bought it. Internal injuries. He... hazed. Emptied out. Refilled with something too complicated for words.

Robert: knxggsvzkqtt...

Pam's not so bad. If she could express how she feels, she'd be motherly even. Apart from her thing for young boys, she's a dyke with an ongoing, serious relationship. Physically she's large, a former fat girl turned comfortably husky, not without a shitload of effort. Her hair's brownish and short, her clothes casual, bland, and male-esque. Like me, she's fascinated by kiddie porn. Unlike me, she can justify making the stuff for a living. Until recently I could justify watching it, period. Now I'm confused. As a way to help Chris overcome his obsessive death wish, I've instigated a project, a kind of pseudo-snuff kiddie porn film to be scripted by me, starring Chris, and directed by Pam. I'm thinking it might be a safe, effective way for Chris and I to semi-act out our intermeshed fantasies once and for all, not to mention making Pam infamous on the kiddie porn circuit, which I believe is her goal.

Mason studied Scott's awestruck or horrified face. "What do you think they're... seeing?"

156

I swallow the pill. "Hard to know," I say, handing Mason his beer. "Luke, Scott? Can you hear me? Hey!"

Luke's eyes are greenish... no, hazel... no, aquamarine, with a spray of brown speckles and kind of, uh, yellowy smears.

Scott heard not words but a million or so little tones that were so beautifully interlinked that he got the idea to record someone saying those words then release it on CD.

Luke's eyes are the immediate clue to his greatness. Without them, he'd just be a sweet looking raver, on first glance at least. They're large, multicolored, and often glazed over in serious thought. That's a guess. Anyway, they seem complicatedly wired. It's awe inspiring to be in his presence. Especially that night, thanks to acid. Luke, meanwhile, was smiling unseeing at my awestruck face, having checked into another reality. He could tell what he'd envisioned was wrong on a technical level. Still, he believed it was real. At the same time, he could think lucidly on his ridiculous state, i.e., Why would my mind construct this? How exactly does LSD work? Then the clarity would erode and he'd be watching a purplish-red orb flash rapidly on a depthless black field, thinking, Wow.

"I'm Goof," says the kid. He holds out one hand.

Chris gives it a shake. "Great name." Then he glances at Pam, who looks much less... well, distant than usual. "What're you thinking?"

"Just..." Pam says. "... about the project with Dennis. Wondering if Goof could play you as a kid."

"Sure, why not?" Chris says, wondering how to change

the subject to heroin. He gives Goof a cursory peer.
"Maybe... if you dyed his..." A yawn eats the sentence.

Chris would rather not crash there at Pam's, but, what
with sleepiness being so fascist, it's not like he has any
choice. So he asks her if he can take a very short nap, half
an hour at most. 'Sure,' Pam says, and kindly finds him
some dope and a clean set of works. Then Chris mock-
salutes Goof, who's too out of it or whatever to notice,
and scuffs into a little room just off the studio where Pam
shoots her porns, kicks the door shut, and whips off his
way stinky t-shirt, jeans, Nikes. Cooking his shot, he
thinks and simultaneously tries not to think about me.
But his hazed imagination keeps ensnaring my face in its
web or whatever.
      "This works fast," I say, turning to Mason. "If I space
too far out, stick around, keep an eye on me, yeah?" And
even as I say this I'm spacing out.
      "Will do," Mason said. He was over by my VCR,
crouched, doing something.
      Donovan: "Looking through crystal spectacles / I can
see I had your fun."
      Scott was... outside, yeah. In a... driveway?

Scott was standing in somebody's driveway. Oh yeah,
Luke's. There was Luke, perched on the hood of a car. He
was talking, gesturing, etcetera, but Scott couldn't hear
shit. No, that's not true. He heard whooshing. Actually,
the sound was extremely refined. Someone had obviously composed it. No wait, Luke's mouth was emitting it.
Shit. Trying to sort out the details, Scott leaned back on

a hedge to his rear. But the surface of leaves was flimsier than it looked, and he plunged into the depths of the plant's slightly springy brown skeleton, then had to claw his way out.

"Hold on," Pam says. "Before you go, I think I owe you some money."

"Cool, thanks." Goof digs around in a pocket. "'Cause I don't know if I'll see you again." He slides out a comb. "I'm going to... change my life."

Pam's counting out twenties. "Really?" She extends about seven, eight. "Well then, am I entitled to one last request?" And she eyeballs his crotch.

"God, you're gross," Goof yells, half-joking. "Allright, allright. But... I get to pick out the soundtrack." And he runs toward a Guided By Voices CD.

I met Chris through Robert and Tracy. Occasionally I'd shop at the store where he worked. Since he was my type, I'd developed a harmless, persistent little crush like one does. I forget how the subject came up, but I told them that I was attracted to Chris, and they told me how Chris had been known to trade sexual favors for dope. One night I dropped by the store around closing time, dropped a few hints, offered to buy him heroin, and we spent an extremely strange night at his place. Sexually, he was open to anything safe, but he didn't give a shit the whole time very obviously. Let's just say he was pliable. And with all that freedom, and fueled by his self-destructive urges, I guess I went sort of insane. I intend to go into the details, just not yet.

Scott stared into something beyond the constraints of human language.

Luke's eyes are so mezmerising they're practically... what? I study their swirly, multiplicitous color for what seems like days, thinking, Wow.

Donovan: Dow dow dow dow... dow dow... dow... dow dow.

Luke stared into something beyond the constraints of human language.

"Mason," I say. He's playing a video. Kiddie porn, I think. "I'm... going."

I'm practically gone. Luke, Scott are gone. There's no point in describing their mental locales. Just accept that they're in two very vast, complicated, non-narrative states. Me, I'm still flashing in and out of what we call reality. Mason has put on a kiddie porn tape that Pam lent me, i.e., three hours of Super 8 films poorly transferred to video. Goof co-stars in eight, nine of them, coincidentally. He's a favorite of mine. In fact, once when I accidentally blink the real world into place for a couple of seconds, Goof's ass is this splayed, perfect, shimmering, televised orb in my peripheral vision. Normally, seeing his ass in that state would fire off a violent daydream, but, thanks to the acid I'm sure, it seems more like a... whatever, bric a brac. Kitsch. So when a finger appears on the screen and is shoved up the ass, I literally don't understand. In other words, I'm in a better place.

Mason spaced out, daydreaming. In his fantasy, Goof's slutty asshole belonged to Blur's bassist. And that

160

finger was Mason's.

Luke, Scott: klvxmhspwwlqhx...

"God," I say. "This is... so... intense." I'm looking at something in Luke's staring eyes that you wouldn't understand.

Mason glanced over at us. All's well, he thought. Still... "You guys okay?" Nothing. So he reburrowed his eyes into Blur's bassist's "body."

Truth is dry. You'll know the truth when everything in your world seems as if it's been cooked until nothing is left but the exact information that separates it from other things in the world. On acid, you look at a thing, any-thing, with complete understanding. At the same time, everything's more mindboggling than ever. And that combination's the truth. It's as if the brain power you normally waste fantasizing sex, love, etcetera had been redistributed to your non-human contacts, i.e., between you and a... I don't know, TV set or whatever. Something finite.

Pam's sculpting two teeny clown hats out of Goof's giant nipples. From the look on his face, he seems very, very into it.

Guided By Voices: "I'm too tired to run from the tiger / I'm too dumb to hide in the bushes."

Suddenly there's this, like, unbelievable pain. Upper chest. "Oh, fuck." Goof gasps, gasps, gasps, balls his fists. "Please... stop."

The very second Pam frees up Goof's nipples, he dies. Empties out. Looks all weird. Crumples up on the floor.

And then there was one. I mean one rational mind in the story. I.e., mine. Everyone else was asleep, dead, in shock, drugged, or horny. Comparatively at least, I maintained a kind of semi-sobriety, by virtue of Luke, who, out-of-it as we were, held my faltering interest, I don't know why. Love, weird. So, hoping to stay in that half-aware state, I pulled out the notebook and pen I always carry around, and began to take notes on my surroundings, occasionally adding a cryptic bit of analysis. Not that anything brilliant showed up on the page.

Doug Lee

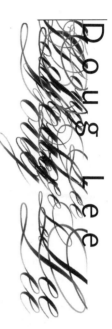

First Name Stella

The shit just rains in and you wish you could escape it. The word 'regret' spells out instant shit stained face and I want to remember but I'd rather forget everything. That's right I can't remember any thing. I just see these fucking patterns that have long since become boring and routine. Fuck them, I'm starting to remember last night and I don't know what it means, but I'm starting to see myself and these people from a distance and they start surrounding me like there's something to see down there like I'm dead or something. Yeah, I'm dreaming and I know if I open my eyes it'll all just fucking disappear, then I'll stop seeing myself and all those fuckers I hate. I'm okay though I think my back and teeth feel stupid and I'm shivering but I don't think I'm cold. I feel like I should open my eyes. I wanna know wherever it is that I am cause I don't recall too much from last night at all. What was I doing? I remember someone dumb looking at my body with big sick eyes. I didn't like it but I was like too tired to move or something. There were more too, with yucky faces, their faces were so ugly, fuck. Their faces...I remember wondering: *Why is everyone so gross?* It was like someone had buckets of their sick greasy faces and was dumping them on me. I can't explain how disgusted I felt. Everyone was looking at me like I was the center of attention or something, I hate that. Why was everyone looking at me? I think I was laughing, I hate laughing. Why was I laughing? Maybe their ugly faces were too much for me to handle, but somehow I doubt that was the case. I'm a good person. Why do these things always happen to me? I don't hurt anybody...they just hurt me. It doesn't hurt though.

I think I stopped crying when I was like 12. I realized crying was a waste of time and couldn't figure out why I was crying to begin with. I'm stronger now. I'm a strong person. They think they can hurt me. They think I'm dumb. Everyone thinks that I am like stupid and just because I'm 15 I'm like gonna fucking die out here or something or get raped or some shit. Who the fuck is going to hurt me anyway not some stupid dirty fucked up old drunken bum, plus I'm never without my friends anyway and it's really not so bad. You know, my dad never thought I was stupid. He knew I could take care of myself. He always understood me. He's the only man I ever really liked. I remember I could tell him about anything, we'd just talk and shit and sometimes at night I'd let him touch me. It was nice. Of course this is well after I realized how ridiculous those little animated commercials are between cartoons that said to tell someone if some dirty old fuck has got his hands down your pants or something, but I let my dad because I liked it too. I wouldn't of let him if I didn't. We almost fucked one time, but that's another story altogether. My dad was total trash but at the same time he was totally honest with me. We had a good relationship. I grew up in a total white trash "atmosphere". Not like a trailer home and shit like that but like this one time when I was 10 in the old house my dad got in a fight with the Robinsons, our neighbors, I can't remember why but he always called them the niggers so I don't know. But anyway they had a daughter, Sissy. She and I were best friends and after the fight I thought my dad wasn't going to let me play with Sissy anymore but he never really said anything or I can't really remember. What the hell am I talking about? Why am I telling you all this shit anyway and why the fuck am I talking like I'm writing a novel and who the hell has got their hand down my pants?

Later:
"... you gotta help me, I feel like shit." I was at Anne's house now.
"Stella, are you okay?"
"Do I look okay? Just let me in." Anne had an unpleasant look on her face. I guess I looked pretty bad.
"What happened?"
"I woke up in the alley again."
"Again? Where are your pants?"
"I-I don't know, I just want to lay down." I didn't feel too bad but I wanted Anne to be worried about me.
"What happened?"
"I don't know, I can't remember. W-what am I doing? I mean fuck. You were there. You probably know better than me."
"I don't know you were like all over the place being dumb. I can't believe you do that shit. You shouldn't shoot smack, that's really gross." I wanted to say shut up, Anne.
"Smack? That wasn't smack that was like some sugar and some other crap. That got me about as high as when we decided to smoke banana peels that one time."
"Still, don't get into that, that's really gross...I knew this guy...he shot up...and...he said...he woke...later...I guess he took Ex-lax but...

Anne is so beautiful. I stopped listening to her and was looking at her face. Anne has short bleached hair that holds the room together and I really like how her bottom lip tucks under her top lip when she pronounces certain words, particularly ones that start with "F". Seeing Anne always makes me feel good about myself. Anne was the first girl. I kissed her first, she was scared. I laid on my back hugging a big dumb pillow and watched Anne walk on the shag carpet ceiling. She ran around the apartment getting ready to go somewhere while yelling at me for acting so irresponsibly last night and mumbling stuff I can't hear but it didn't matter cause I wasn't listening anyway. I was too hooked on the visuals of Anne waltzing around the old room getting ready like in some old movie, like for a second I thought I was watching a movie too. She came out of the bathroom with her big bag that made her fall to one side while she tried to put a jacket on and dragging shoes in slipper fashion across the ground when eventually coming in contact with the wall that kept her from falling flat on her face. I had to check just to make sure that there wasn't a projector hiding in the wall spitting out that flickering cone shaped light thing. When I turned around, I saw it, there it was the bright spot and the diffusing light shaft that caught dust particles like they were swimming around and through it, at first I got scared cause I couldn't believe what the fuck I was seeing, then I realized that there's just a hole in the wall and a tree on the other side that was shaking in the breeze. What I was seeing was probably a residual effect from my multiple experimentations with hallucinogenic chemicals. Then I couldn't help but think about the movie I will one day have Anne star in like "Ms. 45", only with a dyke that has a big dirty mouth and kills lots of boys and politicians and stuff. Only she's not mute and she's not crazy she's just bad and she's dirty cause dirty girls are cool her face is always dirty and she'll shit at least four times in the movie because people never shit in movies...All of a sudden Anne yelled something and slammed the door. It scared the shit out of me. I instantly forgot every thing I was thinking about and watched her head bob up and down outside the little window and the trees turned their heads while she left me and invited the quiet in to keep me company. I got lonely and felt guilty for making Anne mad at me. I really love Anne I don't know what to do. She says I'm selfish and insensitive - I am, but I just fuckin'...I don't know. I know, I'll buy Anne a present.

I left Anne's apartment and shut the door behind me but didn't lock it in case I had to come back. I hate walking in this hallway there's always this smell like steamy pee. Now I'm walking down the alley behind her house. I always look at the ground when I walk cause there's no telling what kind of shit you're gonna step in, one time I stepped in puke and that's worse than any shit or piss cause the smell doesn't go away for weeks. Luckily there doesn't seem to be anything too threatening down there except for the usual black gum stains and some old shit stains. Down in that old lot behind the fence I see a couple of kids poking at what probably is a dead bum. One of them got up by his head and started kicking it a bunch of times. The other kids are watching him and you can tell they're scared of him. It kinda reminds me of the sound of smashing pumpkins on Halloween. We'd stomp on the pumpkins of the people that gave out pennies or peanuts, only that kid's got some serious shit he makes the overcast clouds mean instead of sad because his little leg is working so hard with those clunky boots. Someone should tell him that dead bum's not his dad. I figure I should eat something but I'd rather get high. There's some old crusty guys that look to be concealing something and I know it's crack. I hope they're nice...

"You guys got Smoke ?"

"What? No." He smokes crack cause his teeth are too fucked up for him to eat anything.

"Can I have a hit ?"

"You got green?" The other guy was old his ears were big and I could hear the sound of all the years of disappointment and see the regret in his face. His face was beat but strong, his hair was overgrown and goofy. His milky eyes made me kind of scared. They were dying to fall out of his head and reunite with mother earth.

"No, I don't got none,"I said.

"Well then you ain't getting none." He was protective.

"What's a little girl like you want with shit anyway?" the other one said.

"Why don't you just get the little kid high?" said the protective one, like for some reason getting me high is like teaching me a lesson or he's trying to prove that he just doesn't give a shit about anyone.

"Okay you can have the first hit Shirley." (Shirley?)

I took a very big hit I caught myself trying to be cool. I instantly started racing when it came around again and for some reason I took another big one and that was it, I think I was on the ground for six years or something but those guys took off and left me. My skeleton fused into one bone and I couldn't move, my fucking heart was no longer in synch with my breathing and, my hands were grabbing the ground, little pebbles that left indentions in my palms like I had some sort of fucking skin disease. I'm lying here staring at the edge of the building against the overcast sky with clouds softly going against everything I ever was, like for some fucked up reason they hate me and the city who never gave a fuck about girls and every fucking asshole there ever was whose dick I sucked cause I thought it was cool was now those beautiful clouds and I'm the one who's ugly right? I know, like if for some reason I thought I was right you knew I was wrong because my movie is over and I'm getting the award for best director of the stupidest movie. Fuck, I think every decision I ever made was the wrong one and the shit keeps filling my eyes in the form of the only nice things I ever made that hit the ground in puddles and kills the taste of real life when it hurts the worst. And every one that was ever good to me who made me laugh who I made laugh who I love but was too stupid to say anything: Anna, the kitten, my dad. I wish they knew how much it means to share the same moment in time cause I'm almost all out and I wish I could hear their voices one more time cause right now I can only hear the familiar sound of pumpkins smashing and cruel clouds filled with childish contempt and the words I told you so and their happy white faces falling in the form of rain while they fly over head each eager to catch a glimpse of me crying with the dunce cap in the corner like even then

I would never amount to anything. Well there I am, I'm looking at my body again and I guess I am something to see and there's everyone I hate too (great) and the little kid who's tired of kicking dead bodies and his little friends are all there with the heavy kicks and the angry clouds they just never rest always wanting to smash my pumpkin like it's Halloween.

Halloween was over and I was back at Anne's trying to explain my out of body experience. She was sitting around the apartment attempting to understand me while slowly just becoming another piece of furniture.

"I was like fuck, there must be about a million of them looking at me. What should I do? I hate them. I can't stop crying. I wish they would leave. I think I'm dead," I was saying.

"Really, you were crying?"she said.

"Well, no, but I thought I was dead."

"Oh."

I can't understand her...me...Five minutes ago I convinced myself I would tell her "I love you". I had it all planned out in my head. "Anne I'm sorry I'm so selfish, I love you. I don't want to hurt you. I'm sorry." But what goes on in my head and what comes out of my mouth are two entirely different things. It's like this illness I have. I think too much and whatever I think I can't somehow translate into words. And when I talk it isn't quite what I really want to say. Fuck, now I have to make up some more shit to explain how today was so shitty just because I can't really say how I felt or feel. It's just like this shit you can't escape, right? I'm like so comfortable with shit stains on my face I guess it really doesn't matter. Like I forgot what I look like I wish I could understand what goes on in my round face. I wish stuff was like the movies and that's all there was. Only living is the movies what you think about has nothing to do with it or everything to do with it or whatever.

Sylvere Lotringer

Ball of Fat

he man is standing in the mirror with the grey trench-coat and brown fedora hat cops used to wear in the 40's or 50's. I don't believe he's a cop he looks too much like my father. I can't tell for sure only part of the neck and chin and the thin arc of one ear can be seen floating out of the surrounding darkness. As far as I can tell the face shows no expression. The man's standing against a tall dark curtain — maybe it's a wood paneling the two lines falling vertically on the tip of the hat are much too straight and parallel to be mere curtain folds. Yes it's an old-fashioned wardrobe that's behind the man but the whole thing has a theatrical air about it as if the man was posing there or waiting for some cues. Of course I can't be sure of anything I'm not even certain the mirror is a real mirror it may be the frame of a painting an illusionist painting like Magritte's — the subject standing off center intercepts the frame of the wood-paneling which doubles up from inside the surrounding mirror-frame or its painterly simulation.

The man's looking out — or is on the look-out — but it's difficult to see what he's looking at or for. I can't quite figure out what the angle of reflection is — assuming of course that this is a reflection. The woman in the foreground glances approximately in the same direction but she may as well be looking at nothing just exposing her face to the light which is pouring from a hidden outlet a window presumably. The man may be looking at her — well it would make sense he would — but that would require the presence of another mirror mirroring his own image. In any case both face the same light her from up close him way at the back. His face is lit from below which adds a kind of spectral quality to the scene. I notice he's wearing an arm-band so he is a cop after all or a member of the French militia and not my father. I can't see the inscription on the arm-band since the head of the Greek sculpture sprawled on the mantelpiece is in the way. The sculpture represents a naked athlete throwing a javelin bending backward on the stand his other hand holding a big rock to steady his balance. The javelin is right behind his head and crosses the arm-band which on second thought may just be the reflection of the Greek head in the mirror. The two heads the man's and the sculpture's are not at all the same size or color — one's fuzzy and dark the other of finely chiselled white marble — and they're turned exactly in opposite directions but there is some implied relationship between the two. The athlete's eye is evaluating the trajectory of the javelin. Is the man doing anything of the kind? He may be extending his other arm outside of the mirror like pointing a gun but maybe he's not. The woman's clasping her hands in front of her a strained smile on her face. Is the man threatening her or guarding her against something I can't see?

There's something cold and spare about the whole scene. Although I can't see much of it, the apartment feels empty. Empty and cold. Maybe it's the forced expression on the woman's face her cheeks flushed eyes a little swollen. It must be wintertime she has a cold or something with the kind of smile that verges on tears.

Why does it feel so cold in spite of the light? Suddenly I realize that the man's wearing a coat inside the apartment. The woman's fully dressed too. She's wearing dark gloves and a strange old fashioned hat made of dark material which looks like a French sailor's beret with a fluffy tuft on top. She's also wearing a dark rabbit-skin jacket with broad shoulders and a zipper in front not very becoming at least in today's eyes but obviously quite warm. Yes, it must be winter in Paris early 40's.

The picture is a little tilted to the right as if the photographer didn't have much time to position the camera. The woman herself is standing a little bit off center of the picture a whiff of blonde hair intersecting the mirror-frame — if it is a mirror — situated right behind her. The real center of the picture where the bottom of the frame would have met the top of the mantelpiece is occupied by the woman's chest which hides the man's trunk and the hand holding the javelin. This is the place of her heart. There's something light and geometric directly sewn on the woman's jacket like a direct echo of the man's armband — a piece of fabric made of two overlapping triangles with four gothic letters printed on it — something like "Suif" (candle-grease).

I can't help thinking of a tale by Maupassant which made a strong impression on me when I was a child. It was called "Boule-de-Suif" (Ball-of-Fat) the nickname of a grisette celebrated for her great black eyes and pleasing embonpoint who happened to cross the German lines in the company of Normand merchands and minor provincial nobilities at the time of the Prussian invasion. The carriage with six horses they're in is stopped by a Prussian detail whose officer swears he won't let them go their way until Ball-of-Fat sleeps with him. I remember her companions begging her to prostitute herself Judith-like to the German Holophern and finally treating her like a slut when she accedes to their wishes, well, something of that sort. This atmosphere of danger, suspicion and petty betrayal is forever associated for me with the word "Suif" — although I know, of course, that it is the infamous word "Juif" that is written on the woman's chest. Maybe it is the "greasy" element in Suif that makes it all stick together, an insult I often heard during these years — and after — associated with the Jews.

The woman is my mother. The picture was taken in our apartment in Paris during the German occupation. Why they would have wanted to take a picture of her wearing a yellow star as they were about to go in hiding is really beyond me — such an incriminating piece of evidence. Had the man at the back come to arrest her? It must have been the winter of 1941. The apartment was in Menilmontant a working-class district made world-famous by Maurice Chevallier's soapy songs. 1941 is the year all foreign Jews living in Paris were summarily rounded up at dawn by the French police reinforced by volunteers from the fascist militia and shipped in public busses to the Vel D'Hiv the huge indoor stadium used for sports events in winter time. My mother happened to be in Paris that night — she had come back to buy some food with our rationed tickets. There were rumours of the impending raid but you could never take these at face value. Still she stayed awake all night fully clothed a ladder hanging at the back on top of the concierge's loge just in case. She heard the loud knocks on the doors saw whole families rushed to the sidewalk with a few pieces of luggage. She happened to be at a neighbor's place at the time they forced their way into our apartment. The neighbor too was arrested but they didn't think of checking who my mother was — a real miracle.

It was still dark when the police left the apartment so the picture couldn't possibly have been taken at the time. Did the round-up happen in winter anyway? Although it had this misleadingly innocuous name Vent printanier ("spring wind") it actually took place — I just checked — on July 16, 1941 two days after Bastille day. A few hours after the turmoil subsided my mother ventured to the railroad station and boarded a train hiding her yellow star behind a magazine. In Draveil some twenty miles south of Paris people were peacefully sunning themselves on the beach.

So it might have been my father after all in the mirror. But if so, who took the picture?

My father used to take a lot of pictures before the war. I was just a baby then. In one he held me in his arms in his Foreign Legion uniform. I was so fat I looked like a ball of fur with a fur hat nearly covering my whole face. Ball-of-Fat that could have been my name too at the time. It's only later on when the news from the camps started to filter down to us that I heard about the soaps. Boules-de-Juif I can't help associating the star on the picture with that too.

Daniel Mendel-Black

Pink-9 Has Begun

elcome to Stalingrad where we have just learned that the apartment next door to Stalin's is the gateway to chaos. So says Stalin's mom who is keeping it under the closest surveillance. Stalin's mom, in fact, never leaves her perch by the window. She's absolutely transfixed by all the activity out there. Pink trucks pull up every day. New neighbors are moving in. There's something pink and smooth and lifeless about them. They're almost human-like, the way they move. Except they can't stop smiling. See the way their faces are always transfixed. The way they expose themselves to the light.

Stalin's mom sputters when telling Stalin about the affair next door. She takes a shaky sip from her Bloody Mary. Throws her head back revealing her long soft neck. She smiles ironically to no one in particular.

Stalin's mom remembers quiet children at Stalin's 10th Birthday Party. The sky was fat and gray and a procession of dark clouds came and went all day long. She remembers the lid of a trash can clanking in the tranquil silence of an alley and a revolutionary pamphlet lightly lifting into the stillest breeze. At noon he and his friends will gallop through the factory streets and swarm over chain link fences chasing down all the little girls in the neighborhood. They will tie them up and set every thing they touch on fire. Stalin has never looked so noble. Stalin's mom can still see his dusted coal cheeks and hear his cracking voice. As he stands there in the fiery swirls of black and red, the crackling heat all around him, she remembers him looking up and saying: Fire, I bid you to burn!

Stalin's mom blows her nose into a handkerchief. She thinks his uniform's too big. And she tells him,

"Joseph, you're so pale and skinny and you're practically falling out of your jacket!"

"Joseph, you still comb your black mustache like a Czarist!"

"Joseph, what a pathetic little Napoleon you are!"

To shut her out, Stalin runs the blade of his pen-knife up and down his thumb. What does he care about old stories? He's wondering why a glimpse of squirting red blood in the glint of his blade excites him so much, so he grabs his dinner napkin from his soldier's collar and slaps it on the table, jamming his thumb into it. Stalin grinds it all around. He doesn't stop either. Not 'till his thumb has stopped bleeding and the napkin's good and red.

Either: At precisely 11:30 PM, after sports and weather, Stalin's mom says goodnight to Stalin. He's escorted by three security officers to his waiting red car, and quietly whisked away. Or: At precisely 11:31 PM his security officers don't meet him, and there's no waiting car. Just a dark empty street and all its dark empty shadows. And, either: Stalin waits there a long time. Shuddering in all that cold and dark. Or: At precisely 11:32 PM a pink Impala pulls out behind his red El Dorado and three men in pink ski masks radio in: "Target in sight!" They approach Stalin's car and begin clawing and scratching at his car window until Stalin has to bury his face in a fluffy red pillow. THE PINK CAPTORS laugh electronically, "Hardy Har Har!"

What's definite is that Stalin is taken at gun-point from a red El Dorado or LeBarron at the corner of

Berkshire and Valley Forge or Scarlet and Blanche by either four or five men in pink suits while eye-witnesses clap and shout biting epithets at him at the top of their lungs. As he's carted off they scream "sissy" and "panty-waist" and tell him to go home to his mom. The pink captors shove Stalin, his big red flannel jacket pulled down around his wrists, to the apartment next door, dope him up, and drag him kicking and screaming into a pink cell.

Names! Names! Names! Stalin wants names! The names of all the people who ever laughed at him and called him names. The names of every one of those Capitalist-bastards. There's gonna be hell to pay for every yuppie-child-pornographer-one of them! Only he's having a lot of trouble imagining the executions and mass graves he will have to order for all these names. How can he think about blood baths in such a pink cell? Nothing but pink wherever he looks. Pink floor. Pink walls. Pink ceiling. Pink, pink, pink. Mom! It's revolting. Pink is not a primary color!

Point of fact: The cell is exactly Pink Delight. Otherwise Stalin is right to describe the cell as sparse. Besides the metal frame chair Stalin's sitting in and the monitor on the wall there's little else. Only a cot in the corner, and a pink, metal office desk with a big, pink plastic telephone plopped—dag nab it—right in the middle. No windows to speak of which suits Stalin just fine. Except for a fly won't leave him alone! Lands on his nose.

But who cares?

The boys in pink who file into the room are too busy sporting high-tech safety goggles and other nifty gadgets. They have style. Panache. A flair for the little things that make a difference. All spit and polish. And well groomed, too. Not a hair out of place on a one. Not a dirty finger-nail in the bunch. These boys know how to wear a uni-form. "Glamour Is Fear." That's their motto. Quite the contrast from the kinds of volunteers Stalin's been getting lately. Nothing but Cossacks and hillbillies walking into the recruitment offices these days. How are you supposed to build a brutal war machine with the likes of highway-men and mongoloids? How are you supposed to beat back History with the sloth of today? I ask you: How is the Great Hammer of Progress supposed to smash the swarming enemy when drunkards and perverts hold the trenches?

Once again the door flies open! And this time a large entourage of women in pink file through. Turning their graceful dresses. Staring nonchalantly over their shoul-ders at the helpless host. Step back men in pink. Make room for the girls in their big pink sun hats who talk and giggle amongst each other. Checking themselves in com-pact mirrors they keep in small purses, the women whis-per into each other's ears. Spinning and dancing. Frowning. Batting their long eyelashes. Pointing to Stalin and covering their mouths to suppress their obvious mirth.

At this point I should add that the pink room erupts into spontaneous conversation.

Woman to man: We were following up on reports all day.

Older woman to younger boy: The subject appears calm.

Older man to younger woman: Irreversible damage

to the cerebral cortex.

Girl and boy: The subject suffers from an acute case of Infantilism.

The pink phone rings.

"For Stalin!"

A young man in pink makes his way through the delirious throng with the phone.

"Mom to Stalin, do you read?"

"Stalin, copy."

"Loud noises from apartment next door."

"Copy."

"Over and out."

A pink suit takes the phone from Stalin and, pointing to the gold plated half-note on his lapel, introduces himself as chief science officer, otherwise known as Crawdaddy. He is surrounded by beautiful women and has one at each elbow. Each holding a pink martini glass and smiling forwardly. Crawdaddy hopes Stalin won't mind a little company, and a very long-legged young lady whips out a pad and pen. She brushes back her pink bangs and introduces herself as chief medical officer, apparently indicated by her raised hem-line. "But my friends call me Nurse."

The science officer in her very short pink nurse's skirt addresses Stalin directly. Nurse wants to know about Surgical Experimentation. A topic which brings a little color back to Stalin's horrified face. Now there's a topic worth conversation! No mistaking Stalin's new-found glee. Stalin is very proud of the advances that have come out of the field. Stalin has personally overseen and witnessed countless such operations. At first only animals

were employed. Then the severely retarded. The insane.
Deviants. Vagabonds. Social degenerates are fun to cut up
too. And combinations of any of the above make for a
hardy laugh.

QUESTION: Gene therapy?

ANSWER: Truth serum, nerve gas, and psychological
warfare.

Stalin doubles up. He is really feeling sick. His chair is
too hard. Crawdaddy's head is too large. The pink finger
Nurse waves before Stalin's black eyes is way too long and
cold, and moves way, way too slowly. But wait a sec!

> *Stalin's got a hammer'n'sicle*
> *On his car*
> *And one on his chest*
> *A three-fifty-seven on his hip*
> *And the right to arrest.*

So why's it that the lovely Nurse in pink's lovely nurse's
hand is sheathed in a pink latex glove? And why's it that
all Nurse's attendants who should be saying aloha as
graceful as the lapping waves on planet Why Kee-Kee are
pencil thin and twice his size?

(Of course, the answers to these and other questions
are black-inked from official records.)

At this point I would think the alien cocktail set would
have been fully debriefed. They should probably be
receiving their orders from a hidden intercom just about
now. Commands like: "Don protective pink gear this
instant!" "Prepare to carry out the prime directive at
once!" I might imagine the alien fashion set is supposed
to begin clearing a stainless steel table as fast as they can.

Sharp enamel implements would supposedly get laid out in basins by the alien party set. Hup, two, three, four. . . And a mad scientist would walk through the door with a diabolical smile on his twisted face and a huge syringe in his right hand.

Instead, Stalin simply gets a haircut, a shower, and a shave. The mustache is trimmed. Snot's wiped from his hairy nose. A pink shirt and pink double breasted suit's brought in for him along with a pink cravat, pink cufflinks, and pink wing tips. The Nurse personally offers Stalin a mirror: What a handsome man! And pulls a pink beret over Stalin's square head at an attractive angle. Phase #1: Completed.

Stalin takes off the beret and balls it up in his fist.

OBSERVATION: The subject appears angry.

Phase #2 is implemented. Weekly visits to Stalin's cell by Crawdaddy and The Nurse are designed to monitor the subject's progress.

As was directed the subject has taken up doodling. In an unprecedented move the aliens allow Stalin, who sits at his desk for hours on end, to use a red pen. Nothing Stalin doodles looks red enough. Stalin is all bloody thumbs. So he doodles bloody stumps. Nothing he doodles is doodle-like. Stalin tosses off one scribble after another. The scrawl is wrong. The scratch needs work. The red splotch is an eternal mystery to him.

OBSERVER'S REPORT: The subject is still darn mad.

The light is too bright in Stalin's room, and, to avoid the buzzing fluorescent pink bulbs, Stalin crawls under his cot at night. Apparently, they never turn out the lights in this place and it makes him feel safer!

In the morning the attendants leave his breakfast tray at the foot of the bed and try to poke him out from under the box spring. But Stalin will not come out. The attendants can swat at him all they want with their long pink prods. Stalin likes the feel of cold, surging pain dancing in his stomach.

Later that day he talks frankly with the head attendant: "It somehow makes me feel alive."

Phase #2a: Stalin's phone calls are closely monitored and recorded for further study. They are, of course, heavily censored. Although the affable aliens assure Stalin they only bleep-out the words they think sound the nicest.

STALIN'S MOM: "Bleep the bleeping bleep bleeps!"

Since the subject does not hide under his bed and is observed doodling in a rather light-hearted and carefree manner during these episodes, apparently totally unaware of what's going on around him, the phone calls are encouraged. What Stalin doodles is given the highest priority and deemed invaluable. So much so the doodles are immediately collected and sent by courier phone to the nearest sky lab for study.

In the 3rd and final phase the doodles are hung on a freshly painted pink wall. Crawdaddy and the Nurse inspect them closely checking and double-checking computer printouts. Viewer discretion is advised. The wheelchair crowd has turned out anyway. Not everyone wears the pink uniform. Tonight the doors of the apartment next door are opened to the world. Generals and dignitaries mill about. Businessmen of all stripes and colors discuss the rising markets. Pink Chablis is served at seven.

Stalin sits in the corner tipping a bottle. Let these soft-batches remember the iron fist of Stalin. Let them beg for Stalin's mercy. Let them clutch their stomachs and swallow hard. Let them cry out in pain. Shrink with fear. Whimper. Plead Stalin's forgiveness. Let them pray, "Stalin please cover the terrible red doodles. Please take them away." Stalin will hear little. See less. Stalin, muttering: "I'll wipe my nose on my sleeve and grab them by their bald ugly heads and throw them at the walls; I'll knock them to the ground and crush their frail genitals under my heels; The world will tremble at my. . ."

Stalin looks up. A crowd of candy-apple faces has gathered round him.

Stalin, looking at the crowd, "Worms!"

The gathering multitude steps closer. At the head of the pack a large woman with green hair motions for Stalin to bend over. Stalin does so spitting on the ground. This 'Tree-Woman,' Stalin takes it, is demanding to know more about his doodles.

TREE WOMAN: Mr. Stalin, what do you think of when you're doodling?"

STALIN: Red.

The woman points to a doodle behind Stalin's block-head.

"How about that one?"

At the top of the Post-it there's what appears to be a burning farm house and a barn with crows and vultures gathered on the roof.

"Come gather around, folks."

Stalin, smile coming back to his face...

"If you look closely you'll see that in the barn a wealthy landowner is mounted on a headless woman."

Stalin pauses for reaction and continues.

"Over here soldiers are clubbing the hick farmer and his wife to death."

Another pregnant pause and Stalin goes on.

"Those are two pigs eating a mutilated body while the grandpa farmer is pouring a bucket of pig's blood on his head."

Stalin looks around and starts in again.

"That's a farmhand stoking a pile of burning limbs. While this band of ruffians over here is performing an autopsy on a little girl."

A proud Stalin . . .

"I am cutting out her heart. I call it Twilight Vivisection. And, I doodled it while I was on the phone with my mom."

What a hit! There has never been such a doodle. Examine the craftsmanship. Awe at the expression. Everyone loves it. They can't get enough. Not a dissenter among 'em, either. Which is enough to send Stalin sprawling to the floor kicking and screaming and hammering the wooden boards with his large fist.

STALIN: (clutching his stomach) Argh!

CRAWDADDY: (looking down at Stalin) But you're a hit, son.

STALIN: I am Stalin!

NURSE: The Psychopathic Schizo!

At these words everyone raises a glass, apparently mishearing. "To the Sociospastic Psycho! Hip, hip, hooray!" And Stalin cautiously raises himself to his feet and takes a painful bow, choking down the salt pouring out of his tongue by the gallon.

If he could only focus on something—anything! Stalin tries the pink-ness of a window. But the pink window is no good. So damn pink it only makes him sicker! So he grabs for the wall to hold himself up and bends over to squint at the pink glow of the floorboard. And that doesn't work either. Quite the contrary. It only makes him even sicker than he already was. So he swallows hard. Real hard. But he can't swallow hard enough. His stomach grips him like a Marxist Robot Hand. And he makes for the Men's room.

Mixed red stuff and snot everywhere. Pink tiles covered in red. Long red curls in the water lapping the sides of the pink bowl and the seat is all spattered red.

At first, Stalin's happy. He thinks it's blood in the bowl. His insides floating around down there. Him torn up pretty bad inside.

Only the People know Pink Chablis isn't really red. No matter how much Stalin wishes it was so. The People know there's no sense in pretending. Pink Chablis is pink. And don't put a quick change-up past these folks. The People can tell a good turn when they see it. During a brief huddle they decide to heartily commend Stalin's bold move. Yes, indeed. What a genius! After all, red is really such a blood-thirsty color. So painfully obvious. Who wouldn't think of blood? Now pink, on the other hand! That's what Stalin needs more of. What a friendly color, and what a fine and upstanding message it sends the world! No doubt about it. Pink is a vast improvement over red. And who knows what it could inspire in such an impressionable young man? The People welcome the day with open arms when Stalin's forgotten all about red. In fact, the People are so obsessed with their new and blood-less fantasy, they secretly talk to each other about a world in which Stalin sits by his window listening to the singing birds all day long. Stalin happily doodling nothing but bon-bons and cherry blossoms and all the pretty things.

Lisa Auerbach

Babe
Ms. Paul

s. Paul Bunyan tours the world to promote clearcutting and to drive the woodsmen crazy with desire. Ms. Paul Bunyan is a leggy brunette with a bosom competent enough not to enlist the services of the Wonderbra. She enjoys the attention and prizes that accompany the title, gifts showered on her, invitations to dinner dances, cash, travel, etc.

At 5'11" plus heels, she is almost larger than life, a feature she shares with a certain mythical woodcutter. Ms. Paul Bunyan is sponsored by Raichle, primarily a manufacturer of ski equipment, which recently acquired a small pneumatic tool division and is trying to boost sales of sawing products.

Power tools have always been promoted by buxom broads. In truth there is nothing more exciting than tender naked flesh coupled with dangerous and unwieldy machinery. More often than not, the maidens appear incompetent or just ambivalent toward the dangers inherent in the whirling steel blades they are promoting. The more un-OSHA approved scenario, the better it is for selling industrial products. A poster depicting a bikini clad and sumptuous figure draped suggestively over a table saw is surpassed the following year by a naked virgin, her pearly pink nipples hovering just barely over the blade.

This is not to say that these posters promote the bodily mutilation of young women. They are not a primer for basement dismemberment. Unless the body has been previously frozen solid,the mess would be enormous, as wood or metal cutting blades are not suitable for flesh. A cow carcass is more similar to our own than a plank of pine, and the cutting devices for steaks and chops are widely available and will do the job right. Nobody likes to clean entrails from the ceiling, just because they have used an inappropriate tool.

No, these posters are not about hate at all. They are about love and adoration and this is why Ms. Paul Bunyan digs them royally. She wants to be the Number One Pin Up in sawmills across this great country, posing precariously with the best equipment on the market. With her dark hair and fetching brown eyes, she knows this goal may never be realized. Gentlemen prefer blondes, but she is not about to hit the bleach. She loves herself as is, and wants the world to sink down to their knees for her.

Ms. Paul Bunyan has had her name legally changed to her pageant title, though she will only hold her crown for one year. She will not disclose any details about her prior life, the one she led, according to pageant records, in Iowa. When pressed for details, she fakes amnesia and claims that she was found on a log raft and raised in the forest by lumberjacks and wolves. She claims that Paul Bunyan is her real life lover, and takes week long trips alone into the wilderness to visit his enormous cabin.

Raichle publicity experts go along with her stories, though, off the record, they just shake their heads and smile. She is the best thing that ever has happened to the company. Her likeness appears on almost every product. Her enigmatic cheerfulness has even begun showing up modelling ski boots and bindings. She has posed with the president of the United States while holding a tool.

Her bubbly personality is the hit of every charity ball. When the year of her reign comes to a close, company officials will be hard pressed not to pay off the judges for next year's pageant. She is not officially a company employee. She has signed no contract, and, with her legal name change, she could approach any lumber company in the world, flash a smile, and receive an offer that she might not be able to refuse.

Ms. Paul Bunyan may play dumb, but she is aware of every nuance. She has the body of a goddess and the mind of an eager accountant. She never forgets the bottom line, even while shining her brilliant eyes into the lens of a camera, or heaving her breasts alluringly into the disbelieving face of a potential client. They are just part of her body, after all. She's had them all her life, in one form or another. She checks them monthly for lumps, and at times their weight causes her back to ache. They sprout hairs, which she plucks, one at a time. She encases them in uncomfortable brassieres. The underwire leaves red lines on her skin. After a long day, she lets them loose and they tumble forward, cascading onto her chest. Her breasts are like pets; she names them Click and Clack, after the guys on public radio who discuss cars. When she is driving alone in her 4-wheel drive Ms. Paul-Mobile, she only listens to National Public Radio. If anyone else is within earshot, she cranks top 40 and sings along incessantly.

Ms. Paul Bunyan would like to be in movies someday. She dreams about possible costars, and plots to meet famous producers. She is not yet past her prime, but every day feels closer to death.

I want to be Ms. Paul Bunyan. I want to be the real life wife of the mythical ax man, I want to wield my power over Babe his blue ox, cook thousands of flapjacks and grow to be sixty feet tall. I want to step on cars and smash them into the pavement, sneeze and the windows will break, hold Paul's chainsaw as he yells "Timber" and spend the night in a log cabin at the edge of the lake.

My aspirations are high, but I am confident. I am confident because I have made it this far. After surviving several eliminating rounds, I have finally made it all the way to Dentonville, Iowa, to compete in the Ms. Paul Bunyan pageant. You might think it's just about beauty. Of course, we do have a bathing suit contest, but mostly it's about wood, lumber, and the charm of the heavy forest being mowed down by leggy women wearing short skirts and wielding chainsaws as just another accessory.

My childhood summers were spent in the North Woods, eating at Paul Bunyan restaurants and dreamily gazing at life size statues of the enormous Paul. In Sheboygan he stood 50 feet, in Eagle River 52, in the Dells 60 and in Kenosha only 25, but he spoke there, booming "Welcome" and "Come again soon!" The Science Museum in Chicago, until recently, had a walk-in log cabin, the floor tilted, Paul looking through the window, winking at museum goers walking into the house he held in his hands.

Mom read me stories of the strong and able logger from the day I was born until the day I stubbornly decided that I could read all by myself. There were books of legends on the living room shelf, Jack Tales, Johnny Appleseed, Pocahontas, and Annie Oakley, but I always cried and cried until she brought me the single dogeared drooled over one about Paul. Later, when I began to kiss the boys and make them quiver, I would always look for the ones that were most like the giant lumberjack.

I have a turbocharged 850E Logbuster Pro cordless chain saw with detachable teeth and EZ grip handle. The way I coax it into action makes men drool and trees cower. I walk into a grove of deciduous hardwoods and I can practically hear them shaking with fear and offering to just lie down quietly on their own. Even the ironwood is weak, while I am so strong.

The competitions begin tomorrow morning. Tonight I stay in a small cabin in town with fellow finalist Kat "Kitty" Turner. I have not met Kat before. She has come from the Texas division. I introduce myself to her as "Splinter," which is not my real name. Kat smiles in the semi-darkness of our knotty pine panelled rented room and her teeth positively glow. I can tell that she has had caps and I wonder what other cosmetic surgery she has undergone on her way to Ms. Paul Bunyan, 1993.

My perfect figure was not purchased. From my petite and enigmatic size 7 foot to the top of my healthy, bouncy auburn hair, passing just over 6 feet of flesh uninterrupted by blemishes or scratches, it is all the completely natural and unadulterated me that the judges will gaze upon in the morning. I do not thank the medical establishment for my perfection. I do not even thank my mother. I only thank myself and the spirit of Paul Bunyan, who has driven me to strive for nothing less than optimum.

What will I get as the winner of Ms. Paul Bunyan,

1993? First of all, I will have the honor of being recognized internationally by those who appreciate achieve-
ments in both beauty and logging. Second, I will get a
lifetime supply of firewood and a cast iron wood stove to
burn it in. I will have a chance to become a spokesmod-
el for any one of the great number of chainsaw companies vying for my endorsement. Plus, logging companies
all over the country will be writing me pleading letters,
urging me to come to this camp or that, hoping that my
visit will boost morale and up production. I will also be
offered my choice of a dream date with the winner of Mr.
Paul Bunyan or the equivalent in cash.

Depending on who it is, I will most likely pick the
dream date. I have been seeing some enticing lumberjacks hanging around town all day. I have sauntered up
casually to more than one of them, appealing to his sim-
plicity with my cosmopolitan accent and sophisticated
wardrobe. I do not wear plaid shirts, overalls, red sus-
penders or big brown boots like some of the other con-
testants. I have specially made pantyhose that cut the
wind and keep out the cold. These special fibers are still
in the development stages at one of the country's largest
chemical companies, but I have a relative who works in r
& d and so, on the coldest of midwinter days, I am still
able to prance confidently around town, in a demure mid
thigh length miniskirt.

If Paul Bunyan could only see me, he would tie my feet
to the sturdiest tree in the forest and my neck to the yoke
of Babe the Blue Ox. He'd yell "go" and Babe would pull
as hard as hard can be and I would stretch right out,
stretch until I was just as big as Paul and he would untie

me right there and make me his wife. Our wedding would last 35 days and nights and the celebration would reach from the Mississippi to the Colorado and back again. After the humongous feast, herds of cattle, whole semis full of vegetables, Paul takes me back to his over-sized cabin and he carries me over the threshold and gently drapes me on his bunk. Then Paul, my miraculous, legendary Paul, will undress, leaving on the floor piles of denim and cotton, Gore-tex and silk. As the last tentlike briefs slide over his smooth and muscled thighs and collapse onto the floor with a sigh, it will finally be revealed to me what stories and tall tales have been tastefully left out. But that Paul is hung like that great blue ox of his is no surprise to me. I am prepared for the greatest logging adventure of my lifetime and will have brought my Logbuster Pro in case things get out of hand. But I suspect that they won't. I suspect that Paul's a virgin timber, a competent oak, but one that has not yet been mowed down, sent up river, and milled into a knotless plankdom.

Thinking about Paul keeps my brain in shape. Cutting down trees keeps my body supple until my dreams come true.

And to you, my dear reader, when you sink into your bed this evening, cover yourself gently with eiderdown and quilts. Think about your hard day spent in the forest, cutting and hauling the logs. Feel the scratchiness in your throat, worn out from yelling "timber" over and over again as one by one the great stands of trees are collapsed. Remember how the word would look as it darted shyly from your mouth. It freezes as it hits the air and becomes a cloud, drifting right up into the sky to join the

others. For dinner you ate steaks and potatoes and broc-
coli and then Paul, dear fine Paul, came in carrying 600
six packs of Pabst Blue Ribbon, 579 for himself and the
rest for the others. Look at his strong hands opening the
beers. Spend the night drunk with loggers. Make bad
jokes and imagine that you will be awakened in the
morning by the sound of the Whistling River, whistling
its way past the camp, that is, until Paul brings three bliz-
zards in from up north, freezes the river and harnesses it
to Babe, who pulls it out of the ground just to shut it up.

Kathleen Johnson

A Day in the Life

he only way to properly attach the wings was to solder the very tips to the ends of the handle bars. Tito knew this and I don't know why I, supposedly there mostly for moral support, had to be scrambling with last minute repairs. It stank inside; weeks of fervent preparation, I suppose. If the wings weren't secure, it would be impossible to steer the float, and if you couldn't steer the entry, it would never pass the safety inspection. So, as I strained to get in deeper, I was beginning to think that the basic design was just bad. Tito's encouraging voice pleading the impossible made its way down to me.

"Take them to the outside!" wailed Tito, positioning the wings by hand as I soldered them in place, frantic that his careful planning was about to run up against a brick wall. He never blamed me, but could also not bring himself to consider the possibility that his designs had problems. If the wings couldn't be fastened here, there was no other way to get them to flap delicately in synchronization with the musical score, this score being essential to the overall project. Tito had conceived of this idea one day and although he had never taken a musical approach before, he felt it might be a whole new way to interpret the theme. It made him feel as if he were in band practice again. The problems that arose, however, had to do with the fact that in order to get all of the parts, including the wings, to move in unison to the music, design integrity had to suffer. Tito often said that these compromises were at the heart of what he did.

He had already been through a dry run of the parade route three days ago and was certain that he had established the best stopping points. Experience provided him with certain trade secrets and advantages. "Insider" information, such as knowing that a participant needed to perform not only in front of the Grand Marshall's stand, but also at strategic points along the parade route itself, was the type of insight that gave Tito his infectious confidence. If you became popular with the crowd along the way, word got back to the judges. It actually spread like wildfire along the crowds lined up on either side of the street, and Tito called this phenomenon the 'Lavaliere Effect,' recalling the glamour of his pageant days. Tito would sometimes talk, metaphorically of course, about harnessing the 'Lavaliere Effect' and what great benefits could be gained from its controlled use. Unfortunately he knew of no other instance where the effect happened spontaneously other than along a parade route. There was a file on the Lavaliere Effect in the 'to be researched' drawer in his studio. For now he contented himself with studying and predicting its effects on site at a parade.

Determining the most crowded spots was important not only because of the sheer number of devotees that a winning entry could attract there, but because the most serious parade revelers claimed these spots early. These connoisseurs, above all other parade attendees, could create the buzz that would carry Tito to the podium. This whetting of collective appetites might be dismissed by some but Tito always believed in its vast importance to his chances of winning.

This year at Run About Junction Tito realized that what was required was an entry that reflected some type of 90's one world, global community crap. He had been browsing in all the stores in the mall, doing his usual 'get the pulse of the day' research and he'd seen this type of stuff everywhere, especially in the new Public Television retail store. Curiosity and the need to be thorough—even empirical—in his research usually drove Tito to the world of fashion. Early on Tito was convinced that fashion was a type of window onto the collective soul and pursued this line of research with a vengeance—window displays being the most available sources for this type of overview. A heightened sense of fashion was instilled in Tito at an early age. He came from a long line of pageant moms—women who entered their daughters in beauty pageants as a means of furthering their chances of success in life. His mother, grandmother, and his aunties were all pageant moms and had a passion for it that most could only dream about. Some of Tito's earliest memories were of sleeping in a fully packed car in some unknown, mid-sized city while his mother and sisters would make late night preparations for the competitions the following morning. One summer when Tito was fourteen, the extended family set off on a ten city, five state tour in three cars. The total prize money from this trip alone was nearly six thousand dollars, with a spokesperson gig for his cousin Louisa, three crowns for little Hester, second runner up and Miss Congeniality for Emma in Phoenix, and a carful of good memories. However stressful the schedule of the pageant circuit was on the family, the beauty and glamour that surrounded this world had been worth every trip, or so Tito had always believed. Again here, as in other areas, Tito was a slave to his history. Even before clearly establishing how he might interpret

the given theme or concept of an event, Tito had to completely work out the look of his entry and decide which of
the components could best reflect his keen sense of
design, causing this aspect of the project to be dispropor-
tionately labored over.

Once satisfied with a firmly researched foundation for
Run About Junction, Tito began to build. In the garage,
in the streets, sketching at home and at work. Recently,
he went on a three week binge of building and became so
fatigued that he began to see visions. It was during just
such a vision that Tito's original inspiration for the Run
About Junction parade was confirmed—in spades. He
dreamed or imagined or hallucinated (his version differs
according to his confidence at the moment) that he met
his animal spirit, just like the Native Americans do when
seeking guidance or wisdom. His animal spirit turned
out to be a fox and Tito had always felt really good about
this; the fox was an admirable animal in his mind and he
took it as a direct compliment. So in the dream, or whatever it was, the fox told Tito about creating an entry
around the theme of a global community, one world
ecology, etcetera. The fox also told Tito things like, "If
you build it, they will come," which is hardly original and
thus everyone had their doubts, but Tito remained loyal
to the spirit of the fox and convinced—so much so that
he took the fox's thematic advice to heart and drove to
the "Fox Hills Mall" in Southern California for some
additional fashion research. This might have been too lit-
eral for some but Tito was his own man and he was not
about to let a potentially supernatural, and perhaps
advantageous experience go to waste. He also recalled the

swinging Czech brothers of Saturday Night Live that would say to each other when girls appeared, "Now are the foxes," and the Jodie Foster movie, Foxes, which he'd seen several times as a young man and from which he still had the soundtrack album. He loved these popular culture connections to his dream image and Tito never dismissed coincidences. This, some later surmised , was one of his hidden strengths.

If I am privy to the more intimate details of Tito's creative process it is because I helped him build. I've gleaned most of my insights about him from careful observation while performing my main duty—the upkeep and cataloging of existing, losing entries. This is a devastating archive indeed, causing us to relocate to a bigger building about every six months, but it has yielded a wealth of information.

Stretching deep inside his latest float on site at Run About Junction, I couldn't help but ask myself why more people were not like him. It was my fondest wish at the time—I'm on to other things now—that others be as penetrable as he. At our first encounter, overwhelmed by the sensation that I had known him for years, I realized to both my horror and delight, that I could read this stranger's mind! Enough said. After this enlightening experience, I found it very difficult to be around other people, to be put at such an appalling disadvantage. Thus, Tito quickly became indispensable, for I realized that I could not go back to the darkness, silence and confusion that was interaction with others. I had to step into the sun, step into the light of Tito's world. Except for my day job, I rarely see others; thank god I didn't meet Tito any earlier or I wouldn't have seen much of the world at all. Such isolation and the singularity of Tito's company probably would have made me mean or stupid. Luckily I had seen a bit of life first and can now indulge in my lucky find. Over time my sensing of Tito has become honed to the point where I have to employ it carefully. Not only can I read him completely, but I can see right through him. I can now easily melt him away with a bit of concentration, just unhinge him, cause him to come apart at the seams. Most of the time, in fact, I have to force myself to stop. My newfound talent has awakened a rather violent tendency within me. However, I can usually stop just before he becomes unglued and content myself with a taste of blood and not the entire river.

"Give it to me," he bellowed.

"If you want it so God damn badly, get down here in this shit fire trap you've created for yourself and you attach them!" I yelled.

I know now that I never should have come on site. It's not my style. To see him in his element, his full parade glory—Tito slowly on the move with all eyes turned his way, rounding the bend on gossamer wings—was really the only reason that I had agreed to come; a bit of morbid fascination. How did he handle the pressure, the competition? Was he disappointed in the end and did it show on his face? Mostly, I wondered if his confidence was broken and what it would be like to melt him while he was in a state of nervous anxiety. Emotions had so many different flavors with Tito. I knew that I wouldn't be able to melt him as easily as usual through the bulk of the contraption, although a full dose of him would have been sweet with his adrenaline and excitement up, but I would be able to get some residual feeling at least.

The entry was, however, truly problematic and would not go off without a hitch I was sure. If Tito has said it once, he's said it a hundred times, it is not the stated theme but the personal interpretation of that theme that the judges really focus on. After just a few months with Tito I began to think that perhaps this phrase represented all that was wrong with his approach, his tragic flaw. Thematically, Tito was usually way off. Between obeying his innate, rigorous fashion/design sense and being true to his conviction that a fiercely individual interpretation was always the best approach, he more often than not managed to take everything right over the top and out of sight. In this case, he even overlooked his earlier conviction about the global community-fox hallucination (and backtracking is not something that he usually did) in favor of this winged madness! The mechanized wings were just one ill- fated excess in a sea of many. "Familiar Fantasy" was the stated theme of this event and Tito had had plenty of time to consider it. His reactions were as follows:

"What do you think of birds and angels and other flying things suddenly being stripped of their ability to fly and becoming married to the earth with the other terrestrials?"

"What are you taking about?" I answered, slipping into my usual thoughts of wonder and foreboding that always came with the onset of one of Tito's interpretations.

"Think of it. All the familiar flying creatures suddenly walking about and nothing at all able to get into the air, ever."

"What about airplanes?" I ventured.

"No, no, no, I'm talking about creatures only."

"I don't know what you're talking about," I answered flatly, hoping my incomprehension would discourage him from pursuing this line of reasoning.

"The theme, 'Familiar Fantasy'."

"What are you talking about?" I repeated with trepidation, realizing that the damage had been done, that an idea had been born.

"You see, all of the familiar things that we normally associate with air, flying, space, soaring, would be locked down to the ground—a fantasy world—an earth with no flying anything. That's a 'Familiar Fantasy'," he concluded.

What can one say to that? How could one adequately explain that logic — that interpretation of the theme — on an entry form? How would the abstract read? 'Flying Things Now Earthbound: Your and My Familiar Fantasy.'

"That is not a fantasy, Tito, that's a nightmare. No one wants to imagine a world where nothing can fly," I said.

"Well then, it would scare them, wouldn't it?" he ventured, satisfied.

"This is not my department," I admitted.

I hadn't wanted to think about what got us here, what tortuous machinations of Tito's mind had brought us to this point. I never questioned his final decisions. It was easier that way. Tracing Tito's interpretative path could often be more draining for me than melting him.

Tito called the gathering of entries at the start of the parade route, 'the killing fields', and he called the official who assured that all of the entries were lined up in proper order, 'the keeper of souls.' Drama, just like his use of fashion, helped to make it all real for him. Placement was everything in Tito's opinion, and if you drew a spot at the end and were not able to bribe another entry to change spots or steal another's spot, it was the kiss of death. A bad draw could condemn you to obscurity and mediocrity — the latter being Tito's worst fear. Some officials imposed the order of the draw while others, the corrupt ones, looked the other way for a small fee and allowed the entries to vie for position in a free-for-all that often left the weaker entries really dogeared. Because Tito didn't want me to get caught in the melee, he was resigned to take his chances with the draw this time and hope that the entries immediately surrounding him would be as civilized.

All of the small mechanized bits, especially the wings, were still not working properly at this late hour. The wings, designed to flap stutteringly and haltingly just a few inches above the ground, were supposed to represent the earthbound prison which prevented creatures, great and small, from flying through the air with the greatest of ease. The problem was that the wings were mounted too low to the ground and with each flap, the wing tips would contact the pavement in the most unflattering way and lose bits of their finery. It was a calamitous last minute hitch, and as I secured the wings as best I could from inside and test drove it around a bit, Tito flailed behind me, yelling for me to stop every few minutes so that he could reapply his magic. If the problem couldn't be fixed soon, Tito, operating alone, would have a decimated pair of wings by the end of the route. I had soldered them into a slightly higher position so that they wouldn't hit the ground as they flapped, but when Tito saw this revised version of his symbols of earthbound solitude, a new cloud crossed his face. With this new higher stance of the wings, Tito was now afraid that the message of earthboundedness would not be perceptible to the audience. The wings now appeared more like regular wings in flight, working their way along a shallow plane.

"More like a bird skimming low above the water to catch a fish," I observed, and this confirmed Tito's fears.

He now had a decision to make—go through with the parade, knowing that his interpretation and concept would probably not be clear to the crowd and judges, or sacrifice the whole trip for interpretive integrity and get out of the starting line before it was too late. Had it been a design element, something that didn't look right or an aesthetic problem of some kind, Tito wouldn't hesitate forging ahead. But this wing problem struck at the heart of his entry. I realized that day Tito must have hidden reserves of strength that I knew little of. Perhaps his resolve and true grit were lesser known to me because I had never really seen him in action, under pressure at an event. When Tito's professionalism was at stake, he acted. Fraught with anxiety over the state of the wings and flushing a color that I swear I had never seen on him before, Tito took up his position in the draw and told me to go find a seat.

"Are you sure?" I screamed glancing back, already out of sight. I didn't hear a reply and I wasn't listening for one. My head was pounding. Tito had been in such a ferocious state. The psychic mix fermenting might not ever be this good again, and if I could melt him under these conditions, even partially, during his moment of agitation in front of the crowd and the judges, it would be like nothing I'd tasted from him before. What I didn't know was how close I would need to be in order to get to him through the structure of the float. Usually I can be anywhere near him, even in the next room or up to twenty feet away, but today I would need to be closer because he was covered by the float's thick shell. I couldn't just walk into the street and risk disturbing the progress of the other entries, so I had to find a spot right up front where the entries would be passing very near the crowd. This was the reason why I should have been out here much earlier instead of fooling around with Tito's wings! People never gave up these close range seats. Tito had warned me of that more than once. Even a family going to pee or off for a quick snack would leave behind a loved one to guard the spot like a jackal. I finally got within two people layers of the front and I gave a dad a twenty so that I could trade places with his son sitting right on the curb itself. As I took up my position, I could feel his son spit pink popcorn into my hair.

Regardless, my mind became focused on Tito inside his float — excitement growing, nerves jangling, doubts of failure poking at him, and his adrenaline flowing as if it were a river of honey, sending a signal, exuding a scent for me to follow. It was all well under way, about an hour into the parade and I was getting impatient. The Kit Carson Mountain Men were passing on horseback and I knew that Tito had drawn a position not far from them. I suddenly caught a glimpse of Tito's front end and made myself as tall as possible for his approach. As Tito's entry rounded the bend, I put all that I had into sensing him. With my eyes shut tight in concentration I strained and to my horror I felt nothing, not even a residual tingling, much less the usual reassuring rush from Tito wilting beneath my weight. I knew that something was terribly, tragically wrong, that even from deep inside the structure, something should be making its way to me. Stricken with fear, I flew into a panic and started screaming. Just as people were turning to attend to me, someone shouted from across the street, "Out of the way!"

I looked up to see Tito's float veering dangerously off to the right, ferociously picking up steam and heading straight for the crowd. In an instant, Tito crashed violently into the side of the route scattering the gathered crowd and mauling those unfortunate few who didn't have time to get out of the way. I ran, still screaming and at my wits end to the smoking heap, scaled the structure and ripped open the top. I found Tito's shoulders, caught hold under his arms and pulled him up and out of the float. He was unconscious, and not responding, but as an official helped me get him down to the ground, his eyes fluttered.

"Fresh air," he groaned, and I slapped him.

"Bastard," I yelled as his energy, blocked from me just moments ago, came gushing forth.

I was so relieved, so grateful that the block was not permanent, that the reason for my inability to melt him was due merely to his being unconscious. I danced in the street until the paramedics arrived to treat Tito for heat exhaustion back in their mobile unit at the starting point.

We knew little of the chaos that was left behind. I could hear people being taken away by ambulance and helicopter, and the mess that had been Tito's "Familiar Fantasy" was, I heard from a passerby, being towed to a safe location. I was already tallying the impound lot fees in my head as a group of officials began to discuss whether or not the parade should continue once the injured were cleared from the crash site. Some thought that a continuation would be in poor taste, while others were not prepared to deny the backed-up entries their chance in front of the judges.

I couldn't explain to Tito why I had been so frightened because a) he didn't need to know and b) he wouldn't understand anyway. He thought I was overreacting. If I had somehow lost my ability to get at him... I could always melt Tito in his sleep but apparently my powers didn't extend to unconsciousness. Awash with relief, I hugged the paramedics and Tito promised drinks all around as soon as things calmed down.

Riding home that evening after the promised revelry, Tito told me that he felt I had been a jinx to him and that I probably shouldn't come with him to an event ever again. I could not believe my ears.

"How is that so?" I demanded, " Who helped you put the wings back on, who did the test driving?"

"Regardless of the help you gave me, I believe it would be best if you didn't come along next time," he concluded solemnly.

This I just could not abide by, not when I had been so close to capturing an essence of that high anxiety. Such extraordinary conditions don't come along everyday.

"Listen," I defended, "I had nothing to do with what happened, I was watching from quite a distance."

"You don't understand. I'm very delicate and your presence added an unexpected element to the situation. You know that my work is very mentally demanding. I have to protect my frame of mind when competing. Everything has to be just right. You ruined my concentration. Your energy is too intrusive."

(He didn't know the half of it, I thought to myself with a bit of genuine shame.)

"Look, Tito, if I hadn't been there, God knows what sorry state your float would have been in, and I was trying to lend moral support. What in the hell went wrong, anyway?"

"The last thing I remember was feeling really sick, a heat wave welling up from my stomach and filling my head. When I woke up, I saw you."

"Well I wonder why, Tito. You call me a jinx! I hate to break this to you, but you are your own worst enemy. It's just as the paramedics surmised. I told you weeks ago that it was going to get too hot inside there but you completely dismissed my warning. 'A furnace' was the phrase I used and you serenely ignored me. You allowed a potentially fatal design flaw to go uncorrected, as usual, and you passed out from the heat and fumes of your own locomotion. The paramedics said that when you fainted, you must have slipped down in the seat a bit and wedged your foot on the gas. You went careening into those people at about forty miles per hour, Tito. I don't even want to think about your victims, who cares, but to think that you are sitting there assuming that I had something to do with it. I can't believe you blame me, that somehow I disturbed your psychic balance. It's a ridiculous notion," I concluded indignantly while secretly terrified that I would not be able to convince him I had not caused the accident.

"Perhaps the cavity was somewhat lacking in proper ventilation," he conceded, "but even so, if there is even the remotest chance that your presence somehow affected me negatively in my moment of truth, I cannot bring you along. I cannot possibly gamble like that with my chances. Surely you understand."

"No, I'm afraid I don't understand, Tito. You're being paranoid."

Minutes passed and I wasn't sure what to do next. I had to be allowed to come on site again. I became depressed and put on my most dejected face and stared forlornly out the window as if reflecting upon what I had done. Tito likes to think of me as contemplative. I was beginning to formulate reasons to present to him as to why I would be an asset if allowed to accompany him again, when he grumbled something that told me I would have my chance.

"I don't know, we'll see," Tito brooded. "I'd have to factor in the risk."

Chris Romano

Dreams

une 7, 1993

Alone, I'm in an empty room, with a basketball-sized octopus. It's in a fish tank, in the middle of the room, about 2 by 3 by 4 feet in size. The octopus is orange and black. As I circle the tank, the octopus follows, swimming to whichever side is nearest, reaching with its tentacles. I get the feeling the octopus wants to be pet.

I remember from somewhere that octopi do like to be pet, so I walk to the tank to pet my octopus, even though I'm scared. It's a strange creature with all its legs and lack of skeletal structure, but I overcome my fear and manage to stroke it lovingly.

The octopus then begins to change. The round top part metamorphoses into long, red hair, and the face warps into that of a young woman. She has two human arms and human breasts covered by a bikini-type top. Her profile is exotically reptilian, while her front view is absolutely beautiful in the most innocent way. Her arms change to a sort of normal flesh color, but she has a thin layer of moss or algae on parts of her arms. Her fingernails, claw-like, are a shiny, jet black.

She calls to me and I go. I reach in the tank and remove her. For myself. Lying on my back, I hold her above me. A dangling mollusk. We sit together and I tell her how beautiful she is. How amazing. Modest, she blushes with my repeated compliments. We stay on the floor together for some time where I fall in love with her, completely. She falls in love with me. Happily, I tell her how beautiful her breasts are. She removes her top so I can see them, and they are more beautiful than I could possibly imagine.

But I have to leave. I leave feeling very good about myself because I love my octopus-girl and she loves me. I'm in a car, driving home. The guy who played Maude's husband on the show *Maude* is next to me. He's in the passenger seat and he's apologizing for being such a wimpy guy and terrible lover and I have no idea what he's talking about.

We get to the intersection of Sunset Boulevard and the Pacific Coast Highway. There are some workers who have created a roadblock of some sort. Even though I only live one block past the roadblock, they won't let me by. I turn up a side street, drive over a traffic island, and pass the roadblock. I can see the workers chasing after me, so I speed off and go home.

I'm pissed! Someone told the octopus-woman I'm not coming back for her, and that's a dirty lie.

December 27, 1992

I'm lying in my bed, naked, with Linda. The room is very bright and full of light. I get the impression it's morning and a lot of sunshine is being let into the room. Everything seems happy.

So we're both lying naked and I'm inspecting Linda's sphincter muscle. It's a deep purple-red, sort of like the inside of a plum or a canned prune or something. Whenever Linda flexes her sphincter, it puckers like a set of facial lips. Only a little veinier. I'm amazed, really, because I didn't realize sphincter muscles look like human facial lips.

I roll over and hold a mirror up to my own butt. I remember lying on my back, with both legs in the air and the mirror in my right hand. The position is very awkward, but I manage.

I flex my sphincter muscle and it puckers up just like Linda's. Well what do you know?!?

July 27, 1993

Sherry Y. or Susan Y. is chasing me. She looks very angry, whoever she is. I'm running through an empty bunker in the middle of nowhere. She has a gun.

I'm completely naked and she's really fat. I'd say she weighs well over 200 pounds.

I'm cornered, so she lies on her back, blocking my only escape. I look down and, to my utter horror, she has a very small penis! Wrinkled, her penis is about one fourth the size of mine. She points the gun in my face and orders me to jerk her off.

I'm repulsed by her small, flaccid, partially hairy member. She notices my Johnson is much bigger than hers, which makes her even more angry. She grabs my penis, begins jerking me off, and then forces me to fuck her ruthlessly in the ass.

I don't particularly enjoy it.

September 12, 1993

I'm in an auditorium, on all fours, on a table. The auditorium is dark, and I'm alone except for the guy fucking me up the butt.

I have a terrible case of unlimited and never-ending diarrhea, which is just spreading everywhere. I just can't stop-shit just keeps coming and coming and coming out. It's very wet and gritty.

The guy has my diarrhea all over him. He says he can deal with it, and eats some to prove so. My diarrhea is sort of a greyed-out, burnt sienna.

The guy lets me know he wants to stop, but he's afraid to pull his dick out because the diarrhea will injure him or something. We both know a super-load will rush out like a high-pressure firehouse and blow him over. I try to time it, as maybe I can keep the explosion from being serious.

The guy pulls out and a ton of fecal matter explodes outward. It's almost lethal and it's definitely everywhere. The guy is knocked off the table and he's covered with a thick layer of diarrhea. I'm almost as thickly covered, but not quite.

I get off the table and walk over to the mirror. I'm covered with granules of fecal matter from head to toe and I stink like you wouldn't believe. Looking in the dirty mirror, I smile and notice my tongue and gums are bleeding. What's that all about?

I leave for the bathroom to clean myself up.

September 17, 1993

I'm camping with a bunch of other people. Our camp is right along a very beautiful and somewhat fast-moving river. It's not a dangerous river, but it could present a problem if it's not respected.

Gabrielle is swimming in the river and she seems to be having a problem of some sort. She's drowning! The water is cold and it must have cramped all her muscles!

Everyone just stands at the edge of the water and watches.

Fuck. I'm the world's shittiest swimmer, but I can't let her drown. No one else makes any sort of effort, so I take off my shirt and jump into the water. Some people try to stop me, but I won't let them. I can't.

I swim out to Gabrielle, who can barely keep her head above water. She completely passes out just as I get to her. Now what do I do?

The current of the river increases with speed as I try to swim back with Gabrielle in my left arm.

I can't do it.

The river takes the two of us downstream-our speed increasing the entire way. Gabrielle doesn't seem to be responding and I'm afraid she has a lot of water in her lungs.

Two huge boulders are in the middle of the river. They may be our only chance for survival, but if I do this wrong, I could really hurt myself. I have to hit the rocks feet first, so I can cushion the impact. I feel like the water is carrying Gabrielle and me at 25 miles per hour.
Somehow I made it. But the rocks are slippery and covered with algae and I only have one hand free. The other is around Gabrielle.

I manage to get my hand into a crevice in the rock and I pull the both of us up. I don't know where I get the strength from.

Gabrielle is cold and limp and I'm not sure if she's breathing. I put my head to her chest and I can barely hear her heart beating. I try to resuscitate her, but the rocks are jagged, leaving me no room to lay Gabrielle down.

I look at her. Her eyes are closed and her mouth is slightly open. As she may be about to die, Gabrielle looks more beautiful than I have ever seen her before. Her death is a loss I wish not to suffer through.

I try my best to revive her, but nothing works. I'm in a precarious position, with only one hand free, at the most. It's getting dark and extremely cold, and I am fearful for Gabrielle's life.

I can only hope someone finds us soon.

October 20, 1993

We're working on the CHRIS!(tm) movie. Patti Podesta and either Doug Christmas or Dennis Cooper are the filmmakers. I don't know which is the producer and which is the director.

There's a race scene. CHRIS!(tm) is running to the finish line, and he'll finish first. The huge crowd in the stands is silent, but as soon as CHRIS!(tm) crosses the finish line, the crowd goes absolutely nuts.

All the other runners are Asian females. Yes, it seems we did a casting call for athletic-looking, Asian females who are only mildly attractive. None of the girls are pretty in the least, but even still, each is beautiful and attractive in their own, idiosyncratic way.

I really like working with them. Life is good.

First, we shoot the scene completely wrong. Patti has CHRIS!(tm) run down the stretch and then sends the girls, one by one, at two second intervals. But there's too much space between CHRIS!(tm) and the other runners, making the scene boring. We shoot the scene three or four times, but every attempt fails. Finally, I say, "Let's have us all go at the same time. Everyone should run their fastest." And then I say that if any of the girls are too fast for me, they should just throw the race.

The race is now CHRIS!(tm) versus four Asian women.

Go!

CHRIS!(tm) runs and beats them all. Yes, and the scene looks great. I run my fastest-I think with my eyes closed-and I beat all the girls, making me the super-champion.

Even though everything is great, I want to shoot the scene two or three more times. But as soon as I turn around, I notice the camera is gone. Doug or Dennis says he's sorry, and hands me a small hand-held camera, as if that's going to suffice.

No.

I hide all my stuff from him in the other room because I think he's a big dick.

Norman Klein

The Unreliable Narrator

ears ago, I knew a ninety-three year old lady named Mollie Frankel, who owned a battered Queen Ann Victorian house, about five years older than she was, on what was once a fancy corner lot just north of Carroll Avenue, in Angelino Heights. She had moved in somewhere between 1919 and 1928, had survived two husbands, one a possible suicide. No one knew for certain; or at least her relatives who might know wouldn't say. Even Mollie didn't seem to have essential facts straight.

"My husband was a sporting man," she used to explain, meaning a smart dresser, a john for prostitutes, or a gambler.

"I came to Los An-gheles in 1928, right after the war, and got a job as a bookkeeper. His father saw I was a hard worker, running their business. So he more or less forced his son to settle down with me. I wasn't much to look at, but he knew I would help his boy stay at home more."

"Did you?"

Mollie laughed, remembering something intimate or embarrassing about her first husband. Then she added:

"Now my second husband I kept saying no to. He asked me to marry him five times a week. I exaggerate. He said to me once. He was a lawyer for my business. He says to me: "We could organize very well together.""

"So?"

"So he was home continuously."

Mollie still ran her shop, located somewhere in the warehouse district on Main, near the flophouses. She sold "inside felt" that was used for the collars on suits. "I get my best sleep there," she said.

One Fourth of July, her grand-niece, who now lives in Vegas, came by to drive her to a party. Mollie wore her better wig, had her beaded purse. But she was confused somehow by the entire event.

The next day, a Sunday, I saw Mollie ambling down the hill at dusk, toward the bus. Then she realized her mistake, and told me:

"I must have overslept. I missed a day somehow."

She was beginning to lose track of the difference between sunrise and sunset. Having just had her driver's license revoked, she would take the Temple Street bus into downtown, then get her store ready, waiting for the sun to come up, until finally, it was clear that either there was a solar eclipse or she'd missed a day somehow.

Mollie lived on the second floor, and rented out the rest to a large Mexican family, who seemed desperate to keep Mollie around, because she never raised the rent, and they knew her family coveted her property. I was invited to visit Mollie once at her house, and found her seated in the kitchen, making toast over the stove, using a forties vintage wire toaster that sat on the gas burner.

Her built-in cupboards were literally exploding with depression glass, pink and rose dishes crammed so tight, they were about to spring the lock. Up in her attic, some twelve hundred square feet of raw space, I found a dusty brown bag tied with rope, and hidden behind a lateral support beam. I asked her what this was, and she shrugged, but said I could have it if I wanted.

Inside were four books from the W.B. Du Bois Club, imprints from the early thirties. Was Mollie a thirties Socialist?

"Must have been my sister. She was the reader."

"This has been here for fifty years. Was your sister involved in politics?"

"I don't go up here much."

Later I found out that her husband, apparently the organized one, had hung himself up in the attic. But no one could say for certain.

Across the street, inside a huge Craftsman house, another of the matrons in the neighborhood had died in her late seventies, and left all her clothing stacked neatly, like fossil sediment, one on top of the other, from 1918 as a Temperance activist to 1983.

Apparently, the living room was large enough to hold over three hundred people at her niece's wedding in the early fifties. Now her niece's daughter, a very serious young nurse had moved in, to keep the family interest going, just she and her boyfriend in 7,500 square feet.

The neighbors told her to listen for ghosts. Then after a few weeks, apparently a rattle developed up in her attic. It would wake her up at night. Finally, out of purely secular desperation for a good night's sleep, she walked up the attic steps, and asked her dead aunt for a truce. I'll keep the door closed up here, she offered, if you'll stop waking me up at night. And that was enough apparently.

One early evening I saw Mollie on her way to the Temple Street bus again. I stopped her, and insisted that it was sundown. She laughed at me, but agreed to wait long enough to find out. Then as the sky darkened, and the night breezes started, she finally apologized, saying that ever since that Fourth of July party last month, she kept getting her days mixed up.

That was about ten years ago. Mollie's family took the house, and put her in a senior citizen's home, where she grew enormously fat, and may have been happy for all I know. She died five years later, apparently older than she admitted to, somewhere around a hundred.

It must be strange to live in a world that utterly transforms around you, as if you were an immigrant in your own house. As I explained earlier, from 1928 (or 1919), the area went from mixed Anglo and Jewish bourgeois to prostitutes and drug dealers down the corner in the early seventies. On Sunset Boulevard, there had once been gyms where the young Anthony Quinn in the thirties trained to be a boxer, then thought better of it; and worked on Sundays in the church of Sister Aimee Semple McPherson. Not a whisper of all that remains, except the Jensen center that had declined into a drug contact by the late fifties, and had long since turned its bowling alleys into discount stores.

There are practically no fragments left of Mollie's life, certainly no memories in the house, that has since been sold and renovated into upscale apartments. I have no idea how I would find out precisely where Mollie lied. "I hide a few years," she used to say. I don't even know if her life was dowdy or melodramatic, not really. Like the Vietnamese whom I interviewed, hers is a history of ways to distract information more than erasing it.

That is more or less the spirit of the unreliable narrator. It is a story based on how we forget or repress memory. Clearly it has a literary tradition behind it, from eighteenth century fiction in particular (the Munchausens and Uncle Tobys); in Russian literature after Gogol's short stories; German and Central European fiction after 1880; the Romanticist fascination with demolished historic places as unreliable narrators, the absent presence that in Michelet's words are "obscure and dubious witnesses" (1847). Virginia Woolf's emptied rooms where the remains of memory are displaced; American tall tales that Mark Twain loved; in Roland Barthes' S/Z; in noir fiction by Jim Thompson or David Goodis, where the narrator is a criminal who has to repress what he does, and lie to the reader.

"In old apartments,"writes Bruno Schulz, speaking through the voice of a father, "there are rooms which are sometimes forgotten. Unvisited for months on end, they wilt between the walls and... close in on themselves." "The Father went inside one of these collapsed rooms, and found that "slim shoots grow (in the crevices)," "filling the gray air with a scintillating filigree lace of leaves." But by nightfall, they are "gone without a trace." "The whole elusive sight was a fata morgana, an example of the strange make-believe of matter which had created a semblance of life."

Hanna Hellsten

Sweet Alyssum and Red Diamonds

n our family owned bakery, Papa had been working for thirty-five years, from the time he was a year old. I've heard that when grandpapa led the shop and papa was a baby, grandmama would bring papa into the bakery kitchen every night before bedtime. Grandpapa lifted papa onto the counter and let him crawl and push his round knees into the rows of dough lumps. This practice led him to his trademark technique of using the form and weight of his arms to prepare the "Long-Arm Elbow Bread." His skill not only earned him a considerable reputation as a talented and masterful baker among the villagers but also well-deserved admiration from his peers in the business.

Whenever I'd visit papa's work—whether to deliver a message from mama or pick up some notes of money for food shopping—he would teach me some tricks of the craft. (For example, leaving the "Long-Arm Elbow" dough, covered and protected by a clean towel against any cold drafts, the heat of the kitchen causes it to double in size. The strength of the yeast is then potentialized by a temperature of ninety-five degrees. When finished baking, the bread is taken out and placed on a drying rack to cool, either covered with a clean towel to attain a soft crust, or not covered at all to become crisp on the outside. I also observed that any time he could take a break, he would, to have a cig. He had this habit at home as well—walking out of the room bending so far forward I almost thought his timeworn back would break in half. It always made me nervous to see papa's posture distort so decrepitly although I knew he was only getting the tobacco packet out of his front pocket. It was curious that he did this in the same way I recalled grandpapa moving when he was preparing to smoke. It was as if papa had to reestablish the set of movements he remembered in his papa to prove to us grandpapa had never really died.

So he'd walk outside without saying a thing. I never understood why he even got up out of his seat, for the smoke always drifted back into the room. One early evening he walked out of the kitchen onto the porch. The beginnings of winter had dramatically chilled the air. As papa was pulling the tobacco out of its pouch—the one he always carried with him sewn by mama—our conversation at the kitchen table quickly stopped. Mama, Elma, and I saw him from behind when his narrow, usually crooked, back abruptly straightened. The tobacco between his thumb and index finger flew forward in distinct pieces which threw stripes of shadow onto the flooring.

Under papa's unkempt tufts of hair, perspiration trickled down into his shirt's cotton. The last traces of flush in his cheeks vanished into a pallor that was frightful. My body sat heavy and immobilized. After many taxing moments, papa's head slowly weakened over his chest and then his knees as he lowered his body down onto the top porch step.

We could barely see him now through the hazy glass separating us, but I thought I saw his profiled face bloom blue through its pallor. Then he slumped over the edge of the porch steps onto the pebbled earth. I had an impulse to rush out and catch him as he fell; but as soon as I thought about it I realized it didn't make any sense to try to help a dead body. I'd never been the one to nurse his needs before. Neither mama or I was ever as able as Elma to please him. But now, like me, Elma didn't move from her seat.

People used to say I was exactly like my mama, "the same sour-looking face and ugly disposition" is what I overheard some villagers say. For many years I troubled myself with these words and what they could mean. Previous to hearing this I hadn't thought about my face. I began to seek my reflection. I woke up early in the mornings before the rest of the family and our nearby neighbors and quietly stepped down to the little, narrow river that ran through our backyard. There, I could capture a time of relative stillness before the birds spoke and the morning winds alarmed the leaves. Hopefully, I'd see something distinctly my own—my nose in the ripples that didn't quit but sometimes slowed enough for my special glimpse. I'd patiently wait for the surface to even. I captured one eye—eyebrow—and then a cheekbone. Finally I found my lips and a bit of chin. After these adventures I would watch mama's face intently.

Although I did this for many months and never stopped viewing her thereafter, I didn't see the sameness people talked about. I was furious with what I decided were the villagers' narrow-minded observations. I became so familiar with their ideas that I finally didn't need to actually hear what they said and instead intuited their thoughts. This sensitivity grew stronger each day as I became more comfortable with its possibilities. As I was gaining insight into others' minds as well as strengthening my ability to read their thoughts, I grew exceedingly gleeful. My frog puzzles were barely taken apart and reassembled during those days. I was so excited and caught up in the mental game that I had no desire to touch them.

One spring morning, though, as I was walking by papa's work shed I heard the small cage shake and rattle vigorously. I ran behind the shed to examine the temperament among the frogs and frog parts. Due to my lack of attention, the little live ones had rapidly multiplied on the straw bedding. Yet I was immediately at ease when I realized the stability of the cage. And the careful and specific planning I had undertaken for the construction of their home rewarded me with a deep sense of self-respect. Long and hard I had sought thick, strong branches that would withstand a big wind or our cat's mischievous pawings. For the roof I had stripped shreds of bark from healthy tree trunks. These shreds worked perfectly when weighed down by rocks heavy enough to hold them in place and light enough not to break the bars below. So although the little families played hard as they lay on each other and sprung competitively against the branches and bark ceiling, my building could overcome any of their crazy, ambitious attempts to break the confinement. So I felt truly comfortable to leave them to their games and resume my new and successful habit of joining people in their thoughts.

But then, my sensory skills seemed to have attained their maximum potential and I was hearing the same babble from the same individual minds. I grew increasingly miserable. I was bruised by the villagers' quiet comments between themselves regarding my appearance and personality, and wanted to understand their self-assured interpretations. Yet at this point, after claiming my skill for overhearing personal psycho babble, I was exhausted and really sick of the minds around me; for example, the milkboy with his delusions of priestliness. This simple lad fantasized repeatedly that scores of faceless but adoring village women from his milk route followed him on some retreat into the mountains (what mountain range was never specified). There was also the hired girl behind the Flabbins' Candy Store counter who had creative thoughts on candy-to-wrapper combinations which she never even attempted. I, who put such a great deal of time and effort into my frog experiments, had no patience with a person who merely theorized about things they wanted to do but never lifted a finger to try their ideas out in real life. My tunnel to her head was squeezed so tight I could feel my brain squeal. My spirit grew heavy. Not even their dreams interested me. I knew too much.

To partially solve my misery I discovered a simple way to benefit from the problem of my dreaded resemblance to mama. After papa died a messenger began arriving every Monday afternoon with a note of money for mama. The first time I opened the door to his knock he asked me if I was mama. I answered his question affirmatively, and he handed off the notes of money to me as if I was mama. Thereafter I couldn't stop the game. All summer the lie was so easy and the situation so perfect since mama always laid bare in the afternoon sun in the backyard at that hour and thus never questioned me. The operation was also relieving to my nerves. Mama never found out for all I know. She probably knows now, though, since my leaving the house. I'm sure the messenger still makes his visits.

It seems my younger sister took after papa. That's what others said. "What a wonderful little person Elma is—just like her papa!" said Aunt Britta at every family gathering, said the milkboy who came Sunday mornings to the house, said Joseph the mail clerk at the post office I stopped in at every afternoon, and said Ms. Dia the vocal trainer that Elma and I visited morning and night.

Papa was deemed similarly good tempered but only because he never lifted a fist or raised his voice in dis-agreement with anyone outside the family. He always appeared satisfied and quiet in public. At the bakery, with its undertone smell of cigarette smoke, he worked con-tinuously without speaking or looking up from the dough and took his breaks in solitude and muteness. When someone came to the house or the village had its community picnic papa always sat close to us (usually to Elma)—on the picnic blanket, on the family room couch, at the kitchen table, (or wherever else we may have been sitting)—looking serene, with that expression of satisfac-tion and triumph always present on his face in social situations.

What probably would have shocked the villagers was that as soon as the family was alone again after a social affair, papa usually laughed in his sleeve at what I think he considered the gullibility of the villagers or visiting relatives in misrecognizing his relaxed expression for love and kindness. I laughed with him at first, too. It seemed silly to me that the people surrounding our family were capable of seeing so little. But then his early morning games with Elma would begin again and I would swallow the tickle that had just barely partnered my mind with his.

The aching noises from the other side of the room started. I again succumbed to my obsessional fantasies for recognition by maybe Joseph or Ms. Dia or any other villager, hoping that perhaps they had really taken notice of papa's trickery but couldn't decide what to do about it yet. Or if not that, they would realize his malice on their walk home or as they were falling asleep at night. Possibly they would even have a dream exposing them to our reality. But none of these thoughts ever came true.

Every morning I would awake to the chill running down my arms, thighs, and legs when the wool had been pulled away from my sleeping area and had gathered at the right corner of the opposite wall. I always tried to fall asleep again by covering my head and ears with the sheepskin off the floor. But the muffled sounds of whimpering and groaning always seeped through to my mind—Elma's thin leg with its spidery brown hairs escaping from the bundle of warm wool. Hot air entering my ears and lungs. I can't breathe. Tiny ants crawling up the wall; most of them falling back. The walls wet with perspiration. Papa's dirty hair—bouncing around in there into thoughts and ideas I didn't want to have as part of me.

Supposedly Elma was the beautiful one in the family. That's what most people we knew said or thought; and papa thought so, too. Every morning at breakfast we all gathered—mama, papa, Elma, and I—around the dark mahogany table illuminated only by the candlestick's flickering light. The kitchen was especially obscured during the dim mornings of winter. At those times papa believed that the curtains of dark-day concealed his gestures. He underestimated my attentiveness, though. I was not too sleepy to see or hear the almost unintelligible movements under the table.

On especially dark mornings around Christmas time he reached over and placed the bag of nuts and grains onto Elma's lap in the secrecy of the table's underside. Contrary to his assumptions, I was keenly aware of the affection they transacted as well as my exclusion from it. Then the anxious rattling of her fingertips as they searched for those special surprises he'd thrown into the mix became unbearably annoying to my senses.

Papa knew all too well how Elma and I both loved the gingersnap heart and circle shapes. The bakery displayed these exquisite delicacies only two weeks out of the year for the villagers. Late into every evening papa arranged a batch for us girls so that we would have them for our morning play.

All the mornings that I can remember, papa had broken these cookies into small bits which he laid onto the top of the nuts and grains in our bags. But these gingersnap pieces never remained on the top layer to be easily gathered by hand. As soon as the fragile paper bag was touched or a hand entered its narrow cavity, any possibility of attaining the cookie crumbs was made complicated. Unavoidably, a mix occurred between the ordinary nuts and grains and the special pieces. This was usually a delightful challenge, though. Elma and I had small hands for our ages, but every year that we grew the exercise of the game was more strenuous and so, more compelling.

On the less obscure mornings of the year, papa would have offered the bag equally to Elma and I by placing it at the center of the kitchen table. Then we began our race when papa gave us the sign—he'd signal with a double wink of the right eye and a wave of his right arm over the bag. Elma and I reached furiously to get it. Papa, when convinced of a superior lead, handed the bag over to the one he considered victor. That one of us then stuck our hand into it and took as much of its contents as possible before he hollered, "Wooop!". He called this out at thirty second intervals. Then the other attempted to attain as many sweets as possible from what was left. The final phase was when we counted our individual piles to compare our accomplishments. After that we could enjoy the treasures.

Now, on the darker winter mornings, papa was unfair and seemingly oblivious to the usual methods of the game. Although I sat across from Elma, I was acutely aware of the fact that the rules of our habitual play were being broken. Perhaps papa didn't bother to realize that I was a conscious, feeling being or maybe he had no conscience. And Elma was breaching our bonds of sisterly companionship and love for a few pieces of gingersnaps.

Mama always dearly loved me instead of Elma, though. Thus she was mean and cruel to my sister. She made her eat in the kitchen when we had guests over for dinner; and Elma had to do all the hard work in the house. Twice a day she had to walk to the distant well and bring back a jug filled with water.

One day, while Elma was at the well filling her jug, a

poor little lady spoke to her. The woman begged for some water. Being so kind as Elma is, she filled the lady's jug with the clearest, coolest water in the well. Then she held the jug carefully for the little old lady so she could drink from it easily. When the old woman had finished, she thanked Elma and told her that she was as good and kind as she was beautiful. She wanted to give Elma a gift.

Elma smiled. She probably wondered what a poor, little old lady could give her. She didn't know that the old lady was really a fairy who had taken the form of a poor village woman to test Elma's goodness.

The old woman gave Elma a talent: when she spoke, flowers and precious jewels fell from my sister's lips. Then the little old lady disappeared, leaving Elma alone by the well.

When Elma returned home, mama was cross and waiting for her.

Mama scolded her for being away so long; and Elma apologized. When she spoke, three roses, five black star sapphires, two sweet alyssum, and four red diamonds tumbled from her mouth. Mama cried out ecstatically, plunging to her knees. Her big arms swept the floor clean as they gathered up the jewels and flowers and let them fall into her skirt pockets. She struggled to keep calm as she said to Elma that it looked as if the sapphires and diamonds fell from her lips and questioned how that could be. She even called her dear daughter, which she only ever did with me.

Of course Elma was so pleased to hear mama address her kindly that she told mama about the little old lady she had met at the well. When Elma had finished speaking, a pile of black pearls, baby tears, "string of pearls" lobelias, and clear diamonds was at her feet. Mama threw herself into the mound and cried out, "Frances, come here and see the jewels and flowers that fall from your sister's lips when she speaks! Wouldn't you like to be able to do that?" Mama wanted to send me down to the well.

I absolutely didn't want to do any work that was my sister's responsibility. I had enough trouble with the demands of my puzzle practice. I was sure Elma was calculating some form of humiliation for me, anyhow. Perhaps she wanted to show mama I'd fail at what she could do so well. She had long strong arms trained for lifting and carrying work. I'm sure she thought I'd trip with the load of water. Maybe she wanted to hide or misuse my frog families while I was away. Resentment heated within my belly.

Then my thoughts dissolved as mama forced the best silver jug into my hands. She said all I needed to do was walk to the well and when a poor old woman asked me for a drink to give it to her! But I was not persuaded.

"Wouldn't I look fine—walking to the well, carrying a jug!" I exclaimed scornfully. Mama ordered me to go at once whether I wanted to or not. Her face twisted so hideously that I feared to disobey.

As I walked off towards the well with the silver jug, I grumbled over the inconvenience and tried to imagine ways out of this conflict. I realized I had to come home with something to show so I decided to waste as little time as possible at the well with the little old lady so that I could hurry back to my frog puzzles. Eleven legs were currently drying in my room at home; and they were probably almost ready to be conjoined with other bodies. If I waited too long in the drying process, problems could arise. It was possible that an excessive loss of moisture would occur in the open joints and the hind legs, which drained more quickly, were pivotal to my formations. All other parts rotated about these axes for the realization of new symmetrical arrangements. Those hind legs would be of no use to me if the drying time exceeded nine minutes. Then I would have to begin again the hectic pursuit of amphibians.

No sooner had I arrived at the well than I saw a lady dressed in beautiful, rich clothing coming out of the woods. It was the very same fairy who had spoken to my sister. Yet instead of dressing as a poor village woman, this time she had dressed herself as a princess to test my kindness. Sparkles from her dress and hair, as well as those reflected in my silver jug, were like glaring points which intensified as she came closer. I squinted from the irritating shine and grew increasingly annoyed by the discomfort this caused my eyes.

"Good day," she said, greeting me sweetly. With a voice so soft—it seemed to dissolve her words into such pure, ambient sound that I could barely make out what she was saying—she asked if I would give her a drink of water.

Knowing already what she would be requesting from me, I was prepared to answer crossly: "Oh, now really! Do you think I came here just to give you a drink?! I suppose you think I carried this silver pitcher just so I could draw water for you! Get yourself a drink of water if you want one!" As I was finishing these words, I threw the pitcher at her. It hit the right side of her face so hard that

I thought she should have collapsed violently into unconsciousness. Instead she knelt to the ground very slowly and gracefully. Then she lay still on the cobblestone. Shocked, I watched her brilliant clothing fade into rags.

Although she was a fairy and on the ground, she was not incapable of making rude remarks. Boldly I was told that I wasn't a very polite girl and that I didn't have any manners at all. What troubled me so desperately was not the words themselves but how she said them in the most gentle voice I'd ever heard.

Still I scowled and said, "I don't care." I pointed my nose high in the air just to irk her.

Then she told me she was going to give me a gift. My mind paused a second in anticipation.

"Each time you speak, a snake or a toad will fall from your lips."

As I was going to tell her she shouldn't have frustrated me and that I was not responsible for the chore of collecting water for the house or for passers-by, she disappeared. I was left ill-tempered and alone by the well.

As soon as mama saw me coming, she called out joyfully, "Well, my daughter?"

"Well, my dear mama!" I snapped bitterly. Two snakes and a toad suddenly tumbled from my lips and fell at her feet.

"Good heavens!" cried mama. "What has happened to you? This is all your sister's fault! I'll make her pay for this!" She rushed off to find my unlucky younger sister. Relief swept through me and I sat down on a log outside papa's work shed. My stomach turned and fell in place again.

But Elma was not ignorant of mama's passions. She had overhead her exclamations and knew she would be punished if mama caught her. So she ran deep into the forest to hide. There she cried and cried until someone heard her.

It just happened to be the king's son, returning from hunting, who found her. Standing tall and handsome beside her, he asked her why she was all alone and weeping. So Elma told him how she had been driven from home. And as she spoke, two fire opals, five mallow-worts, one yellow diamond, and three blazing stars fell from her lips.

"Where did these jewels come from?" cried the king's son. And she told him the story of the fairy's gift.

Then he explained how he had fallen deeply in love with her and desired to be by her side for all time. He told her that the gift she had was better than any dowry a princess would bring. The handsome prince took Elma to his papa's palace and married her at once.

Mama grew so tired of sweeping up toads and snakes every time I opened my mouth that she threw me out of the house as well. I was upset at first, but with my cage of frogs and curiosity about what Elma was doing I felt a drive to enter the woods. I haven't seen her yet, though. Over the last few years I've met many who know her and who have stories to tell. After hearing a multitude of facts and opinions, I've finally figured out her story. But I've been too busy to find her. Working with my puzzles is a constant pursuit since I've discovered the rich variety of life in the woods.

My investigation into the potentiality of other forms besides what nature offers has led me to new inventions. Investing the forest with intricate compositions of amphibians and reptiles has demanded my full attention. I feel completely satisfied with my responsibility as a discoverer of new physical shapes and have no time for visits with the past now. Yet I can say that I am truly grateful for fate's chain of events which have brought me to this brilliant place.

Amy Gerstler

Notes from the Ozone

ost nights, the lamp on the nightstand on my dad's side of the bed clicks off at ten thirty-eight. His snores are rattling the headboard by ten forty. My mom doesn't close her eyes for a few more hours. Finally, around midnight, she conks out with a detective novel face-down on her belly. It rises and falls as though afloat on an ocean. On its cover's a sexy blonde, wearing panties and a shirt more see-through than wet Kleenex, with nothing underneath. She's got a snub nosed pistol clapped over her heart as if pledging allegiance. Her eyes are half closed. Books with covers like this end up spending long nights on my mother's lap, contrasting with her high-necked, long sleeved nightgowns spattered with primroses or tiny violets.

When I know they're asleep, I slip out of the shadow-filled cooling house, which creaks like an overheated car, not to meet some boy, but because I'm hoping to lay eyes on a UFO. I'm serious. A decade before I was born, hundreds of people, more than belong to our church, saw a glowing egg-shaped object zoom over a frozen reservoir. What brought it there? Was it tempted lower and lower by the glinting moonlit water, the majestic cement dam and jagged frozen waterfall? Later, when reservoir guards took a closer look, there were big thawed spots on the ice where the object had shone its bright hot light. As with any seemingly random occurrence, all types of people were there that night. College professors and gardeners, kids and their parents, off-duty policemen, a molecular biologist on a date, the usual tourists. There were even a couple of drunks looking for a place to sleep. Certain visitors to the reservoir that fateful night said it changed the way they looked at the world, made them ready to consider possibilities they'd scoffed at before. This reservoir's in the midwest. I've never visited the midwest, but I'm eager to go because from my reading, I noticed there have been a bunch of sightings there, particularly in Ann Arbor, Michigan. I thought maybe I should apply to college in Ann Arbor, so I could be closer to the action. When I mentioned this to my older sister Margaret, she denied there was anything in Ann Arbor that might attract UFOs. "People see flying saucers there because there are a lot of screwed up fools in Ann Arbor who take drugs all the time. It's probably the hallucination capitol of the world." She has no respect for my ideas.

Margaret is married and talks about sex a lot. Not openly, because it would be out of character for her to be straightforward, but she alludes to it constantly. I don't always mind. I know she's just trying to act superior, which I'm extremely used to. From the moment she got engaged, she started saying "we" so much I think she's lost use of the first person singular entirely. Flaunting the fact that she gets laid every night while I am still supposed to be a thumb-sucking virgin gives her a thrill. She happens to be wrong about my status, but for obvious reasons I have to pretend I don't know what she's talking about when she tells my mother nice and loud so I'm sure to hear "Orgasm is the best cure for cramps I've ever found." Whenever she comes over without her new male Siamese twin, she makes a big deal of how exhausted she is, till you are forced to ask Why is poor Margaret so tired? Then it's always "Oh, Will kept me up all night again. He's insatiable". Another subject which comes up every time she visits is blinds. "We absolutely have to get blinds for the living room and the upstairs bedroom right away. Will just loves to walk around naked at all hours of the day and night." Months have gone by and she is always too tired from being a sex slave to actually go out and buy these blinds. But I keep my mouth shut.

In the past, my sister has proven beyond a shadow of a doubt that she will tell my parents whatever I confide in her. She doesn't even let a decent amount of time go by. She will rat on me within fifteen minutes. My parents are very sweet, but they have not checked in with social reality since the fifties and are terrorized by so many aspects of what it's like to grow up these days it's not even funny. If they ever saw a marijuana leaf in one of their ashtrays they'd get so freaked out they'd probably burn the house down trying to get rid of it. Drugs are personal. Sex is personal. Unlike my sister, I am the kind of person who knows how to keep a few things to herself. Once, shortly after she got back from her honeymoon, Margaret came into my room, acting like she could hardly walk, practically waddling. She flopped onto a chair, rolled her eyes and announced with a completely fake blush "I'm soooo sore. I feel like I've been on horseback for days." I guess she made this incredibly ladylike remark just to let me know her husband hadn't been neglecting her. In case I was worried.

At least Margaret blabs different things about sex than girls at school, my parents, teachers, and the man and woman that run the "New You" class for teens at church, where they push books at us with titles like: "Being Born". I would like to announce to those planning future sex

270

education classes, that "Being Born", vile disgusting diseases that leave juicy sores all over your body, as well as how insects and plants reproduce are on the very bottom of the list of things inquiring young minds want to know about sex. VD and spider egg sacs are totally gross and unerotic, unless you're really weird. Being born is something everyone has already experienced, only to have it wiped from our memories, probably because it's too frightening and painful to dwell on consciously. Even mothers don't seem to remember giving birth accurately. If you ask them about it, half the time they come up with wild inflated tales, because it's the only story they know that they're the hero of. My sister's going to be just like that when she has kids, an exaggerating mother who tries to wring gratitude out of her offspring nonstop, from the second they're born. I can just hear her:

I had you in a taxi driving a hundred miles an hour, darling, through terrible areas of town—construction sites where they were jack hammering and steel girders swung through the air, and buildings were being destroyed right and left, with wrecking balls and dynamite./ The pains overtook me as I strolled through a pasture, but the cows instinctively understood and left me alone./ I had you in a park, under a jacaranda tree, my back pressed up against the trunk for comfort and support during contractions. Every so often a breeze would kick up and float a bunch of wrinkled purplish blossoms onto my heaving bosom./ The crows brought you in little pink package with glitter all over it and curled satin ribbons dangling down and silver bells attached. No matter how absurd she gets, you can't contradict Margaret. If you do, she just cries. Then everyone takes her side, and she walks around for hours with her nostrils flared, raw and pink, her lips quivering.

I don't need to remember being born—it's not relevant information at this stage of my life. It would have been much more helpful to know what sex was like when I was trying to figure it out. Now I know, if you can call having done it four times knowing, and no thanks to my sister or parents or anyone else older and allegedly wiser. All they did was mislead me with Latin names and booklets published by tampon companies that reassure you it's safe to shampoo your hair during your period. Big revelation. During the past several years I wasted untold hours trying to imagine having sex, so I wouldn't make a fool of myself when the time came, if ever. I pictured it many ways, none of which turned out to be too accurate. I could have saved myself about two or three solid years worth of worrying if someone had just showed me a film. For instance, I frequently dreamed I had what turned out to be an anatomically incorrect version of sex at the bottom of my parents' swimming pool where I and some faceless boy could suddenly breath easily without oxygen tanks. Just to show you how incredibly dumb I was, a long time ago I used to think people could have intercourse without the woman uncrossing her legs. Sex was sketchily described to me by four or five girls I knew from English or PE last year who claimed to have done it. But the only way I could get them to talk about it was to pretend I had done it too, so I wasn't really able to ask my most pressing questions.

I need something to zoom across my path and leave

me stunned and breathless. A ship that leaves white plumey streaks in the sky, day or night, that travels in spurts, stops abruptly, then darts out of sight. Maybe I'd be alone when I saw it, or with a friend, hiking in a secluded spot, surrounded by great outcroppings of rock with Indian picture-writing on them. There would be a body of water nearby when it appeared, and the UFO would be reflected in it for a few seconds as it hovered above. It'd be terribly hot. We'd both have cameras loaded and ready.

There was a lady minister in church today, because First Unitarian is doing an exchange with Faith United in Woodland Hills. Her sermon was titled: "Life is a Constellation of Accidents, So Be Prepared." Almost as if she caused it by making that declaration, I saw an accident on the way home from the service. A root-beer colored Honda Civic, which doesn't look like it could do much damage, hit a guy on a motorcycle. Or the bike hit the car. It was hard to tell. I don't see how police or insurance adjusters decide these things. They probably just make something up when they write a report, because everything that happens could be anyone's fault, or everyone's. You can't tell where events begin and end half the time, or what really causes most things. Maybe I unknowingly had something to do with that crash just by being in another car two lanes away. Maybe something I was thinking, or the way I turned my head on my neck at that second, or how I licked my finger to rub off a speck on the car window caused the invisible web that holds everything together to tremble, the way it does when you accidentally disturb a spider web and you can see the spider shaking in anger, making the whole delicate structure vibrate like crazy.

My dad is the type who not only carries a first aid kit in the car, but actually goes through the kit every year and replaces all the supplies that have gone bad. Once he proudly called me into the garage to show me how the expired mercurochrome was all dried up, a little bottle full of rust flakes. As soon as the Honda/motorcyclist collision occurred, he was on the car phone calling 911. He told my mother and I, "stay with the car, you two." My dad helped out till the ambulance arrived. His first aid efforts consisted of not letting the motorcyclist move, and stopping any bleeding he could see. We left when the paramedics came, and dad gave them our number in case witnesses were needed.

The only kind of witness I want to be is witness to something utterly amazing that no one ever saw before. A sight that will change me just by flashing in front of my face, something I will think about for the rest of my life. I wouldn't mind if it was a sight that aged me a little: but no more than six or eight months. I wouldn't want my hair to turn white overnight or anything like that, but since I'm fifteen I feel I would be willing to make some other, small sacrifice for great spiritual gain. You never know for sure how long anyone will be on earth, but I am counting on having a lot of life left.

Recently, my father was politely grilling me about why I read UFO books. Why did they interest me so much? Was I unhappy about something? This was another in a series of periodic demonstrations of parental concern. As usual, his questioning began: "Your mother and I were

274

just wondering...". At first I didn't want to talk about it, so I asked him why mom reads so many detective novels. But then I realized I was being rude, not giving him a chance. When I told him I wanted to see something that had never been seen on earth before, that would leave its mark on me as an unforgettable, incredible experience, he said "huh!", making a one-word transition from sounding worried to surprise. He also snorted, which I don't think he meant to do, so I pretended not to hear. Usually I would have imitated him. Then he felt his chin and it made that dry grass noise stubble chins make when you rub them. He never shaves on the weekends. I thought he would laugh at me, which is what my sister does. I made up my mind if he did, the conversation was over. But the look he got on his face reminded me of the our dog, Jupiter: attentive, puzzled, intense. Then he told me that before I was born, when he was a few years older than I am now, he was in the Navy, which I already knew, and that he had volunteered to witness the underwater explosion of an atomic bomb in the Pacific Ocean. This last part was new to me. He said he wasn't sure, but he thought that might be somewhere in the ballpark of the sort of experience I had in mind. He paused and dug in his ear with his pinky. If I did this he'd say "Use a Q-Tip!" Then he asked if I thought that sort of experience might fall into the right category.

I was completely shocked he'd never mentioned this before. I sat up. "You're kidding" I said.

As he sat down on this ugly green leatherette couch which folds out into my bed, the cushion let out a gust of air. "Honey, in some ways I wish I was."

Then it was my turn to ask questions.

My room has a window that looks out over the porch and driveway. Part of a gardenia bush, moved by breeze, was scraping the window screen, like it wanted to come in. Seeing gardenia leaves move in and out of view seemed weird. I guess any regular garden type plant, or hearing the distant sound of a neighbor's power mower and the traffic from up the hill would seem bizzare in its normalness compared to what he was telling me. He looked around my room while he talked. Maybe he was just resting his eyes on different things, books, candles, clothes and posters, like touching them with his finger-tips to get his bearings, keeping in sync with this time while he talked about his past.

He watched from Bikini atoll while they exploded the bomb in a lagoon. Not because he was particularly inter-ested, but because a buddy of his talked him into it. His dead friend Nick, who I've seen snapshots of, was really excited. "Come on, it'll be great. It'll be in all the history books. You'll have something to tell your grandchildren." I asked him what an atoll was, just to stall for time because I was so blown away. He explained it's an island made of coral that's shaped like a ring, with a lagoon in the middle.

"It was real beautiful," he said quietly.

"What, the atoll, or the explosion?"

He forced a little grin and I could see the spaces between his yellow teeth. He refers to them as horse teeth.

"Both, I guess."

I made him tell me about it for over an hour. I made my mother delay dinner. Over a million tons of water flew into the air. A couple of days later, all his hair fell out. The other guys' hair fell out too. It grew back after a while, but my dad said "By the time it grew back, I was used to the idea of it being gone."

He answered every question. Then I said "You have a funny look on your face. Like you kind of regret having seen it. Do you?" I was sitting on the opposite end of the couch from him, on the arm, with my feet on the seat. He tried to tell me how he felt. It's not something he does much, because he's such a careful person. "I have mixed feelings" he said. He talked for a while about doing things without weighing the consequences, which I'm sure was part of a lecture he wished he could give me but didn't have the heart. "Nick died of cancer in his early thirties. He never had kids, let alone grandchildren. Once I told a doctor about having been at the blast and he said I might not ever be able to have children, or if I did, they might come out deformed."

"They did" I said, making a face at him by yanking down the corners of my eyes with my fingers, and sticking out my tongue.

"Honey, I'm serious" he said, not even smiling a little.

"OK" I said, sliding off the couch arm onto the seat. "Margaret's the only one that turned out to be a geek."

He acted like he didn't hear me. "When I met your mother I was petrified she wouldn't marry me if I told her."

"So, did you tell her?"

"Of course. Eventually."

Eventually, we went in to dinner. I asked a few more questions while we ate. "How did this lovely subject come up?" my mother asked, not unkindly, tossing salad. I could tell this was going to be a discussion topic later, when they were alone. My father said "Just apropos of some things your youngest daughter and I have in common."

Later, lying in bed, sweating, braiding and unbraiding my hair, I heard someone cross the living room, go through the kitchen and let themselves out into the backyard. I got up and went to the sliding glass door in the living room. The high louvered windows in the kitchen and above the door were open, because of the heat. My father was sitting on the concrete, by the side of the pool, a piece of the wavy illumination reflected by the water cast on his face, a tattoo of light. He couldn't see me. He was holding Jupiter sort of on his lap, petting him and rubbing behind his silky ears. Jupiter was smiling in the way dogs who have big stretchy mouths do, tongue hanging out, probably dripping. Jupiter's a border collie, very handsome, with rubbery black lips that have a slightly jagged edge. Every time my dad would stop petting for a second, Jupiter would push my dad's hand with his nose. Jupiter has beady eyes, not like a criminal's, but unswerving and to the point. Border collies were originally bred as herders, and it's said their eyes can hypnotize cattle. I believe it. Jupiter could probably hypnotize me. Of course I'm a good subject, staggering around most of the time in the ozone, hoping to stumble across anything spellbinding—a bright silvery object like a giant bullet shooting through the sky the way thoughts zigzag through my head.

I admire dogs. They can seem sweetly familiar if

you've lived with them but remain alien in lots of ways. I read dogs can smell one drop of blood in 5 litres of water. My father says Jupiter is a better judge of character than my mother is. Jupiter barks at things, indoors and out, that are invisible to me—gets mesmerized by bugs or ghosts or flying molecules. His head whips around as they zip by. I wish I had talents like that.

Jupiter licked my dad's nose and then yawned in his face. "Wow" my dad laughed, looking into the interesting canine mouth. "It looks like a cathedral in there." He tried to pry Jupiter's mouth open again to get a better look but Jupiter began to wriggle and whine, so he said "OK, OK, sorry pal", and went back to petting. Jupiter lay down with his head on my dad's pajamaed thigh. My dad was saying "It's alright boy, it's alright", as though the dog needed consoling.

I went back to my room. From inside, I locked the door that faces the way my dad would come back into the house. This was in case he got some sentimental urge to open that door a crack and check on how I was sleeping. The locked door would satisfy him, and I figured he wouldn't bother checking the other door to my room, which I left through.

Very quietly I shouldered open the front door of the house, which sticks, partly because the wood swells in the heat, and partly due to the way dad repainted the door-jamb. I crossed the porch, made of redwood slats and crowded with flowerpots, including a hanging one this not very intelligent bird built its nest in. The little blue eggs hatched OK, but for weeks we had to go in and out of our house by the back door, because the male bird would dive-bomb pedestrians who crossed the porch. Once he knocked Dad's hat off.

Outside, I walked down the porch steps and brushed off a spot about my size on the blacktop. I could hear my dad re-enter the house, and I froze for a second. Then I saw the remaining light go off in my parents' room. I pulled my nightgown off over my head, hung it on a porch post, and lay on my back on the circular driveway to study the sky.

I'm not a nudist by nature like my friend Megan, star of the swim team. Meg is both feminine and muscley and doesn't like wearing clothes. If I looked like she does naked, I might not be such a big fan of clothes either. She's tan all over. She has the kind of optimistic, brownish breasts that point upward, towards her face, like detective novel cover breasts, rather than staring dully straight ahead like good students or hanging their heads towards the floor like morons. I, on the other hand, look like a wax candle nude, so pale I'm practically translucent. At this point in my career my breasts resemble a couple of paraffin drips, so under most circumstances it's better for me to stay dressed. But if I don't take off my nightgown before I lie down on the asphalt, it ends up looking like I repaired a truck wearing it, and my mom wants to know why.

There were a million leaves from the apricot tree on the driveway. They felt pleasant to lie on, dry but not sharp, sort of like stretching out on a pile of torn up paper. I wondered if my bleached nightgown could be seen from miles up, maybe resembling a truce flag. I tried to imagine what I might look like from that vantage point, if aliens were flying over and looking down through a super-powerful viewer. Maybe the one who noticed me first would say, "Excuse me captain, but we're passing over a humanoid, lying naked on her driveway." The guy in charge would say, PF-3383, take a reading to see if she's crazy, or worth contacting. A third guy would fiddle with his instruments, make some calculations. After a minute he'd respond, Sir, she's a little bit grimy but in her right mind.

David Bailley

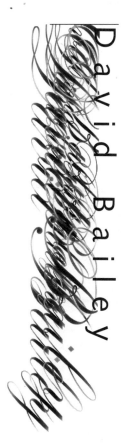

Floater

Something else to look forward to," I say eventually.

My father just looks away. Toward the window for a long time. Then, with an unusually specific, dry gravity he quietly states, quoting someone he forgets and I never knew, "It ain't for sissies, growing old."

"I reckon not," I say, and look down toward the dog, Peg. It's late morning and she's asleep on the floor, laying on her side. Her legs are twitching out the fitful cadence of canine dream-running, her gums parting occasionally to punctuate the sound of scuffling carpet with muffled barks. Some people have one dog all through their childhood, and it's in every family picture. We mostly shot slides, and no one ever wrote notes on the little cardboard mounts, so you have to date the photos by other means. Any picture with Peg in it is from the last nine years. Before Peg there were eight other dogs, usually two at a time, all of the same breed but individually recognizable, like they say about gorillas in Africa or whales in Alaska. More palpable than the abstract numeric succession of the calendar is the memory of nine staggered weanings, trainings, first hunts, shock collarings, best hunts, house days, and putting downs. When looking at a picture, by cross-referencing the signs of these stages against the sequential position of the pictured animal, it is possible to date the image rather precisely.

"Does it hurt when it tears?" I ask when the dog stops dreaming.

"If you mean, can you feel it happen, no . . . No, you can't feel it," he says firmly if absently.

"And later can you?" I persist, reeling him in a bit.

He then draws a distinction: "Well, the surgery's not exactly comfortable, but that's the surgery, not the injury."

"I thought it was all lasers," I protest, figuring it's only light.

"Mostly cryo," he says, tilting his head back and gesturing with his hands, as though holding his eyelids open between the splayed fingers of his right hand, and reaching across his face with the left. In this pose, and holding his bent index finger close to the outside corner of his restrained eye: "They stick this long curved needle around the back of the eyeball and tack the retina down—they just freeze it, like frostbite, your tongue on cold metal. The scars act like little welds." He makes his bent finger make a "zzzzz" sound, then moves it slightly and does it again, "zzzzzzz." He makes three welds this way.

When he moves his hands away from his face I can study his eyelids, his eyebrows, his crow's feet more clearly. "You can't tell by looking—no incision or anything," I observe.

"No," he concedes, as I reach for my coffee, "They about lock your head in a vise."

I consider this. "Cream's gone bad," I remark, studying the ivory curds swirling aimlessly around my cup, "and left eye up, or flat?"

He looks puzzled.

"I thought it was your left eye," I clarify.

"Oh," he pauses, "no." Another hesitation, "The right," then, "But I'm not right-handed."

Waiting all I get is, "And sugar's better for you anyway."

"Right-handed—left-eyed, I don't get it," I say.

"It's just," he explains, "trying to show you righty, I'm liable to poke out what I do got left."

The sink's under an east-facing window, but it's filthy. Early morning sun like this and the view is registered more than it is transmitted by the glass: the shadow of the cottonwood tree out front plays out its repertoire of puppet theaters across the opaque film. Summertime the leaves are full and the sun early, so only the stray speck of light actually makes it through to flit about the window. Dead winter all you get, for breakfast anyway, is the shadow of the trunk making its slow pan, with the occasional speeding silhouette of a truck out on the burmed road. The mailbox is too far north to figure in the drama, save a brief cameo, stage left, around the summer solstice. Just now the leaves' shadows flutter gently, and one occasionally falls diagonally down in the breeze. I assign their density at just below 40%, high thirties, shadows to light, figure to ground.

"One of these last warm days we ought to clean the window," I say, half to myself, as I go to pitch my coffee.

"I wouldn't sweat it," he replies, "if the weather's coming in it's coming in from the west."

His pragmatism catches me off guard. My father is not a formal man, but with him there is a right way and a wrong way. Not fixing what's not broke and tending to what is—these are the two right ways to treat things. Upkeep and preventive maintenance—tending-to-what's-not-broke-yet-because-if-you-don't-now-it-will-be-broke-when-you-need-it—these are borderline cases only from the abstract standpoint of logic. In practice, in Dad's practice anyway, they invariably get conflated into the latter category: b-r-o-k-e.

"Do dogs really see in black-and-white?" I ask, kicking Peg's empty bowl out from underfoot. It clatters stainless steel on tile, gonging into the stove.

"They say that," he replies from the table, "but bulls get mad at red."

I turn toward him to ask, "You talking about real bulls or pit-bulls?"

"No, bull-bulls—Toro! Toro!, you know, bulls," he says, placing his fists against his temples. Extending his index fingers forward at about 2 o'clock he pauses then adds, "With horns."

"But bulls aren't dogs," I object.

"No, they're animals," he argues, rising halfway out of his seat as he makes the point. Crouched and gripping the arms of the chair, he freezes momentarily, then jerks the old wood chair slightly into the air and pivots it ninety degrees to the left, twisting with it at the knees. When the legs catch in the carpet's shag, the joints squeak loudly, and he crashes back against it. Finishing the thought, he coyly stretches his legs out toward me.

"Bees are animals too," I counter, "and they say they see in infra-red—haven't you ever seen those pictures of flowers they take from a bee's point of view?—it's just an old white daisy to you or me, but to a bee the center's bright red with little black specks, and the petals got yellow bases and purple tips."

"Well I ain't seen them, and they don't know that, scientists, and anyway bees aren't animals, they're insects," he complains. "Insects see hundreds of hexagons at once."

"Insects are too animals," I argue. "They sure aren't plants or minerals."

"That's too broad," he snaps.

"Well, I asked about dogs." I say, "And I think you're thinking of honeycombs, the hexagon thing."

"How should I know what dogs see?" he continues, undeflected. "Maybe they do see in color—why shouldn't they see in color? They also say humans only dream in black-and-white, but I know for a fact that I dream in color, vivid color, so you figure it out."

The dish soap has been knocked over in the sink and has all run out into the tangle of silverware. A thin green slick languishes under the arched handles of spoons, holes up darker and thick between the tines of forks. A slotted steel spatula lies on its side, translucent eyebrows of bacon grease rimming the perforations' upper contours before spilling into delicate alluvia. The tendrils gather and congeal where the bottom edge of the flipper rests on the sink's white enamel. This arrangement diverts the drainward course of the detergent glacier toward a clearing between two knives. Opaque pearls of cold fat deliberate in the slipstream, breaking off to drift in its flow or sitting tight and setting up oily little back-eddies below them. I stick my thumb into the clearing and smush a fat polyp. I smear it around in a slow circular pattern, spiraling out slightly, squeegee-ing back the soap. I lift my thumb and watch the viscous contesting of the new border, as the detergent tries to creep over the successive ridges of my thumbprint.

"What about birds?" I ask, crossing the kitchen, stepping over the dog, and slumping into the couch beside the dinner table.

"Black-and-white, I'd figure," he replies without pausing.

"No, I mean this year," I spit out, "birds-this-year."

"Oh, this year?" he queries rhetorically.

"Yes, this year, birds, what about 'em, what do you hear," I say.

"Well," he begins, "could be O.K.—rain kept the equipment out of the fields, but not as late as spring before."

"My shoulder is still bruised from last year," I joke, sticking a pillow behind my head.

"'Bout killed off the old lady here," Dad says, gently kicking Peg's withers with his boot sole. She starts, and raises her head off the floor, eyeing him then me, looking for an explanation; not getting one, she lays her head back down.

"I'd be happy for half of last season," I confess.

"Dog's half the season, half the battle right there," he says to me, then nudging Peg again, "dog's half the battle, it'nt that right, Peg?" She doesn't even start this time, just opens her lids and watches us from the corner of her right eye, the left being buried in the strands of the carpet's beige yarn. A crescent of reticulated ivory emerges as she looks up at Dad, for a moment hangs limply below her tobacco iris, then rotates lazily as her eye swivels in its socket toward me. For Peg, the two things worth getting up for are eating and going outside, neither of which can happen before Dad or I stand up. She knows this, we stay seated, and shortly the whiteness is again eclipsed by the tight graying fur below her eye. After her lids seal she collapses her ribcage and forces out a big breath.

"Afraid Peg's halved her last season—we'll have to see how the-new-half-the-sequel is," I say, referring to my brother's new yellow.

"I don't frankly know if that puppy's got much of a nose on her," Dad replies, adding, "It's kinda pink."

Peg's nose is jet black, with the texture of pigskin, like a football but finer grained. Maybe a calf's tongue. Cow's anyway. The taste buds wrap around and line the inside edges of her nostrils. Her frustration has whipped the thin clear mucus of her nasal passages into quivering bubbles. Each uncertainly clings to a separate bud. With each successive breath one or two burst, until the mucus again pools tranquilly in the twin valleys of her nostrils.

It started because we didn't own enough guns. But even after my brother got the Italian side-by-side, Dad would just carry a camera, just shoot film. Ironically, the first time his retina tore it tore at 5 a.m. the morning he was getting on a plane to Ecuador. That trip was to celebrate his retirement—first non-business trip he'd made in probably twenty years and he bought a whole lot of film to take down there, to stay busy.

"If it doesn't hurt, how do you know it happened?" I ask him.

"The tear?" he states, "You get a bunch of junk in your eye."

"Like bloodshot then," I gather.

"Bloodshot you see the same but you look different; with this you look the same but . . . "

"What's the difference between a cross-eyed marksman and a constipated owl?" I interject.

This is one of his favorite jokes but, because it's vaguely scatological, it's only funny to him when he tells it, which is to say, since we all have known the punch line for years, that the joke's only funny when it's told at the right moment. This apparently was not one of them. Maybe a few other pre-war Boyscouts, Troop 319, Great Lakes Council, have an inkling, but only Dad knows for sure.

"Sorry—you were saying, you see different," I apologize.

"Where the retina tears, there's a flap of it sitting there, flopping around in the vitreous fluid, and all this junk— little torn up bits of retina—winds up just floating around inside," he explains. Then, with care so as not to rouse Peg again needlessly, "In the b-a-l-l of the eye."

A couple of years ago this would not have slipped by Peg. How we knew she was really sick as a young dog was when she would just lie on the floor and let you kick a tennis ball right past her, wouldn't even track it with her eyes, just'd look plaintively up at you while it rolled past. This went on for days. Thought she was dying. Then they cut an abscess the size of a grapefruit out of her flank. Infection, apparently, from where she snagged up on some barb wire during dove season. She wasn't even sobered up from the anesthetic before she was wanting to chase balls again, hardly made it in the front door before she's flipping one at me with her teeth and barking, big old field of stubbled gray skin showing, little beads of

293

blood popping up between the sutures as she strained on them, and her legs slowly, uncontrollably slipping out sideways from under her, drunk on the slick linoleum. Had to catch her before she fell down.

"You mean the hollow part," I say to Dad, staring down at the H-shaped dent where the incision scarred down behind Peg's ribs.

"It's full of fluid," he corrects me.

"And that junk—when you say you see 'floaters,' those are them?" I surmise, looking up again.

"No," he counters, "those are just pieces of junk, debris—like I said, bits of the retina."

I remember the retina is this fabric of rods and cones in some arcane array; I used to know about it in high school. I could describe the pattern, the grid, give the formula, tell you mathematically how the rectilinear matrix of receptors and transmitters conformed to the concavity of the retinal surface, explain the phylogenetic and ontogenetic stages of the eyeball's evolution. Now I can only imagine unmoored fragments of neural sensitivity, still receiving information but unable to transmit it, off-axis and adrift in the eyeball like the Voyager satellite circling Mars. I wonder what those pieces see.

"They have to get that stuff out of there," I insist.

"Maybe they suction up the big pieces, but mostly they just worry about the flap and try to tack it down. The little pieces break down eventually," he says, picking up a decoy he and I carved together, tag-team style, years ago, which the new puppy chewed the tail off recently.

"But I thought you said the floaters were permanent," I say, confused.

"They are," he replies. "But they don't happen in the eyeball, they happen at the flap, the weld," he says, as Peg cocks her ears and he runs his fingers over the puncture wounds and raw pine left by sharp puppy teeth. "Shame about this deke."

"Watch you don't get a splinter," I warn. "So floaters don't float at all, they're attached," I continue.

"Just because she has teeth doesn't mean she has a nose," Dad says. He then draws another distinction: "They don't float in your eye, they float in your vision."

Uncomprehending, I just look at him.

"They're welds," he says with irritated resolve.

"But you said they weren't," I push.

"Of course they're not," he spits out. He has flipped the duck over and has got it by the neck. Agitated, he is slapping the duck's back against the palm of his free hand as he speaks. "All that floats—all a 'floater' is—is the images from where the welds are, they're what the weld sees, what the scar can't see, what the scar does see because you can't see through the scar, they're what you see in the place of the scar instead of what you would normally see if it were still just retina—rods and cones."

His palm is quite whitened now. Each of the decoy's primary feathers is carved in slight relief and their lozenge-shaped tips have beaten the blood out of my father's palm. Color then quickly returns to the ham of his hand as a blush of red. I watch as the hue fades slowly, stealing intermittent glances at my own palm. When his color again matches my own I continue, "So you see these scars on top of everything?"

"You don't see anything on top of everything," he says

putting the decoy back down gently. "The scar erases the image from the retina, like a burn erases fingerprints."

"Then you see nothing on top of everything?" I ask, a little ingenuously.

"Well, points of nothing anyways—blindspots." He replies matter-of-factly.

"Burnt fingerprints," I offer.

"Most of the time," he says, then pauses, his voice lifting slightly as he continues, "you don't even see them, they just blend into the scene."

"Camouflage," I say by way of encouragement.

"You maybe see them when you're looking up at an overcast sky, or maybe you've come in from the sun and are staring at a white wall," he explains in long breaths, "You can't pick them out till your vision is very blank, plain, nothing to see."

It's sort of a joke with my brothers, about how you can train a dog to be still but you can't keep Dad from fidgeting in the blind. He's constantly scanning the sky for ducks, geese, anything that flies. Half the time those specks on the horizon turn out to be planes. The rule is, by the time you can see a bird it's seen you, so we tell him, "You don't even need to see them till their wings are set: you can hear them and your face will flare them, keep your head still and brim low, frame the space above the river and below the treetops, keep the decoys on the upstream border of your vision, just watch for birds to appear at the downwind edge of your visor—they'll be close, there'll be plenty of time, they won't be specks, you won't miss them . . . swing through them."

We say that every time, but every time—even before

the tear—he squirms, pans, jerks, twitches, flares them—
he can't seem to stand the suspense of waiting for them to
fly from his peripheral vision into sharper focus.

"Floaters are the opposite of roadkill," he says.
"Roadkill move along, grazing on the shoulder or just
ambling across the blacktop, heading for the river or back
across to bed down, taking their sweet time, fluid, till the
headlights hit them, till they know they are seen, then
they look up, freeze up, lock down, can't move."

"And you can't stop," I say, supplying the inevitable
and imagining the day after: the heat of the sun, the bel-
lies bloated and legs distended, the flies swarming wounds
and eyes, the far too late to salvage the meat and send it
wrapped in white paper bundles to an orphanage somewhere. "Horses are the worst," I add, "except in winter."

"Floaters aren't like that at all," he says looking at me
but raising his left hand off the arm of the chair and holding a loose fist in the air off to the side. "They sit tight at
the fringe of your vision, in the edges, hold up in the
cover of the peripheral textures, but the second you focus
on them . . ." he pauses for a second, then simultaneously
jerks his head toward his hand as he flicks the fingers
open, "Gone - they race away from you."

"Quail, then," I say, staring at his splayed open fingers,
still hovering next to his ear.

"Quirkier," he replies, turning his face back toward
me. "Fly zig-zag, sort of. Flit. Bats maybe."

"But outta hell fast," I qualify, remembering his
demonstration.

"Maybe a little slower," he says, lowering his hand at an
illustrative pace. When his palm again meets the arm of

the chair he wraps his fingers around the end of it and slips out, "More like Utah bats."

"Couple of them came 'round door-to-door the other day," I quip, but my timing is apparently no better than before.

"These are more than two," Dad barks out. But an apology follows shortly: "And they don't wear suits anyway."

"A lot, huh?" I surmise.

He sits there, breathing.

"More than you can count?" I press.

"Hard to say," he says soon, his eyes making twitchy pans and darts all over, though mostly to the left it seems. Eventually he summarizes: "The scars are on the retina, off-center, so when you try to look over at them, the whole eyeball moves, and of course the scars move with it, so the floaters are always "X" number of degrees ahead of your focal point."

"You can focus on blindspots?" I ask.

"That's the point—you're exactly trying not to focus on them," he says, irritated, "You try to not even notice them at all, you notice them, you fix on 'em, they drive you nuts—you try to ignore them."

In grade school they'd occasionally show us anatomy movies where they would enter the body and the camera would dissect it. Soft tissue didn't bother me—I could tour the organs all day, and muscles just looked like dinner defrosting. But bones: all of a sudden you'd be in a joint, watching tendons slide over cartilage, and suddenly I couldn't stand any part of my body touching any other part. If my ankles were crossed it was as though the skin and flesh parted and I felt only bone-on-bone. I'd move them apart but the weight of my legs would drive the bones through the meat of my heel till they rested directly on my insoles. I'd lift my legs off the floor in an attempt to relieve myself of gravity, but this would just fuse my tailbone into the chair's crenulated avocado plastic. Soon I couldn't move.

"Lemme tell you," he adds, "scars lose their charm real quick when no one else can see 'em."

"You mean the floaters drive you nuts because they look like the scars, the welds?" I ask.

"No," he says unequivocally. "Actually mirror images of the scars."

Like a woman checking her nails, I stretch my hands before me. I spend a moment studying the irregularities of the albino traces past mishaps have left on them. "In the same pattern?" I ask, trying to mentally transpose the more abundant scars from my dominant right hand onto my left.

"Reversed," he answers. "I said 'mirror.'"

"But regular," I say, looking at the suture marks.

"Not really," he says as he shifts his weight slightly. The shrillness of the squeaking wood cuts short my imaginative subjection of my left hand to the various blades, the car door, and the tire chains the right has endured.

"But a particular formation, like a marching band at half-time," I suggest.

"An 'M' in a mirror is still an 'M,'" he rebuts.

"Then pick a better letter," I insist. "No offense to your alma mater."

"They're more like a constellation," he replies quickly.

"But looking down on it from deep space, you mean," I infer.

"Beats me, ask NASA," he says, tiring, "but not a letter."

I adjust my pillow once, then again, before asking, "Do you think they'll make it to the Rose Bowl this year, Michigan?"

At this he tilts his head back slightly and raises his hand to his beard, scratching at his jaw under the whiskers. The house was built in the early seventies, and has a white plexi skylight over the dining area. The bubble reflects milkily in his upturned glasses. "More like hair in a drain," he responds after a long pause. With conviction he draws out the words: "A bunch of squiggles."

"People hair?" I ask with equal deliberation. "Or dog hair?"

Peg's ears prick at hearing the word 'dog.' She rises, first to all fours, then dips her chest all the way back down to the floor, stretching, with her butt up in the air and her head down low, between her bandy front legs. The curve of her tail follows the concave arc of her spine. From that posture she cocks her head at me, looking up from under the graying line of her brow.

"You remember all those old pictures of Peg, how her eyes would glow red in the flash?" I ask.

"They make cameras for that now," Dad replies.

"They only work on people—maybe dog pupils are too big," I hypothesize.

"Have you tried your mother's?" he suggests.

"No, it's only a problem for the new pup," I say, continuing my deduction out loud.

"She doesn't like the flash?" Dad asks, not following.

"I mean red eyes—Peg's come out kinda blue."

"Blue?" he asks. "Blue-blue?"

"Well pale blue anyways," I maintain, "slate-blue."

"Pale," my father says. "Then that's not the camera."

"I'm talking about the flash," I clarify.

"No, it's not the flash either," he says, dismissing my pedantry. "She's got cataracts."

Peg's still stretching on the floor. She hasn't moved her feet in the carpeting, but she's shifted her pose. Her tail is still curled the same but now it's her butt that's down low and her rear legs that are stretched out straight. Her torso juts out forward toward me on the couch and her collar shoves forward large jowls of black fur. I grab them with both hands and peer closely into and beneath her cornea, trying to focus on the hazy layers of their patina. It's like trying to locate the surface of mother-of-pearl, and I'm making her nervous, looking at her so closely; I'm making her think I think she's done something wrong. She and I both look away quickly. "Is a good kid," I say, and jingle her choke chain as I release her.

"I'd better put my boots on," I say to Dad. "She's giving me the look."

"Better get her out then," he says, "before she starts sending smoke signals."

"She can be pretty articulate," I comment, reaching for my jacket.

"It's not the way they smell . . . " he begins.

Taking the bait, I blurt out another standard: "It's the

301

way they burn your eyes."

He laughs and stands and turns toward the north window.

Still seated, I struggle a minute with my coat.

"Feeder's empty," he states while I search my pockets. "Birds'll be looking."

"Seen my gloves around?" I ask, checking under the pillow.

"Tell you what," he says abruptly, "I'll take her—you clean this kitchen up." Peg has already made for the door and he follows her out.

After the screen slams I look down at the hourglassed impression the dog's torso has left in the shag, deepest under the haunches and rib barrel, shallower and lighter beneath the flank. Matted black fur lines the sockets created by her twitching hips and shoulders. Detached semicircles raked into the carpet record the outer limen of some oneiric hunt.

I go to the screen door. She's nose to the wind and he's scanning the west for weather. "Walk her on the blacktop," I yell after them, "her toenails are getting long."

Amanda Greene

Do Not Call Me a Toenail

was at the beach with my friend Phoebe and she accidentally cut me with her toenail. My wound bled for a while, and sand stuck to the dried blood on my leg. I walked into the water to rinse off the blood. The salt water only made things worse. My cut started to sting and bleed some more. Live with it. No one should have toenails long enough to cut people and make them bleed. Phoebe never cuts her toenails. She is carefree. Other things are more important than toenails. One time she scratched herself with one of them. It seems like she would take that as a hint that her nails should be trimmed.

I enjoy clipping my toenails. I use the scissors on my Swiss Army Knife to do the job. I usually sit in the bathroom with my foot on the side of the tub. I always cut my pinkie toenail first. It is so small and unimportant. I like to get it out of the way like an appetizer. I make my way up to my big toe, saving it for last. I get a kick out of clipping that big toenail. It is so thick and stubborn, and when it finally surrenders to the scissors, it flies across the room like it never wants to see my foot again. After I cut both of my big toenails, I go back and even out the smaller ones. I get really excited when I realize that I haven't trimmed my nails in a long time, because they are real long and thick. That is, except for the second toe on my left foot. I do not have a toenail on this toe. When I was little I dropped the hot iron on my left foot. I got a juicy burn and the little toenail turned purple, then black, and fell off. Since then, I have been without one of my toenails. I still trim this toe, though. I cut off some of the hard, dead skin from the part of my toe that should be a toenail. I do this on my other toes if I am in the mood for some serious trimming and there is not much to cut. I begin ripping off hard bits of skin from around my toes. This makes my feet feel better. If I have a lot of spare time, I cut the top layer of skin off of the bottoms of my feet. This does not make my feet hurt. The new layer of skin that is exposed is pink and healthy. After I trim my nails and skin, I take a hot shower. Right when I step out of the shower I feel the pain. I cut off too much skin. I always do this. When I am cutting the skin it doesn't hurt. After a few minutes it becomes nearly impossible for me to walk. I get the rubbing alcohol and pour it all over my feet. I love to watch my skin sizzle as the alcohol cleans the dirt away. For a few days I limp around in pain. After about four days, a new, thin layer of skin has grown over the raw, pink skin. The new layer reduces the pain.

David Patton

Supreme

As if on some unspoken cue, they simultaneously commanded some of the muscles supporting their heads to go slack and others to tighten which allowed their skulls to swivel so that they faced me. Jeff seemed more than anxious. I swear I didn't mean to, but apparently I had interrupted the rhythm of this morning's lecture. This was demonstrated by Jeff spitting onto the dusty tile of the service station's "waiting room" and drawl-bitchin' at me, "Sheeit Lar-vey, c'mon boy!" Saliva and cobwebs swirled together at his feet.

Big Terry just smiled at us. His face shone, more so because with my entrance he now had reason to re-tell his sex tale.

Preparations for the re-telling were made. After all, his audience had just grown one-hundred percent. A pull down on each leg of his dark blue trousers, a quick ball hustle followed by a sucking in of his spare tire and tucking in of the front of his lighter blue service shirt. Jeff and I shifted on our asses until our spines settled into reformed arcs and the small wooden step ladders we sat on cupped our cheeks just right.

Terry started slowly. I guess it had to be spelled out to the newest, which was me "The...woman...that...I...fucked ...Lar-vey..." This is my name at the filling station, larvae. It was pretty much created by me when I opened up my big fat mouth soon after being hired for this summer. The snack/junk food machine that is in our waiting room is very old and I think the display candies, which are never actually dispensed, are part of the original equipment. The samples are old enough to be covered with a protective layer of what appears to be dust and the Zagnut bars have a wrapper style that I had never seen before. Where the various chewing gums are displayed in the machine is a pile of dead and dried up insect bodies and/or cocoons. They had lived out their short lives next to the doublemint. The first time I was noticed looking at the dried carcasses my fellow service attendants had asked what "them bugs" were. I said I couldn't tell because, looking all wormy and mummified, they appeared to have died in their larvae stage. I guess we had a winner, they loved this. I didn't hear the end of it all day and still haven't. I still don't get the mispronunciation (intentional?) but I am goddamn glad that I didn't say pupa. My name is now a constant reminder to never volunteer information.

Terry went on "...was the dark-haired one in the black Chrysler with that fucked up antenna that comes in every other morning." I squinted so I would look as if I was thinking hard, but had not quite made the connection. Actually I knew exactly who he was talking about when I interrupted. We all had seen him struttin' around and flirtin' with this one for the past month and it didn't take a mental heavyweight to figure out who he had had. I was playing dumb on purpose. Bullshit is loose and fast and some of its most important elements are the giving, taking, and giving back of, well, shit. My approach was that playin' dumb is a good way to toss someone's story back at them, sort of like bluffing in poker. They have to add to their story, work a bit more, turn up the "h" (as in heat) a little bit. This is only true, I think, if the dumb playin' is convincing. If one is not recognized as a participant one might get told to shut the fuck up, or worse, be ignored completely. I wanted to hear how Terry would tell the story more than I wanted to hear the story itself. Who cares why or what the hell happened, the how of the telling is the best part.

"Long curly hair...real talkative...with the kid." Jeff started giggling at this point, tickled by unseen hands. I rolled my eyes back in their sockets to demonstrate recognition. I sagged wearily on my makeshift seat. My back curved a bit more. My shoulders rolled forward slightly as my stomach rose in my throat. I noticed pain resulting from my poor posture as an image formed in my head. Terry was a fairly large guy, 'bout six foot, a little over two hundred chunky pounds with his belt having to handle a good portion of it. Very relaxed and usually smiling, at least at work. I didn't want to think of him buck naked, going ape...or maybe he wasn't buck...what kind of wacky shit would Terry wear...a blindfold?...his work clothes?

The familiar da-ding of the pneumatic service bell sounded. Normally taking silently designated turns, all three of us lazily rose as several more cars drifted through the heat of the intersection and into the gas station lot. Our quadricep muscles constricted, bunching and swelling closer to the tops of our knees and pulled on their other anchors to the pelvis, straightening out our legs. The inside was the best chance we had against the heat. Two small, dust covered metal fans kept the office/waiting room of the station slightly cooler than the outside oven. Cooler may not be the best word. But in 90 percentile humidity you'll take every degree you can get.

At least the fans kept the heat and smells of sweat, grease and oil moving. With the front and one wall of the station waiting room being mostly glass we could attempt to stay calm and slightly cooler inside while keeping a lazy eye on the pumps and an ear out for the bells that meant work. The sun was not picky today. There were no clouds in the sky. The yellowish white ball would have none of its efforts snatched out of flight by some lollygagging moisture. At least not on our block.

Hot. Since I was newest I was lowest on the gas pumpin' totem pole. As the gamma pumper I knew that I was to take care of the self service pumps when all three of us had to work at once. The self service pumps were put in years after this old station was built. For some reason they were left without the carport style roofs that are prevalent nowadays and indeed shielded "our" full serve island. It, the self serve island, was located about the same distance as the full service stand from the garage proper, just on a different side of the main building. For some reason, the lack of roof, maybe the heat, it seemed to me to be farther away than it really was, not as much part of the shop.

I cross the ten yards of bright shining cement with the growing feeling of moving even farther away from where I just was. I am passing through seemingly countless waves of light and heat. I am the spot where the eight minute old waves from the sun crash into their slightly older siblings that are returning from a meeting with the earth's surface. It is me, the cement, the regular, the unleaded and the super unleaded. I am approaching some fossil getting out of his Cadillac while thousands of gallons of gasoline sit under our feet and a giant ball of flaming hydrogen hangs over our heads. The old timer has that "shake" thing that happens to some folks which makes his head and hands appear to be connected to some sort of springs. I am trying to remember what causes this disorder as he pauses to line up the nozzle with the hole in the side of the car. I am watching the nozzle's spring wrapped metal tip gently shake, launching a drop or two of golden fuel into space. He carefully inserts the dispenser into the body of the El Dorado. His hand squeezes the rubber protected lever and the sound of dispensing gasoline rises. I'm squinting and my face is holding a slight grin because of the glare out here. He is talking to me, something about the fuel injector additive or is it the "Stop Apartheid, Boycott Shell" button hanging off the front of my uniform, I am not sure since I am only half listening. I am watching his mouth move but my thoughts are drifting back through the heat to the conversation that was interrupted. Apparently this woman, now a regular in more ways than one, I guess, was flirting with big boy for a couple of weeks and then buh-bam. The only part of this story that fucks with me is that she is married and has a kid. It don't make no mox-nix to me if I get to hear about Terry spending his nights over at her place and as he says "...driving her like a truck..." swear to god, he said it. I couldn't make something up like that if I had to. But I always end up thinking about what sort of screwed up relationship I think she must have with this "husband" that I never hear about, and of course what will ever happen to the kid? Hell, it's none of my business anyway...shit, the top of this pump is one hot ass piece of...damn, my arm feels like fried bologna.

The valued customer detaches the nozzle from the car and, shaking of course, returns it to its perch on the pump. He is handing me exact change for his fill up. I listen to the heavy-winded purr of the Cadillac as it inflates to idling speed. I am walking toward the garage as I hear the huge machine pull away and fade into the constant ruusshh of traffic. It is so damn bright out here on the lot. I have always loved the smell of gasoline and I am right now as I am slowly walking through an invisible cloud of the sweet vapor raised off the concrete by the temperature. My suburban tastes are reminding me that the metallic syrup of gas is best complimented by the aroma of freshly cut lawn, but for today "straight up" will have to do. My brain is gone now. It is floating to the top of my head as I am reaching the full service island where Jeff and Terry are fully servicing. Instinct is guiding me through the automobiles as my mind is drifting on its heatfuel ride. Terry is expressing no emotion as he is saying "Car wash" to me. What this means is that the customer he is finishing up with wants a car wash and that I am to guide her over to the wash bay and take care of business. I motion to the elderly woman in her dusty but otherwise seemingly mint condition Mercedes Benz to pull her around by extending my index and middle finger and swinging my arm from pointing directly at her to the general direction of the wash to my left.

Just past the garage bays is the added on car wash tunnel. The control panel, basically one round red knob about the size of my palm, is set just inside the machine's front entrance. Window up, aerial down. I am guiding the woman into the hydraulic powered "Hydro-Cleen" unit as I see the black Chrysler pull up across the lot. I am determining that it is her. I can now confirm this by Terry's shit eatin' grin and his swagger around the hood of her car to the driver's side. They look like they're flirting, at least a little. I see Jeff washing the windshield of a Toyota on the other side of the island from the Chrysler. It looks like he is keeping an eye on this rendezvous just like I am. I am beginning to feel nauseous. I don't want to know. I wish I had not seen this women pull in. I am attempting to concentrate on washing this damn Mercedes but between the gas/exhaust fumes rotting my brain and the fact that this task is so fuckin' simple, I am becoming bored and losing control. I am constructing a mental picture of them slappin' into each other, rollin' around on some tiled kitchen floor. On tile I imagine your skin would catch if it was freshly cleaned and mopped or else it might slide like crazy over a layer of household dust. What would this old lady do if I asked her to roll her window down so I could tell her the history leading up to the events behind her? Spread this sexual image around. "'Scuse me ma'am, see that woman in that there black car, talking to that big blonde fella? Well, she is married to some other fuckin' dude but comes here three days a week to flirt with this one. But wait ma'am, there's more. Some nights he goes over to her place and they screw the hell out of each other. At least that's what he says because he walks around here tellin' us about every little detail. And now lady, the scary part is that this crap is cranked so hard into my brain that I have to tell a complete stranger about it."

As I look out from the tunnel I can only see the back of "Mrs. Terry"'s head through the rear window of the K car. Her hand is lazily stroking his forearm as I activate the car cleaner by pressing on the giant red button marked "Start". The woman's little boy is waving to me silly out of the window as a spray of old hydraulic fluid coats the right side of my body with a black oily film. The crusty old pipe, newly broken by dry rot is spinning, twirling and lashing about frantic with half-freedom. The flying hose comes so close with each lash to the beautiful machine it was to enhance, but touches it not. It appears to be settling for coating the car's surface rather than scratching its enamel and sealer. The hydraulic mechanism of the "Hydro-Cleen" car wash machine (used to) move the large rotating brushes back and forth over an automobile. Oil filled pistons would lift, stretch, push and pull. Today this connection tube has decided it is through. The tube has broken away from one of its two mooring points on the machine and, because of a lack of an ability to communicate, the rest of the machine is still forcing fluid through it. I am turning to my right, the six foot tall spinning brushes, though not moving forward now but still a-whirling, their cloth strands now a blur, are filling the whole space with a blinding field of soap, water and oil. I am now reaching the on/off switch and can feel my entire body covered with my now clingy, oil soaked uniform. I think the rest of the staff is running over here to help, at least that is what I think I am hearing.

I am now watching the Mercedes Benz. The old lady must have been daydreaming along with me because she apparently seems to think that that was it for the wash. Maybe she is thinking that the "Hydro-Cleen" is quite a remarkable custom wash and wax system to have treated her car so quickly. Maybe she is just not paying attention. Not missing a beat she is pulling away from us and exiting on the far side of the "tunnel". Windshield wipers on high, tossing sheets of finish ruining liquid onto the cars parked in the lot behind the garage. We are watching her drive off slowly and I am imagining her being completely unaware of the corrosives that now coat her fine car and with the heat, are working on destroying years of carefully applied waxes and polishes.

Timothy Martin.

"Will that be all?"

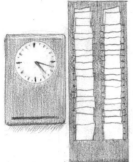

wonder if we might pause for a minute here, dear customer, as I see your hand reaching over the counter so confidently and eagerly proffering these notes of renumeration and I worry, you being new around here and we two strangers, whether we understand this transaction, a conventional exchange by most standards, your hard currency comes chasing my somewhat harder yet comparably valued wares; I worry whether we are or can ever be in sufficient agreement here. Or perhaps only I need to pause to counter a pang of conscience, not out of a merchant's guilt over profit, but over you, a person, personally, about your eagerness or resignation to this exchange, where this little piece of yourself is handed over to me unmourned. Every dollar is a little death, you see, a receipt for the time you have served, however served, at your labors. The thousand heartbeats, the inhales and exhales that stoked the furnace that put your energy to work, the legions of cells laid to rest for the cause and their replacements conscripted into service, only to share the same fate. Your eyesight and posture to pay, your bones abrading in their sockets, harrowing marrow into full production. Time spent away from home, segregation from your spouse or whomever, your children's fleeting childhoods left unguided to the extent of your absent gender. Or your own vanishing freedom, should I wrongly presume this family life, your vitality dribbled like plasma from a pre-sealed container, a prescribed and fixed volume, as we all know, non-refillable.

Don't worry, you say, there's more where this came

from. But how much more? If I were a charity I might ask you to dig down deep, and you would have to consider this very seriously: how deeply can I dig? How far down is deep? You roll up your eyes and dig. So far, okay. Further, you experience some pressure. Further still, symptoms of vascular compression, faintness, shock. How far will you go for Lou Gerig or for lupus? Further than bulimia, not as far as Armenia? An entire hemisphere is unclothed and needs its shots. Tell me your limit.

This complicates things. The need dwarfs what you can offer so you must measure yourself by a different standard. How much are you if you aren't enough? You hesitate, perspire. Miraculously, you will come up with a figure. This is what makes you a charitable person. It's more than the desire to give. It's your willingness to submit, to assess yourself in this humbling, indeed abnegating, fashion. You know you have one life to give for your country, one body for science, and so on, but recognize it's only on condition of your death, the ultimate condition of expenditure. Is there plenty more where that came from? Of course there isn't.

Still, you say, there is more where this came from. This you can easily afford. You are sure.

I know you are sure. Everybody is. That's what troubles me. You don't apply the same standard so that burden is placed on me by default. You come to me with this paper, these apportionments of your abject finitude, expecting me to take them without a second thought, understanding full well that they cannot be replaced with something or things of equal value no matter what I give you in return. It's like you're indenturing yourself to me - or the other way around - as if upon receipt of this paper I assume the contract for your time and all the perpetual false accounting that goes with it. Now you are laboring in my fields, so to speak, so I become the responsible party. Do you have enough water? Food? Clothing and shelter? Health insurance? Are you satisfied and comfortable with what you do? Is the work I have given you suited to your potential? Do you need some time off to pursue hobbies or passions? Are you loved? Don't be proud, you can tell me. That's what I'm here for. It's my business. Please, put yourself in my shoes. Considering all of this, if I offered this cash to you could you take it without giving a thought to what you would then owe me in return? Dig down deep. How much are you? You would owe me my life. Do you have that much? Could you afford to accept my hard-earned tender?

So you agree it seems like an ominous proposition. The way I put it, you don't think you could afford such a transaction. But you object. Isn't it enough that I give you the thing you pay for, granted, with a portion of your finite life? Just give you what you want because you want it? Maybe throw in a guarantee or something if my conscience demands it? Let it be your choice? After all, the customer's always right. And if the customer's always right, except that he's wrong, then the customer's always wrong. Right? Haven't I contrived this problem then?

Only if giving you the thing you want were an even vaguely equivalent exchange. If I could somehow give back in kind what I collected, or fool myself into believing such an exchange were possible, I would do it. But even this dubious bit of intercourse eludes me primarily because if I give you the thing you want, then I give you nothing which is mine. As this absent mineness would appear to be the only valid basis of equivalence to your present yoursness - the yoursness you present to me through your cash - the fact that the thing you want is not mine, that it is in effect only consigned to me, is certainly no relief to me nor a solution to my problem. Indeed it makes my problem worse. Because morally, ethically all I can ever do is make change, which is not what you're asking for. And when I'm not making change, I am making a mistake.

Let me show you a contrivance. This thing you want is itself a receipt for the time wasted by some other thriftless slave like yourself. Heartbeat for heartbeat, grunt for grunt, it is a quantity of wasted life roughly equivalent, as you yourself assert, to your pallid currency here. It does not belong to me in any real way, even though I own this place. I am only the carrier. I know it and you unknowingly rely upon it; it is what gives you this quaint impression that I am somehow working for you, that I am an agent of your wishes. I take these pieces of paper with which you indenture yourself to me, or others which the bank has laundered to a fresh and crisp anonymity, and with them procure the servitude of the poor slob over there who makes the thing you want and who is happy to give me little quantities of his wasted life, which pass into my hands in the form of products, his products, as he refers to them. I have no use for them. They just lie around here making me nervous until I pawn them off onto other poor squanderers like you, who are only too anxious to fork over receipts for their wasted time for the privilege of consuming somebody else's wasted time. It is a food chain consisting of two mouths opposite one another alternately chewing on the same wad of over masticated vegetable matter, a wad that passes back and forth between them, growing paler and paler, more and more tasteless. You don't even have a clue who this other person might be, your intimate wad-chewing, saliva-exchanging partner. It's like Christmas in the fourth grade. Everybody must buy a non-edible gift of a certain predetermined value - say, under a dollar - that no kid that age would ever want - that is, anything non-edible under a dollar - which gets tossed into a big cardboard box and is later drawn out by a kid you don't know or don't like or don't even get to watch, but everybody feels kinda good anyway, because, who cares, it's Christmas!

Yea, who cares, it's Christmas, you say. What a pleasant sentiment. Everybody's telling themselves that. The whole world is lined up at my counter - in a surprisingly generous mood for the living dead - holding out their hands full of cash, staring straight ahead, marching in place, chanting: WHO CARES, IT'S CHRISTMAS; WHO CARES, IT'S CHRISTMAS. It's the giving, dear people, the giving and the sharing. The big green commonality. The woof and warp of community life. And it sounds so beautiful that way! Only where am I? Behind the counter, dumb struck, looking at all the hands full of paper and the mouths mouthing please and thank you. Either way I look at it, I'm in trouble.

If the whole thing is okay, it's okay because it's okay to convert your life into paper chits and swap them around like coupons for government cheese, as long as everybody else is doing it, as long as we're all settling for cheese. In which case I've got a problem, because I'm supposed to be passing everybody else's for them, handling everybody's cheese, and don't have any of my own, that is, unless I take my cut. No commonality there, just business. And if the whole thing is a waste - of this I'm certain - then I'm the one standing here accounting for all the damage - I mean literally, calculating a response to each and every utterance of that cheerful, excruciating question: What's the damage? - and feeling somehow responsible. Here comes your hand again, drifting across the counter without you. Look at that thing. Pitiful. I have to agitate; there is nothing else to do. I will not accept this from you. For your sake, for mine. Keep your servitude. But go ahead, take what you want. I'm not unreasonable. Take it. It doesn't belong to me. Take two. They just make me nervous. Here, I give them to you. Why don't you just owe me? I'm tired of owing. I'd rather be owed to. Go. Take. Owe me. What could it hurt?

What's this? A bribe? You can't bribe me to take your money. I don't care if it's not yours. It's the principle. Please, just pretend you're putting it on an account. Take what you want, and if you're so inclined you can send whatever you think is right to the bank. Just don't make me see it. Here's the address and account number. No, a check is no good. Too personal, it has your signature on it. No plastic either. Same reason. Besides, I couldn't bear to pull an impression off your card anyway. That carbon paper is so tactile, you know, so fleshy.

No, it's your life, dear customer, and if you insist on a

transaction, thank you, please understand that I cannot be personally involved.

II.

Hold on. You don't work for a living? You don't have to, you're set? That's what you meant when you said the money's not yours. I thought it was just a figure of speech, or an attempt to placate me, or I don't know what I thought. I wasn't listening. You meant you don't work for it, so it's not really yours, so it can't represent you personally as it would if you did. You meant it's not really yours in much the same way that this thing you want is not really mine. Huh. A person who doesn't make a living. That is different. Kind of liberating, isn't it? Not for you, of course - by which I mean unfortunately. Liberating for me! I don't know about you, but I think - and I'm genuinely surprised by the thought - I think I can live with this, this particular set of circumstances.

No, don't bother. Cash will be fine.